King of the Bottom

a novel

by **William C. Gordon**

Bay Tree Publishing, LLC
Point Richmond, California

Calligraphy by Ward Schumaker
Cover design by Lori Barra and Sarah Kessler
Interior design by mltrees

Library of Congress Cataloging-in-Publication Data

Gordon, William C. (William Charles), 1937-
  King of the bottom : a novel / by William C. Gordon.
    p. cm.
  ISBN 978-0-9836179-0-7 (alk. paper)
  I. Title.
  PS3607.O5947K56 2012
  813'.6--dc23
                                              2012005135

This book is dedicated to Isabel Allende, who created the space for me to hear the voices.

Table of Contents

1

The Dump

THE SECOND WEEK of December 1961 was the coldest weather on record for the Bay Area in almost fifty years, even though it had been a year with little rain. That morning the fog inched its way up San Francisco Bay from the Golden Gate all way to the Richmond-San Rafael Bridge, and you could hear the constant groan of the foghorns breaking the silence of the dawn. It was still dark when the phone rang at the Richmond Police Department, and it took several rings before the sleepy officer on duty was shaken from his drowsiness. It was the last hour of the night shift and, for that reason, the most difficult.

"Richmond Police Department. Dispatch, Officer Malcolm speaking."

The voice on the other end of the line was hysterical. "There's a man hanging from the gate out here!"

Officer Malcolm was seated in the middle of the three stations positioned in front of a large radio transmitter filled with dials and vacillating needles. The other two stations, which could be independently operated in case of an emergency or extra heavy workload, were empty.

Now fully awake, Malcolm focused on what he'd just heard, knowing the details he gathered now would be important in the future. He turned on the tape recorder.

"Calm down now, just calm down," he said.

He took a pad of paper out of the top drawer in front of his position and, with a shaky hand, wrote the date and time on it. He cleared his throat.

"Who are you, sir?" he asked nervously, pulling at the open collar of his now-wrinkled shirt.

The agitated voice came back at him. "I'm a truck driver. I was heading—"

"Hold on, hold on. Give me your full name, man."

"My name don't matter none. Ya better get someone out here."

"Where are you?"

"The dump at Point Molate in Richmond," the man shouted. Then he hung up.

"Hello, hello!" yelled the officer, but it was no use. The caller was gone.

Malcolm grabbed the dispatch radio microphone in front of him and began broadcasting.

"Calling all available patrol cars. Report of a possible 187 at the chemical dump at Point Molate. Give me—"

He counted on his fingers, aware that he was responsible for a city of over a hundred thousand and that he only had six patrol cars available that morning.

"Give me three cruisers to the scene. Over."

"Car 5 responding," answered a voice over the radio. "We're in Point Richmond, just around the corner."

"Car 12, downtown Richmond, responding," said another voice.

"Car 27, heading west on Cutting Boulevard," said a third.

Point Molate was a promontory that jutted into San Francisco Bay near the Richmond-San Rafael Bridge. Reached via an access road off Cutting Boulevard, Richmond's main drag, it offered a last exit before heading westbound onto the bridge.

King of the Bottom

Situated at Point Molate was an industrial chemical dumpsite. A massive steel gate with an arch rising some twenty feet above the ground blocked the entrance. Both were painted white. Next to the gate was a guardhouse painted the same color. The gate was open and a man's body hung from the arch, a rope around his neck. His hands were tied behind his back and his feet were bound together. He was obviously dead.

The driver of the first police cruiser to arrive focused the car's spotlight beam on the body. "Is he carrying a gun?" his partner asked. "There's a bulge on the inside of his suit."

"Don't know. Hope he's not rigged with a bomb or something. We can't tell until we cut him down, and we can't do that unless we say we're trying to save his life—and no one would believe that story."

They shook their heads in shock and the driver aimed the beam at the ground to avoid having to look at the body. The officers noticed the guard shack on the left side of the gate, but there was no one around. They got out of their cruiser but remained some distance from the gate. After a few minutes, the driver stuck his hand inside the car and focused the spotlight on the body again. The bright yellow beam pierced the early morning darkness.

The officer who had been riding shotgun looked more closely. "Have you ever seen that kind of a knot before?"

"Can't tell from here. It looks weird, though."

"Better get a detective and the coroner."

The driver reached in and grabbed the hand receiver of his radio.

"This is Car 5 calling Central. Are you reading me? Over."

"Yes, sir," answered Malcolm, now full of adrenalin and perched on the edge of his swivel chair. "What's the situation out there? Over."

"This guy's a goner. We need a detective and the coroner

PDQ. The sun's not out yet, but if the fog lifts and it comes out today, he's gonna get pretty ripe. Don't remember seeing any clouds around the eastern hills, so you can bet on it. Over."

"Roger. I'll get right on it." Malcolm clicked off the microphone, reached for the telephone and dialed the detective bureau.

"Detective Bernardi speaking," answered a fresh-sounding voice. "What can I do for you?"

"Lieutenant, we have a 187 at the chemical dump down at Point Molate. Car 5 just called for a detective PDQ."

"Can you give me a rundown?"

Bernardi listened intently as Officer Malcolm told him a dead man was hanging from the arch at the gate. He put down the phone and stood up, taking another bite out of his glazed doughnut and a swig from his cup of hot coffee. He licked the crumbs off his lips, adjusted his pistol in its shoulder holster and checked to make sure he had his handcuffs. Then he sat down again and dialed the crime lab.

"This is Mac," the man at the lab answered.

"Mac, this is Bruno. I've got a 187, and I need a tech. Are you available?"

"I will be in about ten minutes. I've got to finish the report on the one you gave me last week."

"Okay," said Bernardi. "I'll wait for you."

He clicked off the receiver, waited for the dial tone, and called the dispatcher back. "Get me the officer in charge at the crime scene."

"Yes, sir," answered Officer Malcolm. "Car 5, this is Dispatch."

The officer was standing by his squad car. The two other vehicles had arrived by then, and five of the officers had spread out to block access to the dump gate. The dawn sky was brightening and workers were already arriving for the morning shift. As a crowd gathered outside the gate, they began shoving to get a better look at the body swinging in the morning breeze. The policemen pushed them back, away from the scene.

"Yes, sir, this is Car 5. Over."

"Hold on. Detective Bernardi wants to talk to you."

Malcolm patched the detective in. "Go ahead, sir. Car 5 is on the line."

"This is Lieutenant Bernardi. What have you got out there? Over."

As the policeman described what he saw, including the small crowd-control problem that was developing, Bernardi took notes.

"Don't let anyone contaminate the scene," he told the officer. "Stop 'em from coming in or going out. Get the name of everyone who shows up and spread 'em out. We'll be there in ten minutes. Over."

"Yes, sir," responded the officer. "Out."

Bernardi then dialed the coroner's office. "This is Lieutenant Bernardi at Homicide in Richmond. We need a meat wagon at the chemical dump at Point Molate. We're working on a 187. I'll meet the coroner there in half an hour."

There were now six officers at the scene and several more workers had just arrived, all of them Mexican. The officers were taking their names and addresses and then separating them so Detective Bernardi could question them individually when he arrived.

The driver of Car 5 moved his spotlight to the ground beneath the body to see if he could identify any footprints around the area, but he saw none. There was no blood on the ground either, even though the dead man's pant leg was drenched in it.

The other officers weren't having much luck with the Mexican workers, so the driver called Malcolm. "Have the detective bring a Spanish-speaking interpreter. Only one of these workmen speaks English. Over."

"Thanks for the tip," said Malcolm. "Out."

He picked up the phone and called Bernardi again. "Better get Sergeant Jimenez out there. We need someone who can speak to the Mexicans."

"Shit," said Bernardi. "Can you call him at home? He doesn't usually get here until after eleven. He spends the mornings at the county jail in Martinez."

"Yes, sir," replied Malcolm, who then contacted Sergeant Jimenez and told him to report directly to Point Molate.

* * *

Lieutenant Bernardi pulled his dull-brown suit jacket over his white shirt, which had a plastic insert in the pocket for his ballpoint pens. He adjusted the gun holster on his stocky, five-foot-eight frame, which still weighed the same one hundred and seventy pounds it did in high school. Then he walked out the door with his technician.

When the two men arrived at the gate, the sun was creeping over the top of the East Bay hills. The spotlights from the three squad cars illuminated the crime scene, which included two officers corralling five Mexican men off to one side of the gate. Four large dump trucks filled with sludge were lined up behind the squad cars, the drivers inside and their headlights on. The arc of lights from the many vehicles made the place look like a carnival, complete with an effigy of a barker in an expensive gray suit hanging from the entrance arch—its face pale, tongue protruding and eyes bulging from their sockets. The corpse had a full head of black wavy hair, a few strands of which dangled onto its forehead. Two Coke bottles poked from its jacket pockets, and blood drenched the front of one of the pant legs.

Bernardi approached Car 5.

"Put your spot on him, Officer," he said. "And hand me

your radio."

The policeman reached in, grabbed the receiver and stretched the coiled cord out the window. Bernardi took it and depressed the talk button.

"Dispatch, this is Bernardi. Call the fire department to send some kind of a lift with a long arm so we can cut this guy down without disturbing the ground underneath him. Over."

"Yes, sir," replied Officer Malcolm. "Out."

Bernardi turned to his tech.

"Get me photographs from every angle. I also want prints off everything in sight, including those Coke bottles and that rake that's leaning against the gatepost. This looks like a murder, all right. And it looks ritualistic—almost like it was part of a ceremony of some kind."

Mac nodded and began taking flash photos, popping the spent bulbs into a pocket of the apron he wore around his waist.

As the scene lightened, it became apparent that the ground beneath the victim had been smoothed over. There were both parallel and perpendicular rake lines in the dirt, as if someone had been attending to a baseball diamond.

Bernardi made fast work of the truck drivers who were lined up waiting for the dump to open. He took their names and addresses and asked if they had seen anything. Since they claimed they hadn't, he sent them home. He wanted to talk to the man who had originally discovered the body, but nobody knew who had made the call.

Bernardi then turned to the Mexicans, who were short and had skin tones in various shades of brown. They wore faded overalls, work boots and an assortment of straw hats.

"What is your name?" he asked the one who spoke English.

"Mauricio Chavez, *señor*."

"What are you doing here so early in the morning?"

"I work here, *señor.* I am the foreman."

"How long have you worked at this place?"

"Two years. *Sí*, two years. But I only been foreman for six months."

"Who made you foreman?"

"The boss, Mr. Hagopian, the guy who is hanging there."

"Did you have any problems with the boss?"

"No, *señor*. He was good to me. He even made me foreman when Juan Ramos left."

Bernardi noticed that the small man never looked him in the eye, and that bothered him. He didn't know what to make of wetbacks. They came into the country illegally by crossing the river. He knew they worked hard, but because they stuck to themselves, they were a mystery.

"Who's Juan Ramos?"

"He was the foreman, but he left with three other men."

"What are the names of the other men who left?"

"Miguel Ramos, Jose Ramos and Narcio Padia."

"Are Miguel and Jose related?"

"*Sí, señor*, they are, how you say, *primos*."

"You mean cousins?"

"*Sí*, cousins."

"Are they any relation to Juan, the foreman?"

"*Sí, señor*, he is their uncle."

"You say they left. Where are they now? Do you know?"

"I think Jose went back home. I not sure."

"What about the other three?"

"They all took jobs at another company in Emeryville."

"What's the name of the company?"

"I don't know, *señor*. They mix chemicals is all I know."

"Are all you guys from the same city in Mexico?"

"We all from San Juan de los Lagos.

"Where the heck is that?"

"It is outside of Guadalajara, in Jalsco."

"Are any of you guys legal?"

"*Sí, señor,*" stammered the worker. He shrugged and looked down at his steel-toed brown work boots, which were caked with a chemical residue. "But I can only speak for myself."

Another squad car arrived, its lights flashing. A neat-looking Mexican police officer with sergeant stripes on his sleeves turned off the lights and got out of the driver's seat. He was of medium height and build, with black hair and a neatly trimmed mustache. He approached Bernardi and the group of men. Bernardi shook his hand and motioned for him to take over the interrogation of the workers in Spanish.

After talking with them for about fifteen minutes, Sergeant Jimenez approached Detective Bernardi. "There is something that's come up that you should know about," he said.

"Okay, let's hear it."

"None of these guys except the foreman have been here very long, but they all tell me the same story. There's a lot of anger in the Mexican community against the owner of this dump. Some former workers sued the guy hanging from the gate, claiming he "ruined" their children. They were born deformed. As soon as they sued, they were fired."

"Yeah, I learned that from Mauricio," said Bernardi. "I want to know where I can find the guys who were fired. Will you follow that up for me?"

* * *

Bernardi climbed up on a rock overlooking the entrance to the dump. He scratched his salt-and-pepper brown hair, which was short-cropped and parted off to one side, and rubbed his noticeably flattened nose. There was a strange odor in the air.

The sun had risen, but it didn't provide any of the anticipated warmth to the cold December day. The waters of the bay splashed gently against the sand just below the rock. As he sat on his perch, Bernardi tried to make sense of what he had before him: the carnival-like atmosphere of a dead man hanging from an arch over a gate, a line of dump trucks full of chemical sludge, a group of workers who didn't speak English, and a foul smell that was getting worse as the sun came up. He also noticed the complete absence of bird life along the shore.

The coroner arrived with the meat wagon, followed by the fire department, which showed up with a crane that contained a platform surrounded by railing.

Bernardi descended from his rock perch and approached the coroner.

"We need to get him down from there, but first we have to gather the evidence. You go up there with Mac so we can detail everything with photos."

The two of them got on the platform as directed by Bernardi, and the firemen elevated them so they could examine and retrieve the body. Mac took close-up flash photos of the decedent's face and neck and of the unusual knot that was tied around his neck. They examined and photographed the clothes he was wearing, in detail, focusing in particular on the bloody pant leg.

"You see that crushed blue insect on his pant leg?" asked Mac. "It looks like a beetle of some kind."

"Yeah, I do," answered Bernardi from below. "We need to save that. It may be important,"

Rifling through the pouch pocket where he kept all sorts of things, including spent flash bulbs, Mac pulled out an envelope and removed the bug with a pair of tweezers. He wrote "blue insect" on the envelope, noting where on the body he had found it. Then he put the envelope in his evidence pouch.

Mac motioned to the firemen to lower the platform and he and the coroner watched as it slowly came down beside the body and then moved directly underneath it. Once the platform was in position, he indicated that it should again be elevated. When the victim's feet touched the bottom of the platform, Mac called out to the firemen to stop. The two men could now walk freely around the body.

"See anything like mud on his shoes?" asked Bernardi.

"Yeah, there's a little."

After photographing the shoes, Mac searched for another envelope and scraped some of the mud into it. He wrote "mud" on the outside and deposited it in the pouch next to the envelope containing the insect.

"Now we have to remove those Coke bottles," said Mac. "But we have to be careful to preserve any fingerprints, as well as the contents."

Mac demonstrated his skill by reaching with gloved hands deep inside the two suit jacket pockets and gently lifting the open bottles out.

"This stuff stinks. It must be a chemical of some kind. But each bottle has something different in it. You can tell by the smell."

"Be careful," said the coroner. "You see those bulges inside the suit? It looks like there is something in there, too."

Mac unbuttoned the suit jacket. When he opened the left side he found another Coke bottle with still another liquid inside. He also noted the tailor's label stitched to the inside pocket. It read "La Roche et Fils, Paris." After taking photos, Mac skillfully dusted each bottle for fingerprints and then removed them, putting stoppers in the tops to ensure that none of the liquid spilled. He then placed the bottles in the evidence box so he could have them analyzed by the toxicologist.

"We've done everything we can up here, Chief," said Mac. "Can we take him down now?"

"Yeah," said Bernardi. "But first get some pictures of that raked ground underneath. See if you observe anything unusual from the platform that might help us figure out how they got him up there."

Mac gave instructions to the fire crew and the platform was lowered to within a couple of feet of the ground. He studied the terrain carefully and photographed it.

"Take a look at the edge of the raked area," he called over to Bernardi. "There's a suggestion of a footprint. When I come down, I'll put some plaster of Paris on it so we can make a mold. I've already got photos."

"I'll wait for you and we'll look at it together," said Bernardi.

"Okay," said Mac. "Move the platform back up underneath the body."

The fireman complied. When the platform was in place, the coroner cut the rope above the knot and he and Mac slowly laid the body down on the deck of the platform.

"It's stiffening," said the coroner. "It's the beginning stages of rigor mortis. This will help us determine the time of death." He busied himself taking notes while the body was lowered to within a few feet of the ground and the crane moved slowly away from the gate area. When it was near the coroner's vehicle, his crew put the corpse in a body bag and transported it by gurney to a white panel truck.

"We need to analyze what's in those bottles," Mac told the coroner. "Do you think any of this stuff contributed to his death?"

"I can't tell you that until we do the toxicology studies on the corpse. If he was poisoned, it'll show up. But you'll have to tell me what's in the bottles."

"Sure thing, as soon as I know. When can you give us a time of death and a cause?"

"I can give you the approximate time of death this afternoon," answered the coroner. "The rest of the studies are going to take longer, maybe as much as a month. I'm not sure what to make of that insect you found on his pant leg right now.

Maybe nothing. But you analyze the chemicals, and we'll try and figure out if hanging is what really killed him."

"You mean he may have already been dead when he was put here?"

"Anything's possible, Mac. We just like to cover all the bases."

"Can you tell what kind of a knot that is around his neck? My boss says he's never seen one like it before."

"Okay, I'll put my assistant on that one," said the coroner. "He's an old rodeo rider."

The coroner climbed into his truck on the passenger side and motioned to the driver to leave.

Bernardi, who had been watching intently near the gate, moved closer to Mac.

"Let's get a mold of that footprint," he said, pointing to the edge of the raked area.

Mac took a jug of water and a bag of white powder out of his utility bag and mixed the plaster of Paris in a paint pan until it was a thick, gooey consistency. Then he poured the material onto the ground. While he was waiting for it to dry, he took fingerprints from the rake.

"They got his body up there the same way we got it down," said Bernardi. "For some reason, it seems too neat, too contrived to me. It was obviously a well-planned assassination."

"I pulled pretty clean prints off the rake and the Coke bottles," said Mac. "You would have thought that whoever did this would have wiped them clean. Especially when you see how meticulously everything else was done."

"Not necessarily," said Bernardi. "If they were really pissed, it could be they didn't care who knew it was them. Of course, why did they rake the ground then?"

"You say *them*," said Mac.

"Yeah, one man, or even two, couldn't have pulled this off. There had to be a team. I don't have any answers right now, but

I'll bet my boots on that."

"Do you think it could've happened in the heat of passion?"

"No way," said Bernardi. "Unless you define passion in the broader sense—long, simmering anger for something that he or his company caused. I would say this was a cold-blooded, calculated execution. So the question is, who did it and why?"

"There's an attorney in San Francisco named Janak Marachak who represents the employees of the dump in a lawsuit," said Mac. "It was in the paper a couple of weeks ago. Do you remember that?"

"The lawsuit came up a couple of times already this morning," said Bernardi. "I guess I wasn't paying attention. But now that you mention it, I do remember they were talking about it at the Rotary meeting the other day."

"The employees claimed that their kids were born with birth defects," said Mac. "Their attorney, Janak Marachak, inquired at our office if we had any environmental complaints against the dump. I actually talked to him. I told him to go to the State Health Department. He subpoenaed their entire file on the dump."

"Maybe we should do the same...and maybe we should talk to Marachak ourselves," said Bernardi. "By the way, don't you think it's weird that there's no bird life on the shoreline down there?"

"You're right," said Mac. "I hadn't noticed."

* * *

The early-morning radio traffic between the police dispatcher and the patrol cars was picked up on a police scanner by one of Samuel Hamilton's bird dogs, who then relayed the information to him via telephone. Thanks to this sort of monitoring, the reporter had published several scoops for his paper.

King of the Bottom

It was still dark outside, and the call startled him as he struggled to wake up in his small Powell Street flat. His one-room apartment, located on the edge of Chinatown in the heart of San Francisco, had a fold-up sofa bed, which occupied most of the space when it was open. The underwear and socks that he'd washed the night before were drying on a thin wire he'd strung between two walls, and a pair of greasy cardboard cartons sat on the table in the miniscule kitchen, filling the air with the smell of stale Chinese food.

Samuel was aware that he didn't live in a palace, but since he didn't have the slightest hope that Blanche would ever honor him with a visit, he had no incentive to clean it. He often wondered what Blanche's apartment looked like. He imagined it to be as impeccably clean and bright as she was, but he figured he had no chance of ever seeing it from the inside.

It was only a few months since Samuel, who was short and whose receding red hair hinted at his Scottish-German heritage, had started his job as a reporter at the morning paper. He'd won the job by breaking a big story about murder in Chinatown, which was published in a series of daily articles. Before that, his job had been selling advertisements for the same paper.

The first thing Samuel did was reach for a cigarette, but then he remembered that he'd given up the habit several months before with the help of a Chinese sage who'd hypnotized him. Or, at least, he'd tried to quit. Samuel still cheated when he was feeling desperate.

As soon as he'd gathered his wits—he wasn't used to getting up so early—Samuel dialed Marcel Fabreceaux, his photographer, who accompanied him on his assignments for the newspaper and who, fortunately, had a car. They agreed to meet in forty-five minutes at a Chinese restaurant near Samuel's flat.

Samuel quickly showered, shaved and dressed in his usual

attire: a cheap khaki sport coat and pants, a white button-down shirt and brown penny loafers. The only difference in his attire from when he was an ad salesman was that now he had fewer cigarette-burn holes in the sleeves of his coat and his clothes were a little less wrinkled.

He'd asked Marcel to get details on where they were going and what they could expect. Samuel knew Marcel would have plenty of time to fill him in on the details, since they would have to cross both the Golden Gate and Richmond-San Rafael bridges, a route that would take them through part of Marin County.

When they arrived at Point Molate in Marc's green '47 Ford coupe, the sun had risen over the East Bay hills and now cast plenty of light on the scene at the gate. Samuel's alert blue eyes took in the surroundings. He arrived just in time to overhear the conversation between Bernardi and Mac about the lawyer and his Mexican clients and made a mental note of it, since Janak Marachak was a friend of his. He flashed his press card and called out to Bernardi.

"I hear there was a hanging. Can you give me some background?"

Bernardi and Mac walked over to the area where Mac had placed all the evidence he'd gathered in a cardboard box.

"Can't say too much right now," answered Bernardi. "All we know is that it looks like someone took care of Armand Hagopian, the owner of this chemical dump."

"I see we're too late for pictures," said Samuel. "Will you make available the ones your men took?"

"I think not," said Bernardi. "You guys in the press always want the sensational. And photos of a man hanging from the gate here are certainly sensational, and if they were out in the public, they might jeopardize our investigation. But I'll let you stick around, if you don't get in the way. That means be an observer and don't butt in. Later, I'll brief you on what we think is appropriate for the public to know. You understand—we're trying to find out who killed this prominent citizen."

"Can you give me some background on him?" asked Samuel. He noted the remnants of the rope hanging from the arch of the gate and the carefully raked ground underneath, making sure his photographer got pictures of both. He also observed the same barren shore Mac and Bernardi had commented on.

"He was a big shot in Richmond, the owner of this chemical dump," said Bernardi. "Most major industrial companies in Contra Costa County use his facility."

"That's all you know right now?"

"Yep, I'm afraid so."

"Can you give me anything on motive?"

"It would all be speculation," Bernardi said, not wishing to discuss what he had learned about the Mexican workers' lawsuit. "It could be anything. Robbery? Maybe jealousy, maybe even a business deal gone sour? Who knows?"

Samuel watched Mac organizing four bottles in a paper box and craned his neck to see if he could recognize anything else. He saw a piece of rope and several white letter-sized envelopes, but he couldn't read what was on them.

"What do the bottles have to do with all this?" Samuel asked.

"Don't know yet," said Bernardi. "I can tell you they were found on the decedent, and that they're filled with some pretty vile-smelling stuff. But we'll have to get them to the crime lab before we know what we're dealing with."

"You looked for prints, though, or they wouldn't have all that powder all over them. Did you have any luck?"

"Depends on whose prints show up." Bernardi's tone sharpened. "Look, I'd like to spend more time with you, but this is a police investigation and I've got work to do."

Samuel shrugged. "Can't blame me for trying to get information. We're the cops' best friends, so don't be stingy, Detective."

Bernardi didn't answer. Samuel watched as four policemen under Bernardi's supervision carefully walked the gate area with flashlights in hand, even though the sun was now high. Mac took flash photos of them as they worked.

Samuel tried again. "When can we get an update from the coroner's office?"

"Nothing for a couple of weeks. You can call me this afternoon and I'll fill you in so you can meet your deadline."

"Can we come with you to the dump's office or whatever is up that road?"

"Not a chance."

Samuel had gotten as much as there was to get, so he went to talk to one of the officers he knew. The officer gave him a description of the body and how it was cut down from the gate. Samuel and his photographer left just as a number of other reporters began to show up.

* * *

Bernardi stationed two squad cars at the gate with instructions not to let anyone on the premises. He took two officers and Mac and headed toward a bend in the road where the actual dump was situated, a few hundred yards away. When they were half way to a pair of white trailers, he received a call on his walkie-talkie.

"We have some office employees here. Do ya wanna talk to 'em or should we send 'em home? Over."

"Send 'em up the road," said Bernardi. "Out."

Soon three women appeared in the distance. He called on his walkie-talkie. "Did someone tell these women what happened? Over."

"Yes, sir," a voice answered. "From the description I gave them, they were pretty upset. It seems that the victim is a relative of theirs. Over."

"Okay. Thanks for warning me. Out."

By now, Bernardi was feeling sick from the pungent odors. "What's causing all that smoke and that smell?" he asked.

"Piles of chemical debris on the other side of the office," said Mac. "They're decomposing or just *brewing*."

"The smell alone could kill ya, don't you think?"

"I wouldn't let my kids play here," said Mac.

Bernardi took a handkerchief out of his pocket, wiped his running nose and blotted the tears from his eyes. "This place feels like the Hiroshima bomb hit it," he mumbled.

They finally reached the office, which was comprised of the two white trailers. Bars covered the windows except where the air conditioners stuck out. In back was a steel tower that went up fifty feet in the air and had a radio antenna on top. To the side was a Coca-Cola machine with six boxes of empty bottles stacked next to it. Bernardi noticed that some of the bottles were missing.

Bernardi turned to Mac. "We need prints off that Coca-Cola machine and those empty bottles. Photograph them in place and get an officer up here to confiscate all those boxes and take them to the lab. Don't do anything to compromise the prints. Then look around and see if there's anything else out here that might interest us."

"Okay, Chief," said Mac.

The three women had walked quickly and were now in front of them, seemingly indifferent to the stink of their surroundings. The eldest, who was in her fifties, had a round face and coal-black hair. She was about five-foot-five inches tall, had a slender build and carried herself gracefully. She was dressed in a nondescript blue wool dress and a gray overcoat. Once at the office, she opened the double-locked door and let everybody in, then turned the air conditioners on, even though it was cold outside.

"Can I use your restroom?" Bernardi asked. He and Mac

had tears streaming down their faces and were coughing.

The slender woman pointed him toward the rear of the double trailer. Once inside the tidy space, he turned on the cold water and washed his hands with the bar of Borax soap next to the basin, then splashed his eyes and face several times. He saw in the mirror that his eyelids were red and swollen.

Suddenly, Mac burst through the door. "Jesus Christ, this is hard to take," he said, rushing for the basin to douse his burning face with cold water. "I can't believe that people actually work here. This place is hell."

"Yeah," said Bernardi, "We need to pull ourselves together, though. Otherwise, we might miss something."

"It's one thing to pull yourself together," said Mac. "It's another to do the job without proper protection." He began to cough and spit into the urinal.

"Did you notice that the employees seem to handle it without being bothered?" asked Bernardi, blowing his nose on toilet paper.

"That may be true, but there's a short haul and there's a long haul," said Mac. "And I'm only here for the short one, so I don't want to get used to it."

They walked down the narrow hallway to the main part of the office complex, where they found the three women talking softly. Two of them were crying. Mac couldn't stop coughing and had to escape while Bernardi tried to do his job. Looking at them, Bernardi deduced that all the women were probably Armenian, as was the decedent.

"You ladies can start your daily routines," said Bernardi. "I'd like to talk to each of you separately if you don't mind."

"This is terrible!" said the slender woman, who had a slight French accent. "Armand was related to all of us. Who would do something like this?"

"What's your name?"

"Candice Hagopian. I'm Armand's sister.

Bernardi nodded sympathetically. "I'm sorry for your loss, ma'am. I'll try and make this as painless as possible, but I need information." He motioned for her to follow him to a side office. "Can we talk in here?"

He closed the door behind them. "Did you know that we found your brother hanging from the front gate this morning?"

"Yes," she sobbed.

"Do you have any idea who might have wanted to hurt him?"

She went to one of the desk drawers, grabbed a box of tissues and blotted her tear-streaked face. "Armand didn't have any enemies," she said. "Everyone loved him. He did so much for the community, for his family and for Armenians. I can't understand this horrible crime. What will become of us without my brother? He took care of us!"

"We were told that several of the Mexican workmen were suing him. Is that correct?"

"Yes. Those people were so ungrateful. He did a lot for those men. He gave them jobs when no one else would have them. My brother believed that they were being manipulated by someone who was trying to make money."

"Do any of these men still work here?" asked Bernardi.

"They all quit or they would have been fired. After all, they couldn't be allowed to bite the hand that fed them."

"Can I get the names and addresses of those workers?"

"Yes, I'll have someone get that for you right away." She picked up the phone.

"Do you have their fingerprints on file by any chance?"

"Yes, that's part of our hiring process. We fingerprint all of our employees, and we check with the police to make sure they aren't in trouble."

"Well, that might be our first break in this case." Bernardi smiled. "Are the other office workers part of your family, too?"

"Yes, we're all related," said Candice.

"Is there one in particular you think would be more helpful to me than the others?"

"I am in charge of the office, so I know more than anyone." She answered in a shaky voice, straining to hold back more tears.

"Thanks for all your help, Miss Hagopian. I know this has been hard on you. I'll be back in touch."

Bernardi called Mac to the office and they went over the evidence they'd collected, piece by piece. Once Bernardi decided they had everything they needed for the time being, they said goodbye to the employees. Before stepping outside, they both took a deep breath in the air-conditioned trailer. Then, covering their mouths and noses, they rushed to the front gate as fast as they could.

2

Marachak and Deadeye

AFTER SIX, SAMUEL WENT to Camelot, his neighborhood bar, which was located on the lower edge of Nob Hill. With a front window that overlooked a park and had a view of the city and the bay beyond, the bar was a welcome home for the tired news hunter.

Samuel's life had changed dramatically since he got the job as a reporter on the morning paper, and he owed it all to people he had met at Camelot. Now he pondered the irony that, once again, there was a connection between the new story he was working on and his favorite watering hole.

He and Janak Marachak had met at Camelot several years earlier. Samuel had injured a young woman while driving drunk, and Janak had steered him to another young attorney, who ended up representing him. Samuel should have gone to jail, but because of the attorney's skill, he was only put on probation, though he did lose his license for three years. Since his narrow escape, he and Janak had struck up a friendship of sorts, but it never deepened into anything more, mostly because of lack of opportunity and the fact that the lawyer was a man of few words. He was actually sort of rough. But Samuel was grateful. Without Janak's help, he would have been incarcerated.

He saw Melba, the owner of the bar, sitting in her usual place at the round table—Samuel always thought of it as a Round Table— just inside the door, her pathetic dog, Excalibur, at her side. The dog, an Airedale with a missing ear and no tail, got up from his spot at her feet and greeted Samuel like a long lost friend. As always, Samuel put up with the mutt licking him and chewing on his shoelaces.

"Hello, ingrate," said Melba. "I haven't seen you for days."

"I came in yesterday, but you weren't here. Blanche told me that she's worried about you. She thinks you're sick."

"Don't pay any attention to her. I'm in great shape—"

Suddenly she began coughing, unable to continue.

Samuel thought she didn't look so good. Despite her well-lived fifty-plus years, Melba normally radiated vitality. The fact that she smoked and drank like a sailor, and that she only ate the hardboiled eggs and olives that were on the hors d'oeuvre table at the rear of the bar didn't seem to do her any harm. She always coughed, but now she had a wheeze in her chest and her nose sounded plugged, suggesting that her head was congested. In addition, her blue-tinted white hair, which she usually whipped up like meringue to give it volume, lay flat against her head.

Melba waited for her coughing to subside before taking a deep drag on her cigarette. Then, to refresh her itchy throat, she took a couple sips of beer. Just as she finished, however, she had another coughing attack.

"Jesus, Melba," said Samuel, slapping her on the back. "What's wrong?"

"Nothing," she said, picking up a comb with her free hand, a rare gesture of vanity on her part. "I just have a touch of bronchitis, which I can't seem to kick,"

"You shouldn't be smoking then, should you?"

She laughed and coughed at the same time. "Look who's talking," she retorted.

"What do you mean?"

"You started smoking again, so why are you lecturing me?"

"How do you know that?"

"The burn holes in your sleeves are back, just like old times." Melba laughed.

Samuel turned red and put his hand over the crease in the left elbow of his sport jacket.

"Yeah, but just once in a while," he said. "I'm not back on the old habit again. Really."

"Sure, that's what they all say."

"It's just when I'm real nervous, like right now."

Samuel told her about the crime and what he'd learned thus far.

"What do you think about all this, Melba?"

"Too early to tell. What does the police report have to say?"

"I'm waiting for the attorney right now. We're supposed to go over it."

"What attorney?"

"The attorney who can give me information about the case. Maybe you know him? His name is Janak Marachak."

"I see him around here once in a while but Blanche usually waits on him. I've seen them talking. I think they're friends. What's he got to do with it?"

At the thought of Blanche and Janak talking in the dimness of the bar, Samuel began to itch all over and his temperature rose.

"What an idiot I am," he murmured under his breath, but Melba didn't hear. She was coughing again.

"Janak represents some workers who were suing the owner of the dump. The owner was the guy who was killed."

"What do you mean the owner of the dump?"

"A rich Armenian guy owned a chemical dump over at

Point Molate."

"Rich guy? Chemical dump? So he was king of the bottom."

"What do you mean?"

"I mean he got rich doing something that no one else wanted to do," she said. "And once he was rich, everyone wanted to do what he was doing, so the shit hit the fan."

"I like that phrase. Mind if I use it as a byline for the story on this guy?"

"About the shit?"

"No, king of the bottom."

"Be my guest, Samuel. You know I can't deny you anything." She laughed. "Except my daughter."

Samuel changed the subject.

"You haven't heard the worst of it. If this guy was the king, the police are interested in talking to his vassals. The suggestion is that they did him in."

"Sounds like a proletariat revolt against the ruling class."

"I'm afraid that's what the cops are saying," said Samuel.

"Well, make yourself comfortable and have a drink and a smoke." She pushed her pack of Lucky Strikes across the table toward Samuel.

"No thanks," he said, pushing the cigarettes away. "Don't tempt me, woman." Calling to the bartender over his shoulder, Samuel ordered his usual drink, a Scotch on the rocks.

That afternoon he'd called Janak's office, but the lawyer hadn't been in. He told Marisol Leiva, Janak's secretary, that the Richmond police were interested in talking to Janak's Mexican clients, the ones who were suing Hagopian. She promised she would have Janak get back to him as soon as he returned that day, but Samuel hadn't heard from him.

He took out his reporter's notebook and tapped his pencil on the drink-stained oak table. Then he ran a finger around several of the rings left behind by years of wet drink glasses. With the eraser end of the pencil in his mouth, Samuel watched the lights of the financial district twinkle in the distance. In his mind he formed an outline of what he needed to investigate. Lists helped him organize his ideas.

1. Find out about this guy Hagopian. Where to start?

2. How much hard evidence was there about who committed the crime?

3. Was it really an execution, as his article (which would appear the next day) would suggest?

4. Was there a bigger picture here? Prominent businessmen don't get bumped off without a good reason. Were the Mexican workers really a part of it?

5. Was there something romantic between Janak and Blanche?

While Samuel was lost in his thoughts, Janak walked into the bar. He caught Samuel's eye from a distance and waved.

"Wait, I'll be right back," he said, and ambled off toward the men's room in the back.

On his return, Janak picked up a drink at the bar. The mirror behind caught his reflection, showing a man who was tall and strong, with a rugged face, gray eyes, a severe expression and disheveled, chestnut-colored hair. The white scar on his cheek, earned in a fight during his university days that ended with him being cut with a broken bottle, contrasted with his skin, tanned brown from all the tennis matches he played to burn off excess energy.

Janak moved to the front of the bar, drink in hand, and muscled himself down at the Round Table with Samuel. He smoothed the sleeves of his wrinkled gray suit and loosened his red tie.

"Janak, this is Melba," said Samuel, introducing the two. "Melba is the owner."

Melba nodded and started to stand, ready to leave them alone, but Janak stopped her with a gesture.

"Glad to finally meet you, Melba," he said and he held out his hand. "I come here a lot and shoot the breeze with your daughter, so you're no stranger to me."

"Same here, Counselor. I've seen you around. Glad you feel at home." She got up.

"Come on, Excalibur. These boys have work to do, let's get out of their hair." And she went to the horseshoe bar to talk to the bartender, closely followed by the scraggly mutt , which never let her out of his sight.

"Marisol said you were trying to get ahold of me," said Janak, adjusting his chair so both had more space at the table. "I called your office, but you'd already left. They told me I could find you here."

"I'm glad you got my message. I guess you already know about this thing in Richmond?"

"Only what you told Marisol. I just got in from Los Angeles, so I haven't had time for anything."

"The big boy over there is history. They found him hanged this morning, right on the front gate of his dump."

"Shit," said Janak. "I didn't even get a chance to take his deposition. I sued him and his company for the mess they made out of their workers' lives."

"The detective told us all the workers who sued got fired. Will you make them available to me for interviews?"

"We can arrange something," said Janak, arching an eyebrow. "I'm not sure how much I want them to say in public, in light of what's just happened. Maybe it'd be better if I gave you some information on background—you know, off the record. That way, you'd never have to give up the source, and I can be more frank with you."

"That'll work," said Samuel.

Janak's mind had already shifted. If the Mexican workers were convicted of this crime, they could get the gas chamber.

"Did you get the feeling that the cops were trying to blame

my clients?"

"My impression was that they're the ones they're interested in right now. But, honestly, I couldn't find out what evidence, if any, they had that would implicate 'em, other than that they got fired for suing the owner."

"That, by itself, isn't enough to charge 'em with anything," said Janak. "I wish I could listen in at the Richmond Police Department. I'd like to know what they got on 'em."

"Bernardi—that's the detective in charge—said he'd let me know in a week or so."

"I need to figure out what to do before then," said Janak.

"What're you worried about?"

"Are you kidding? Do you know who we'll probably end up with in Contra Costa County?"

"Nope, you'd better educate me," said Samuel.

"None other than Deadeye Graves. He'd send his mother to the gas chamber just to get another conviction if he thought it would bring him political gain."

"I never heard of him," said Samuel. "Sounds like a bastard. What makes you so sure he'd be after your guys?"

"It's easy to figure out. Five Mexicans, or however many, and a dead businessman they just sued. I can see Deadeye licking his lips. He must be thinking this is his ticket to becoming the D.A. of Contra Costa County, or maybe even governor."

"That big an ego, huh?"

"That's only the beginning. But I'm not a criminal lawyer. I'm a specialist in chemical torts. That's the field I know."

"Who's going to represent them if they're implicated in this mess?" asked Samuel.

"That's a good question. I know for a fact that none of them have any money to hire a lawyer. So what do I do?"

"What do you want to do?"

"Right now, I'm going to protect them. When I see how this thing develops, I'll decide what to do."

"So, for now, you're the boss as far as this case goes," said Samuel. "I'll do my best to keep you posted."

"When are you going to talk to this guy?"

"You mean Detective Bernardi?"

Janak nodded.

"He said to give him a week."

"Do you think he's a straight shooter?"

"I like him," said Samuel. "I think he'll tell it like it is. But you know better than I. Doesn't the D.A. call the shots?"

"Yeah," said Janak. "Fortunately, Deadeye isn't the D.A., but I bet he'll do whatever he has to do to get the case."

"Maybe you should come with me to talk with Bernardi."

Janak laughed, looked down at his drink and squinted.

"You think the cop is going to open up when he knows I'm there to find out what he's got against my clients?"

"Yeah you're right. But it doesn't matter, I'll be your inside dopester."

"Can we talk before you go to see Bernardi? That way I can give you a list of specifics, so we can see where he's coming from."

"Sure. We can cover that when we get together to discuss your clients."

"Speaking of them, I need to get back to the office and find out where these guys have been for the past few days."

Janak swallowed the last of his drink and put the empty glass on the table. He got up and left the bar, straightening his tie and buttoning his suit jacket as he walked.

It was now well past eight.

* * *

Once Janak had gone, Samuel went to the bar and confronted Melba. "I want you to come to Mr. Song's with me."

"You mean the Chinese albino?"

"Treat him with more respect, woman. He's a wise man. I'm sure he can do something about that tubercular cough you have, and maybe he can even help you to stop smoking."

She laughed. "You mean the way he helped you?"

"I'm serious, Melba. Will you go there with me?"

"Yeah, sure. You arrange it and I'll make the trip with you."

Samuel felt better. He had blind faith in Mr. Song and was sure he could help his old friend using hypnosis and his mysterious herbs. Samuel was ready to leave, but he vacillated a moment, not knowing how to ask the question that was on the tip of his tongue without sounding like an imbecile.

"Do you want another drink?" asked Melba.

"No, I've already had two."

"I suppose you want to know where Blanche is," said Melba, caressing her glass of beer. "She's not here and she won't be back tonight,"

"Hey, Melba," stuttered Samuel. "Janak and Blanche…I mean…"

Melba started to laugh and instantly began coughing. Samuel didn't wait for an answer. He left Camelot quickly and rushed back to his apartment. He went directly to bed, ready to forget all about Blanche; he knew he couldn't compete with Janak. It wasn't as if the lawyer were an Adonis, but some women liked rough men, and Blanche could be one of them. Shit. But the next day he would get Melba an appointment with the albino. He wondered if Mr. Song had herbs in his exotic shop that would induce love? Maybe he could give them to Blanche…Samuel added that item to his list, determined to find out.

* * *

After leaving Camelot, Janak went to his tenth-floor office at 625 Market Street, across from the Palace Hotel. He pushed his way through the small, cramped waiting room full of sec-ondhand furnishings, past the two secretarial desks, and into his messy office, which had files spread over every piece of furniture in the room. There was a raincoat and an umbrella on the floor, and a fichus tree without leaves withering in its pot next to the window. Janak flicked on the wall switch, which only accentuated the chaos. He then turned on the desk lamp so he could focus on the file on top of his desk. First, how-ever, he looked around, amazed at how busy he'd become—and how messy—since he opened the doors of his California practice a few years earlier.

While Janak organized what little information he had on the crime—most of which came from newspaper articles—he thought back to his origins in Cleveland, Ohio, and to his Czech father, who worked in the steel mills after escaping the horrors of the First World War in Europe. He also thought of his mother, who'd been his father's piano teacher. He knew he had the rugged look of his husky father; he hoped he'd also captured the quick intellect of his mother.

He'd started to get to work on a Ph.D. in chemistry at Kent State University in Ohio, but stopped midway through and instead went to law school. After graduation, he decided to specialize in chemical torts because he already knew so much about the subject.

Janak grabbed the phone and called Juan Ramos.

"*Hola, Juan,*" he said in pidgin Spanish. "*Como está?*"

"*Muy bien, señor Licenciado.* I got a new job. It's not so smelly like the dump."

"You heard about what happened over there, eh?"

"*Que pasó?*"

"The boss man Hagopian was found hanging this morn-ing. They killed him."

"*Santa María. Que Dios lo tenga en su Santo Seno.* Who would do a thing like that?"

"That's what the police want to know. They will be coming to ask you a lot of questions, Juan. When they come, you tell them you're saying nothing until your lawyer's with you. You understand?"

"*Sí, sí,*" answered the man, frightened.

"Where are Miguel and Jose?"

"They went back to Mexico last night."

"No kidding? What time did they leave?"

"I took them to the airport in San Francisco. There was a Mexicana flight that left at midnight. We got there about eleven."

"What time did you leave Oakland?"

"Around ten, I think."

"Why'd they go now?"

"You know, *Licenciado*, they wasn't working and Miguel's got those crippled kids. He figured he should be home helping his wife with them. Jose went to keep him company. It's like those two is always together."

"I wish they'd gone a week ago," said Janak.

"What you mean, *Licenciado*?"

"It just doesn't look right that they left town right when this happened."

"You don't think they had nothing to do with that guy hanging?"

"No, I sure don't," said Janak. "But I'm not the one who counts." "What about Narcio Padia?"

"He works with me at the new job in Emeryville."

"You saw him there today?"

"Today? No, he didn't show up for work. But he was there all day yesterday."

"Do you know why he didn't show up?"

"I ain't got no idea, *Licenciado*. That has to do with his personal life, you know."

"What time do you guys get off?"

"Five o'clock, every workday."

"Was he there until five?"

"Oh, yeah, *Licenciado*. We walked out together."

"Did you hang out with him after work?"

"No, no."

"Do you know where Narcio lives?"

"Somewhere in Richmond."

"Shit, that's not good," said Janak. "I wish it was farther away. Have you talked to him since then?"

"No, *Licenciado*. Haven't seen him since five o'clock yesterday."

"Okay, Juan, *muchas gracias*. Remember, don't talk to anyone without me being there. Do you have a way to get ahold of Miguel or Jose?"

"No telephone at Miguel's house in Mexico. I can write him and tell him to call you, but the mail is slow over there."

"Thanks, Juan."

Janak hung up. His thoughts raced as he made some quick notes. He rubbed the scar on his cheek, something he always did when he was nervous. He wondered if the cops would claim that Miguel and Jose or even Narcio and Juan would have had enough time to perpetrate the hanging between five and ten o'clock and still get to the airport in time to catch the flight to Mexico.

He called Juan back.

"Juan, this is Janak again. Were Miguel and Jose with you all evening before you took them to the airport?"

"Yeah, *Licenciado*. You know they live here. They were both home with my family when I got here. We had dinner like we do every night, and then we watched TV until it was time to go."

"Do you remember what you watched?"

"Yeah, it was that show about the detective guy. What's his name?"

"You mean *Perry Mason?*"

"Yeah, yeah, that's the one. I like that show. We watch it every week."

"What time does it come on?" asked Janak.

"Eight o'clock, every Thursday. It helps us learn English, *Licenciado.*"

"Your watching it also helps me, Juan. We'll talk some more."

Janak then called Narcio. His wife answered the phone and told him her husband was working the night shift at the Seafood Merchant, a restaurant in Point Richmond near their house. She said he started at six-thirty and wouldn't finish until after midnight.

"Juan Ramos told me that Narcio missed work today at the place in Emeryville."

"Yes, we took our youngest child to the doctor at the University Hospital in San Francisco."

"That has to do with the problems I'm representing you for, right?"

"It's for the deformed leg he was born with, *Licenciado.* You gave us the name of this doctor."

"Yeah, I know about that. How is your child doing?"

"It's hard on him, *Licenciado,* and it's hard on us."

While Janak listened, he unbuttoned his suit jacket and wriggled out of it, leaving it lying haphazardly over one arm of his secondhand red leather chair.

"Did he come straight home every night this week after finishing up his work at the restaurant?"

"What kind of a question is that, *Licenciado?* Of course, he came home. He's a married man with responsibilities. And, you know, Narcio ends up very tired. Imagine working day and night."

"Okay, *señora.* Can you have him call me tomorrow? And by the way, if the cops call, don't tell them anything except that you have a lawyer and give them my number."

Janak gave her his phone number and hung up. He took off his tie and rubbed his hands, staring out the window at the reflection the neon sign from the nearby branch of the Bank of America made on the empty winter street below. He knew he was in for a fight; he just didn't know how much of one, and he needed to anticipate as many obstacles as he could before it started.

Janak scribbled the name "Hagopian" in pencil over and over again on a yellow legal pad. There was a dull ache in his head and he was tired. He rubbed the scar on his cheek and wondered where Marisol kept the aspirin.

After a while, Janak called the reporter.

Samuel was asleep. He'd gone to bed after eating a reheated carton of Chinese food from the day before. The telephone woke him from a bad dream with a jolt, and Janak's voice brought him back to reality.

Janak quickly told him what he'd found out about the Mexicans' whereabouts.

"If all these stories pan out, are your clients protected?" asked Samuel.

"Depends on what the evidence is," said Janak. "Do you know when Mr. Hagopian died?"

"Not yet, but I'll find out as soon as I can," said Samuel.

"The reason I'm calling you is because of Hagopian. Do you know anything about this guy? There has to be a reason for his death. He had to be mixed up in something."

"I asked myself the same question. Tell you what I'll do. I'll make him the subject of my inquiries over the next few days. Are you available to follow up on anything I find out?"

"You bet, Samuel. I'll make it my business."

* * *

King of the Bottom

Contra Costa County comprises an out-of-the-ordinary combination of bucolic rolling hills and extensive San Francisco Bay frontage. It stretches all the way from Richmond in the west to the Carquinez Straits and beyond to the east. The city of Martinez, located on the Straits, is the county seat and was an important port in the nineteenth century. Two-mast sailing ships able to navigate the Sacramento River, which empties into the San Francisco Bay, would stop overnight, and the bigger ones, which couldn't go much further, came for dry-docking and repair. Many of the city's buildings, with the notable exception of the courthouse, were from that era, and more than a few had seen better days; some were even falling apart.

In the sixties, the seamen coming off the big ships from the ocean-going trade collided in the evenings with the blue-collar workforce that poured out of the oil refineries and the sugar plants dotting the landscape along the water's edge. They were a hard-drinking, hell-raising bunch of mavericks, and many were inclined to imitate the bandits they saw portrayed in old Westerns. No question about it, the place needed order, and Martinez officials took a tough stand on enforcing the law whenever they caught a wrongdoer. More often than not, however, the only one caught paid the price for the two or three that got away.

It was a perfect setting for Deadeye.

Earl J. Graves was born in South Dakota, but he considered himself a Californian because his parents came to California in the thirties when he was ten. It was the middle of the depression and times were lean. The family settled in the lower Central Valley, near Bakersfield, where Earl finished school. He then enrolled in Fresno State College and got a degree in education. But teaching didn't suit Graves, so he enlisted in the Navy, just in time for the Korean War. Afterward, he made use of the G. I. Bill to attend law school at the University of San Francisco. Upon passing the bar, he took a job as an deputy district attorney with Contra Costa County.

Graves liked the county's rural atmosphere; it reminded him of his home around the Bakersfield oil fields. It was wild and woolly—full of bums waiting to be picked on by someone with apparent authority.

Deadeye was tall, with prematurely gray, wavy hair and eyes the color of steel. He got his nickname following an accident as a child when, one evening at dusk, he ran full speed into a thin wire stretched at eye level between two posts. The nerve in his left eyelid was damaged, leaving it permanently half-closed.

He showed his great admiration for the American West by always wearing a black suit with matching black cowboy boots, each of which had a sharp-pointed silver plate on the toe. His attire included a bolo tie, which was held in place with a Navajo-design centerpiece featuring a hunk of turquoise. He would have worn his gray Stetson on a daily basis, but even *he* knew that would have been overkill, so it only went on when he was up to something.

The district attorney's office was lodged in the new courthouse, which was built in 1932. It was a low-slung building and looked like a poor imitation of a Greek ruin. Imposing pillars suggested there were attributes of justice to be discovered inside its walls, which wasn't always true.

It was just seven-thirty when Deadeye walked up the stairs to his second-floor office and plopped down at his desk with his coffee, pastry and morning paper. The more he read of Samuel's piece on Hagopian's death, the more excited he became. He forced down the rest of his pastry, wiped his lips with the back of his hand, and washed down whatever was still stuck in his throat with the rest of the hot coffee. He then headed down the hall and burst into the office of the District Attorney.

"Sir, I just read about this terrible crime in the morning newspaper and I'd like to talk to you about me handling it."

Surprised by the interruption, the D.A. put down the budget report he was studying and looked over the rims of his glasses at the nervous man standing before him.

"What are you talking about, Graves?"

Deadeye regained his composure.

"The hanging of our Mr. Hagopian," he said in the slight Texas drawl he had polished over the years. "You remember him. He's the gentleman we could count on every Christmas to pony up the shortfall for our Children's Toy Drive. Lovely man. Lovely family. A real tragedy."

"Hanging, you say? When did this happen?"

"Looks like the night before last. Let me read you a few lines from the morning paper." He proceeded to read some of the juicier snippets that Samuel had included in his article.

"My goodness, that's a terrible shame. Isn't Richmond P.D. in charge of the case?"

"Yes, sir, Lieutenant Bernardi," said Deadeye, looking out the window so his boss wouldn't pick up on his eagerness. "One of the best."

"You're right about that," said the D.A., now totally engaged. "One of the best! But why are *you* telling me all this now?"

"Because I'd like to handle the case, sir," Deadeye said, turning his head from the window and giving the old man his *I can whup any cowpoke* pose.

"This sounds like capital murder, Mr. Graves. We need to contact the Richmond Police and get some more details before I decide who's going to handle it. You know it's a Richmond case. I'll reward your interest by allowing you to be in charge preliminarily, but clear it with the deputy district attorney over there."

The D.A. sat back in his chair and took off his glasses, putting them on the ink blotter in front of him. "Do you think you have enough trial experience to prosecute a case of this magnitude?"

"You bet! I appreciate your confidence in me, boss. I'll show you that I'm up to this one."

"Very well, then. Get what you can from Richmond and report back to me. Let's say tomorrow, and we'll decide what has to be done."

"Yes, sir," said Graves.

"And leave me your paper," instructed the D.A.

Graves backed out of the office and swaggered down the hall to his own small office. He entered whistling "The Streets of Laredo" and looked over the paintings on his walls, smiling when he saw the one depicting a cowboy on horseback chasing a group of young Indians riding bareback. The cowboy was aiming a Winchester rifle at them. Deadeye cocked his finger and squinted his drooping eye, pointing his extended digit at the painted Indians.

"Pa-choo," he said in a low voice.

* * *

Deadeye moved the Louis L'Amour pulp fiction cowboy book he was reading in his spare time to the side of his desk, dialed the Richmond Police Department and asked for Lieutenant Bernardi.

"This is Earl J. Graves from the D.A.'s office," he said in his soft, unhurried accent. "The old man asked me to inquire about this Hagopian murder case."

"Yes, sir, Mr. Graves," said Bernardi, who happened to have the file open on his desk. "What does he want to know? I was just looking over what we have so far. But isn't this a Richmond case?"

"Sure is," Deadeye said smoothly. "But the old man asked me to give it a preliminary look."

"Okay by me," said Bernardi.

"Any evidence?" asked Graves.

"We have fingerprints from the Coke bottles that were found on the decedent's body."

"Coke bottles?"

"Yes, sir, there were four of them, all filled with chemicals."

"That's weird," said Deadeye. "What d'ya make of that?"

"Don't know yet. We're testing the chemicals. We think that might explain why they were in the bottles."

"Any match on the prints?"

"Looks like they belong to some former workers of the dump where the body was found."

"Isn't that enough to make an arrest?"

"That'll be up to you fellows," said Bernardi. "But I must tell you, I'm pretty skeptical of that evidence." He took out a pad of paper from the top drawer of his desk and, in strong, clear handwriting, scribbled the time and date, prepared to record the details of his conversation with Deputy D.A. Graves.

On the other end of the line, Deadeye was congratulating himself for his good luck in having both hard evidence and someone on whom he could pin the crime. He could hardly wait to get off the phone and get back to the old man.

But Bernardi wasn't through with him. He explained that the evidence seemed too pat. The fingerprints and chemicals in the bottles would probably point to the same persons who had filed a civil suit against the company. It seemed to him that the perpetrators of such a sophisticated crime wouldn't leave those kinds of clues.

"You think it's a setup by someone else?" asked Deadeye.

"That's exactly what I think, but I haven't decided where else to look yet."

"The old man wants to see the evidence and get your full

report. When can he have it?"

"Just as soon as I'm done," said Bernardi.

"By the way, do you know where these suspects are?"

"I wouldn't call them suspects. Let's say we have an eye on them. We have names and addresses. We'll take statements today, if we can find 'em."

"What do I tell the old man?" Deadeye was insistent.

"Tell him he'll have a full report in two days, minus the toxicology stuff. The autopsy showed the victim died of hanging. But that's verbal. We don't have a report yet."

"When did the man die?"

"Hard to say exactly. When the coroner did his tests, he figured the victim had been dead for several hours, but he couldn't be more precise."

"Where'd he die?"

"Right now, the guess is he died where they found him, but I'm skeptical of that, too," said Bernardi.

"Why?"

"I'll explain that later. Like I said, there's no report yet."

"If it's not in the report, don't bother," said Deadeye. "That means it's speculation."

"I wouldn't say speculation," said Bernardi, bothered by Graves' tone, "I just haven't ironed it out yet. Let's say I'm working on an educated guess."

"We'll be waiting for your report. Detective. Thanks for your time."

Deadeye got up, stretched his long frame and sat down again. Fingerprints. That's all I need, he thought happily. He put his big boots up on his desk and reached for his Louis L'Amour novel; opening to a dog-eared page, he began to read. He'd already decided to wait awhile before sharing what he'd learned with the D.A. The reports wouldn't be in their hands for a couple of days. Knowing the old man, if Deadeye showed too much interest in the case, he wouldn't get to handle it.

3

Samuel Goes to Bat for Janak

JANAK KNEW HE HAD to act fast to defend his clients, but first he needed to know who was being accused of what. He couldn't be the person out front on the investigation; once he was recognized, sources would dry up. He hoped he could rely on Samuel to get a broad view of what was out there. Having already called Juan earlier that morning to ask him to tell Miguel and Jose to stay in Mexico until further notice, he now called Samuel to explain his dilemma.

"I already told you I'd keep my eyes open for you and report back," said Samuel. "I'm on my way out the door this very minute to go across the bay to Hagopian's funeral. I'll have a photographer with me. I'll try and get some photos of the important players in this drama, and maybe some idea on where we go next. I'll see you tonight at Camelot. I should have lots to tell you."

"Right now I can't see how I can do this without you," said Janak. "Thanks for your help."

"Nothing to it," said Samuel. "See you later."

The truth was, Janak was broke. He was bringing in just enough to cover his overhead but some days he didn't know where his next dime was coming from. On more than one occasion, the loyal Marisol, who had become his right-hand "man," would loan him her own salary so he could finish out the month. Janak didn't charge by the hour because none of his clients—all marginals—would have been able to afford his services; instead, he worked on a percentage fee basis if he won the case. The contingency fee system was risky but it had the advantage in that it usually paid off when he least expected it. Luckily, the rent on his office was cheap, and Marisol maintained tight control of his expenses. But he was worried that he wouldn't be able to raise enough money to properly defend his new criminal clients. That required hard cash that none of those poor Mexicans had, so his decision to have Miguel and Jose stay in Mexico was easy.

Samuel had no idea of Janak's financial problems, but it wouldn't have made any difference to him. He was willing to help him because he admired him and had confidence in him—even though he couldn't avoid a pang of jealousy when he imagined him talking with Blanche in a corner of Camelot. What did they talk about when they were alone? Better not to think about it, he decided. He was curious about the crime, and it was turning into a damned interesting story for his newspaper. Since the murders that he'd reported on earlier in the year, which he named *The Chinese Jars* in the story he'd written, he hadn't had anything so sensational to write about.

* * *

Samuel and his photographer, Marcel Fabreceaux, arrived at the Armenian Orthodox Church in Oakland a half hour before the ten o'clock service. There was already a big crowd of people outside the church—hundreds, really. The men were dressed mostly in dark suits, and many of them had beards. The women, also dressed in dark clothing, wore hats; some also had veils covering their faces.

Samuel spent the first fifteen minutes examining the

crowd and pointing out specific individuals to the photographer, who then made sure he got the right shots. He saw Detective Bernardi—who was wearing the same dull-brown suit he had been wearing when Samuel first met him at the scene of the crime—talking with a tall man wearing a gray Stetson hat and cowboy boots. When Samuel approached the detective and said hello, Bernardi smiled slightly.

"Hello, Mr. Hamilton. Here to give the public more information?"

"Yes, sir. That's my job."

"This is Earl Graves from the District Attorney's office. He's handling the preliminary investigation of the crime."

Samuel extended his hand to the stranger. His smaller one disappeared into the other's long-fingered grasp. He looked at the man and concluded that he was smartly dressed, although Samuel wasn't generally one to judge style. Nonetheless, the hat and chunk of turquoise that held his bolo tie in place impressed him. Seeing the one drooping eyelid, he figured that this was the man Janak called Deadeye.

"How do you do, Mr. Hamilton? The name is Earl J. Graves. E-a-r-l J. G-r-a-v-e-s." He spelled out it slowly so the reporter would get his name right in the newspaper.

"Can I get a statement from you, Mr. Graves?" asked Samuel.

"Right now, I've nothin' to say," said Deadeye. "As soon as Lieutenant Bernardi gives us his reports, the District Attorney will hold a press conference. Here's my card. Call me tomorrow and I'll tell you when that'll be." He tipped his hat to the two men and strutted off to be noticed by other mourners who he felt were more important to his cause.

"That's gotta be Deadeye," said Samuel.

"Sure is," said Bernardi. " I see his reputation precedes him."

"Is he in charge of this case?"

"He says no, but I bet he ends up with it."

"I heard he was sniffing around for it."

"Who'd you hear that from?"

"Sources," said Samuel. "Sources…Was the decedent married?"

Bernardi nodded, knowing he wouldn't get any more information on Samuel's sources.

"See that group of women huddled together over there? The shorter one in the black dress and hat with the heavy veil is his wife. The taller one in the dark gray dress and the expensive-looking hat—her veil is less heavy than the wife's—is his sister, Candice. The rest are other family members."

Samuel pointed to the group of women, and the photographer began snapping away.

"Did Hagopian have any children?"

"Yes, two daughters, but they're away at school in France," said Bernardi. "There wasn't any way to get them here in time for the funeral."

"Have you talked with any of the family members who are here?"

"I had a long talk with the sister the day the body was found, and I'm scheduled to meet with the wife this afternoon."

"Can I go with you?" asked Samuel. "I need to know something about the family to include in the story I'm writing."

"You know I can't speak for them, Samuel, but I will say that what they tell me is going to be in the police report and that's a public record."

"Can I call you later and get some more background on all this family stuff?"

"Sure, I'll tell you what I find out. But as I said, it'll all be in the police report."

"I know that, Lieutenant. I just like to be a little ahead on these things. I've got deadlines to meet."

"Yeah, I understand," said Bernardi, his tone ironic. "The

public's right to know."

"What about that group over there—all those bearded guys in the dark suits?" Samuel pointed his finger, triggering another series of flashes from the photographer.

"Those are the elders. They represent the Bay Area Armenian community."

"There must be hundreds of people here. Are they all Armenian?"

"I'm not sure, but probably most of them are. They've come from all over—from Fresno, Los Angeles. I understand there's even a contingent from France."

"Why France?"

"'Cause that's where the family went after the genocide, according to what his sister Candice told me,"

"I see," said Samuel, stroking his chin, realizing that Bernardi was referring to the Ottoman Empire's systematic killing of more than one million Armenians during and immediately following World War I. "How can I get in touch with the family?"

"Through me. I'll let you interview 'em after I'm through. Do you speak French?"

"Pidgin," said Samuel.

"Then you'd better bring along an interpreter, although I've been told they speak pretty good English."

"Who told you all this?" asked Samuel.

"Candice."

"Have you gotten any dirt on Hagopian at all?" asked Samuel. "He couldn't have been perfect. He must have some blemish on his record, or at least some enemies, don't you think?"

Bernardi thought for a moment and scratched his head. A slight smile appeared on his usually expressionless face. "You know, I've wondered about that. All these people are Armenian, and they really stick together. There has to be another side. Maybe you can help me. If you find a dissenting voice, will you let me know?"

"Sure thing, Detective."

Samuel unbuttoned his blue suit jacket and took in the plain façade of the church. Orthodox churches were usually more architecturally ostentatious—more rococo—but this one had a Spartan simplicity. The bells began to toll, indicating that it was time to enter the sanctuary for the funeral service. He and Bernardi could hear the chorus, which was singing an unfamiliar but melodic chant.

"My only problem is I don't know where to start looking," continued Samuel. "Is there a Turkish community around here? They'd probably have a different view of Hagopian, don't you think?"

"No doubt there is, but I haven't had time to look for it," said Bernardi. "But I'll be square with you. I'd like to know if there is another side to this guy's life."

The two men walked slowly up the cement stairs. The crowd was now gathered at the wooden doors of the entrance, waiting their turn to enter the church and pay their last respects. Once Samuel and Bernardi were inside, an usher directed them to the observer's section, located at the rear of the church.

Hagopian's closed coffin was in front of the altar. The sun streamed through the arched stained-glass windows, highlighting the larger-than-life saints in the colored glass. On either side of the altar were stands of lighted votive candles.

"The idea of digging up something on Hagopian wasn't originally mine," said Samuel, thinking of what Janak had said to him. "But I will find out."

"I'm interested in any information you can provide," said Bernardi.

"Even when the D.A. takes the case away from you?"

"Always. That's our job, to get the facts."

King of the Bottom

The service was presided over by a priest, a tall man with a neatly trimmed beard. He wore a brocade robe, ornately decorated with gold and lavender stripes, and his head was topped by an ancient miter, an elaborate ceremonial headdress. The service, a mixture of song and verse, was conducted in Armenian and was accompanied by a chorus in the balcony singing what sounded like Gregorian chants. Throughout the ceremony, Samuel kept an eye on the small family group clustered in the front pew near the altar.

When the service was over, he slipped out the side of the church and stationed himself by the front doors at the top of the steps. Once the family group had exited, he made a beeline for Hagopian's widow, who'd stopped to talk to one of the elders.

"Excuse me, ma'am," he said, handing her a card. "My name is Samuel Hamilton. I'm from the morning paper. Can I get an interview with you about all this?"

In spite of the hat and the heavy veil, Samuel was surprised to see that the woman looked twenty years younger than what he knew to be her dead husband's stated age of fifty. She was slim and just under five feet tall, but had a well-proportioned figure. Her dark hair hung almost to her shoulders, and she wore a very black dress. When she lifted her black veil momentarily and looked up at him with big, chestnut-colored eyes, he saw that she was heavily made up, which he thought incongruous in an inconsolable widow. In fact, there wasn't a trace of sadness on her young face.

"It's very difficult for me right now," she said in a thick accent. Then she turned to her sister-in-law and spoke in rapid French.

"Perhaps you can call on her in a few days?" said Candice, translating.

"Where can I reach her?" asked Samuel, smiling at the taller woman. "You're the decedent's sister, aren't you?"

"Yes," she said softly. "We can talk with you, but not today. I hope you understand that this is not the right time."

"Of course, ma'am," he said, blushing.

He took down the phone number where both could be reached, and the women turned and walked toward the Cadillac hearse parked nearby. He motioned to his photographer to accompany him, so they would be in position to follow the entourage to the cemetery.

"Did you get photographs of all those people I pointed to when we were at the church?" asked Samuel.

"Yes, sir," said Marcel, taking out the keys to his car.

"Good. By the way, how old is this car?"

"I've had it for ten years but it just keeps rolling along," said the photographer proudly.

"How can you afford to have a car in San Francisco?"

"Don't live in San Fran. That would break me. I'm out in South City."

"That explains it," said Samuel. "Okay, the next thing we need to do is to figure out how to identify the people in all those photographs. How many do you estimate we got?"

"I'd say about twenty-five. I can have 'em ready for ya by this afternoon, but I can't help you identify anyone."

"Did anybody in particular catch your eye?" asked Samuel.

"Maybe. I'll show you a couple of photographs I took on a hunch."

* * *

That evening, when Samuel arrived at Camelot, he didn't see Melba at her usual place at the Round Table. He was surprised instead to see Blanche, dressed in white sweatpants and a matching sweatshirt, standing behind the bar earnestly talking to the bartender. His heart began to flutter just as it always did when she was around.

No one could say that they were a compatible couple. He was short—just five-feet-six in stocking feet. He was also shy and lazy, and he'd never participated in any sport in his life. Blanche, who was very sure of herself, was at least five-foot-ten, slender and physically fit. She was the picture of health, a vegetarian and an outdoor fanatic. She had blond hair, which she usually wore pulled back. What Samuel liked most, however, were her luminous, pale blue eyes—eyes in which he thought he could see her soul, but which he felt never looked upon him as anything more than a casual friend.

"It's great to see you, Blanche," he said, beaming as he approached her. "I thought you were working as a ski instructor up at Tahoe."

"I was," she smiled, clearly happy to see him, too. "But Mom came down with bronchitis and will be laid up for a month or two, so she asked me to take charge of Camelot until she gets back on her feet."

"It's probably because she smokes so much. Sorry for the bad news. I'm trying to set up an appointment for her with Mr. Song. Do you think she's up to it?"

"I think you'd better wait until she gets better."

"Okay. How about us having dinner?"

"Love to, but let me get things under control first. How's it going at the paper?"

"It's not bad. Right now I'm investigating a case of an Armenian who was found hanging from the gate of the dump he owned."

"Was it suicide or murder?"

"The latter." Then, in a tone of feigned indifference: "I'm working with someone you know, Janak Marachak."

"Janak? He's a great guy," Blanche spoke with more enthusiasm than Samuel wanted to hear from her.

"Why do you say that?" asked Samuel, annoyed. "He seems

to me to be very rude and not at all simpatico."

"Rude? No way, Samuel. He has the heart of a missionary and he's an idealist. He works for the poor and he's done me a lot of favors. We're good friends."

"Just friends?"

Just then, the bartender interrupted, announcing a telephone call for her, so she didn't answer his question. In any event, Blanche didn't have any more time for him, so he drifted back to the Round Table where he and Melba often sat and talked. He ordered his usual Scotch, thinking that he missed seeing Excalibur, too. That flea-bitten mutt had personality.

* * *

By the time Janak arrived at Camelot, Samuel had almost finished the second of the two drinks he allowed himself each night. He'd had enough problems with alcohol in his youth.

"Jesus, you look like hell," said Samuel when he saw Janak, who appeared in a rumpled suit, his hair disheveled and his ears purple.

"Yeah, it hasn't been a great day."

Blanche approached and, under the keen eye of Samuel, she and Janak kissed one another on the cheek. She then rushed back to her work without giving Janak a second look. He, too, made no further effort at conversation. Maybe they're just friends after all, thought Samuel. Or—Samuel couldn't help thinking—maybe they were being careful to hide something more.

"I thought you were going to cooperate with me," Samuel said with a sour expression. "I heard they arrested two of your clients, so I tried to reach you before my deadline, but there was no answer at your office. I had to write a one-sided story with just what the D.A.'s office gave me."

"Hold on. Let me tell you the whole story. After the police

report came out things began to happen—fast. Deadeye made sure he got the report first and manipulated the situation so that the old man gave him the case instead of entrusting it to the deputy district attorney in the Richmond office, which is the usual protocol. My clients Juan Ramos and Narcio Padia were taken into custody and charged with murder. Miguel and Jose Ramos were also charged, but they couldn't be found."

"Shit," said Samuel. "Deadeye promised he'd cooperate with me on the release of the police report. I tried to call him all afternoon but, like with you, he didn't return my phone calls. When I tried to talk to Bernardi, he said he'd been instructed by Deadeye to turn off the information spigot unless the details were approved by him. So now you're my only source."

"Because I represent two of the charged defendants, I demanded and received a copy of the report," said Janak. "I spent the rest of the day going over it before coming here to meet you this evening."

"It must be a big report. It's well after seven."

"Look, I told you this was a tough day," said Janak, impatiently. "The crime was terrible. They mutilated him."

"They what?" said Samuel, sobering up quickly.

"They cut off the guy's penis and testicles. Whoever did this crime was one angry motherfucker."

"Does the report blame it on just one person?"

"No, no, I told you. They arrested two of my clients and they're still looking for two more." Janak sat back in his chair and folded his arms. "It's all in the report. But I've got to warn you: it makes for graphic reading."

"Will you go over it with me?" asked Samuel.

"Let's go in the back where we won't be interrupted."

They headed to an isolated table near the restrooms.

"Want a drink first?" asked Samuel.

"No, thanks. Too much work to do later. I need a clear head."

They sat down and Janak unfolded the voluminous

document. "It says here that Miguel and Jose Ramos's fingerprints were found on the Coke bottles that were in the decedent's pockets."

"There were four bottles, right?" asked Samuel.

"Yeah. And Narcio Padia's prints were found on the rake that was used to smooth the ground underneath the body after it was hung."

"Is that why they're charging 'em?"

"As far as I can gather, that's all they have against any of 'em. But the the sister's statement that they were ungrateful workers and that her brother was a saint is pure bullshit."

"Anything else? I can see you're fuming."

Janak was slumped down in his chair, breathing hard through his nose.

"I already told you, they emasculated him. I can hear Deadeye arguing at trial that since my clients claimed they were rendered sterile by the chemicals at the dump, this was their revenge."

"Your clients were rendered sterile by working at the dump?"

"That's the most recent thing that happened. It was a slow process. First the chemicals got into their systems, so when they conceived children, they were born with birth defects. The injuries to their children are very severe. One of Miguel Ramos's kids was born with a withered leg and the other with no hand. Narcio Padia's is crippled and has all sorts of neurological deficits that the doctors at U.C. attribute to the chemicals at the dump. I had the men tested and all three are now sterile. Mind you, these guys aren't even thirty yet."

"What about Juan?" asked Samuel.

"Nah, he wasn't injured that we're aware of right now, and he doesn't have any children. He was never tested for sterility because we didn't file suit on his behalf. I'm not even sure why they've charged him, unless they have some kind of evidence that doesn't show up in the report. My guess is that they're trying to get him to snitch on his nephews. I guarantee that won't happen."

"How did the charges come down?" asked Samuel.

"What d'ya mean?"

"Indictment? Information?"

"Information. The D.A. couldn't get the grand jury to issue an indictment against Juan Ramos based on the facts."

"What about the pictures?" asked Samuel.

"I'll get 'em tomorrow morning, and then I'd like to put 'em together with the ones you took at the funeral yesterday."

"Is there anything in particular you're looking for?"

"Any clue whatsoever, but I'm particularly interested in the French clothing label on the inside of Hagopian's suit, the footprint at the scene and the photo of the insect."

"Insect?" asked Samuel.

"Yeah, insect. The report said there was a blue insect on his pant leg. So I'm going to see an entomologist at U.C. Berkeley tomorrow afternoon."

"Really? What for?"

"You were out at the dump. There's no life at Point Molate, so the insect had to come from somewhere else. If we find out where, it may lead to where he was killed, or it may lead to who actually killed him."

"Do you think that he wasn't killed at the dump?"

"The scene of the crime was staged, like a play. For one thing, there's no sign of a struggle. I think he was killed and castrated somewhere else and then they hung the dead body on the arch over the gate."

"Does the report say that?"

"No, but I bet I'm right. The insect may prove that."

"I remember the eerie feeling I had at the gate when I noticed there were no shorebirds anywhere around. What about the French label? What's the interest there?"

"Don't know yet," said Janak. "But it's worth looking into."

Janak went quiet. He seemed to be somewhere else.

"What are you thinking about?" asked Samuel.

"A curious coincidence. I knew an Armenian girl in Paris a few years ago."

"And?"

"I fell for her in a big way, but it didn't work out. She was a very special person. I doubt if I'll ever find another like her."

"What was her name?"

"Lucine. I've thought a lot about her. I wrote her several times, but she never answered."

"Does Lucine have anything to do with all this?"

"Absolutely nothing. When we started talking about the French label, I thought about Lucine, that's all. What's important here is the connection between Hagopian and France. One of us may have to go over there and investigate. I'm including you on my team, Samuel. Am I being presumptuous?"

"Not at all. I wanna help. First, 'cause I'll get the inside scoop on the story, but also because I believe you're right. Your guys are being framed. Are you sure you'll get the photos by tomorrow?"

"Yeah, Deadeye gave Bernardi the okay, so he'll release them to me in the morning. Do you want to come to my office around ten?"

"Sure. I'll bring the photos from the funeral."

Janak got up from the table and Samuel followed him, glass in hand, back to the Round Table at the entrance to the bar. Once again, Samuel noticed how tired his friend looked; seen from behind, his broad shoulders were slumped, his head bowed. After saying goodbye, Janak pulled up the lapels of his suit jacket as a defense against the chilly winter evening and headed out the door, lugging his two heavy leather briefcases.

Samuel felt a new sympathy for the man he was just getting to know. From what he'd hinted, Samuel thought that Janak had experienced an impossible love situation, just like the one he was currently in with Blanche. He wondered how profound the relationship had been in Paris and why it didn't work out. If Janak still thought about Lucine, perhaps he had no real interest in Blanche. That calmed him a little, but not much. It was a shame that Lucine lived on another continent. He looked out the window at the lights of the financial district shimmering in the distance and swirled the last piece of ice in his glass, wondering if he should have another drink. No, definitely not. Samuel reluctantly left the glass on the Round Table and looked for Blanche, but she was too busy to talk much. They said their goodbyes, agreeing they'd get together in a few days.

4

Lots o' Troubles

THE WAITING ROOM OF Janak's office was full when Samuel arrived the next morning. Workers with an array of chemical injuries—some with blisters on their faces, a bandaged arm or leg, or even blind—were gathered there in an atmosphere that touched on hope. It was a place where people came to get answers about what had happened to them in their workplaces and why. Janak Marachak was one of the few attorneys in the Bay Area who had answers and could help them untangle their diminished lives.

Marachak hadn't arrived yet, so Marisol Leiva, Janak's secretary, met Samuel as he came into the reception area. Although originally from Managua, Nicaragua, Marisol had been in the U.S. long enough that she spoke English without an accent. She spoke Spanish with clients and acted as an interpreter for her boss when necessary. Janak had hired her almost as soon as she answered an ad he'd placed in a legal newspaper. He didn't even ask for references; the intelligent look in her hazel eyes and the precise manner in which she answered questions was enough for him. Marisol was tall for a Latin; she had a nice shape and was pretty even without makeup. Her clothes were simple and without pretension, perhaps because her budget was limited.

King of the Bottom

Marisol had no experience as a legal secretary, which was a break for Janak in terms of her salary, since he was chronically short of money. His hunch paid off, however, and within six months of being hired she was running the office like an old hand. She also managed his private affairs as if she'd worked for him for years. Marisol became so involved in the legal cases that within a year she'd become a lawyer without a license. There was nothing she didn't know how to do, and Janak would tell anyone who would listen that she was the most important person in his life.

Marisol escorted Samuel to the library, which was crowded with bookcases filled with tomes on California legal cases. In the middle of the room was a six-foot table with three overflowing ashtrays littering its surface. Shaking her head, Marisol picked them up and carried them out of the room.

A man sat hunched over a document at one end of the table, law books piled high beside him. Small, with drooping shoulders, he was probably younger than he looked. Dressed in shirtsleeves and a tie, a worn sports jacket hanging limply over the back of his chair, he paid no attention to Samuel when the reporter walked in, and Samuel ignored him as well.

The man's name was Bartholomew Asquith. Once a partner in a big San Francisco law firm, where he'd been in charge of the appellate department, he'd developed a phobia of public speaking. He grew incapable of taking on the role of lead attorney in a courtroom, or even of making any oral arguments at all. It got so bad that he stopped talking altogether and quit making court appearances. Soon after, Asquith suffered a nervous breakdown. Following psychiatric treatment, he decided to leave his firm. After not working for six months, however, he found he'd burned through his savings and he reluctantly answered an ad that Janak had posted for a book lawyer in *The Recorder*, the Bay Area's legal newspaper.

Janak immediately saw his talent and hired him, putting

him at ease by assuring Asquith that he himself would make all court appearances and do all the talking. Asquith's only jobs would be doing legal research, writing briefs and riding shotgun in court in case there was a complicated legal problem that Janak couldn't solve. Asquith could whisper the answer to Janak; he would never be responsible for answering to the court himself.

While Samuel was going over the list he'd made a few days before, Asquith went out to get a cup of coffee. Soon after, Janak walked in with the package of photos he'd picked up from Bernardi. He slapped Samuel affectionately on the shoulder.

"What'd the detective have to say?" asked Samuel.

"He was pretty tight-lipped, as I told you. I pried until he told me that Deadeye cut him off. He wouldn't say more."

"That's too bad. Just the other day, he was open to other suspects and possibilities."

"Maybe. But for now, he's sticking to the company line."

Janak wore a neatly pressed gray suit, a starched white shirt and a striped tie. He looked more rested than he had the night before but he still had bags under his eyes from lack of sleep. He spread the crime scene photos on the table. They featured close-ups of Hagopian from all angles, showing each piece of evidence and the scene in graphic detail. Both men perused them closely. Janak set aside the one of the blue insect, which included the bloodstain on Hagopian's pant leg.

"We'll deal with that one later."

He placed another photo in front of Samuel. "This is a knot that's used by vaqueros around San Juan de los Lagos, where my clients are from. There's no doubt about that. But it's not a hangman's knot. And look at the photo of the dead man's neck. You see that rope burn? That's not even from the same kind of rope."

"How do you know that?" asked Samuel.

"You can see the indentation on the man's skin, right next to the collar. See those marks on his neck? They're different. Whatever it was, that's what killed him. I bet he was garroted and then strung up after he was dead. Whoever's trying to stick my guys with this is either an amateur or just didn't give a shit."

"I'm not sure I follow you on that," said Samuel. "But I'm willing to listen and maybe I'll learn something. Can I make that point in my article?"

"Not yet. Let's do some more investigation. I don't want them to know what I'm thinking right now."

"Speaking of investigation, don't you think we need to look into the fact that he was emasculated?" asked Samuel.

"I wonder if that's a cultural thing, like a ritual, or if it's a red herring thrown in to emphasize the fact that my clients are sterile. The question is, who's going to look into it? And where do we start? There sure is a lot to do."

"I'll see what I can find out," said Samuel.

Janak breathed a sigh of relief.

"And what about these Coca-Cola bottles?" asked Samuel, picking up one of the photos. "Look at this one of the Coke boxes stacked outside the trailer. You see where the bottles are missing? It's the box next to the bottom. There are four on top of it. That means someone with an intimate knowledge of the employees' work habits was keeping a pretty close eye on 'em. Otherwise, how would they know what bottles to fill with chemicals so that your clients' fingerprints would be on them?"

"I see what you mean," said Janak. "If there was a spy at the dump, watching everything and taking notes, I betcha he was watching Hagopian, too."

"Yeah, that's exactly what it looks like. The question is how can we find out who that person was? Bernardi's out of our reach for the time being, thanks to Deadeye."

"Poor bastard, I don't envy him having to take orders from that jerk," said Janak.

"The other thing I've got to do is talk to the coroner," he continued. "Even if the D.A. has him in his pocket, he's still a public official. I want to show him what he's in for on the witness stand if he's going to claim that the man was hanged with the Mexican knot. That's why I don't want you to say anything about those marks on Hagopian's neck, at least for the time being."

"Fair enough."

"Let's look at the photos you took," said Janak.

Samuel spread them out on the library table. "This one needs no explanation," he said, pushing a photograph across the table to Janak. "It's of the church and the crowd. There were hundreds of people there." He pointed to another picture. "This group here is the family."

"You're going to have a talk with them soon, right?"

"Maybe as soon as tomorrow."

"Which one's the sister?"

"She's the tall one. The short one is the wife, and the two young ones are his nieces."

"Where are the man's daughters?"

"I was told at the funeral that they were in school in France and that the family decided they couldn't get them here in time."

"Doesn't that seem strange to you?" asked Janak. "They could have postponed the funeral for a few more days."

"One of the many things that's strange about this case."

"Aside from background, we need to get a list of all the employees," said Janak. "If the family won't give it to us, then I'll have to get it by way of discovery in the civil case. In fact, I'll just send out interrogatories. That's a better idea than us showing our hand right now."

"I think I should ask the family anyway," said Samuel. "If I remember right, interrogatories take thirty days to answer, and we need the information faster than that if we can get it."

"Okay, give it a try. What about the group of men in this photo? Who are they?"

"I don't know, but my photographer said these guys looked suspicious."

Janak laughed. "Why? Because they all have beards?"

"It was something about the way they huddled together. They looked isolated from the rest of the crowd, almost like they didn't belong there. The photographer's a pretty savvy guy. I'd listen to him if I were you."

"Okay, who do we ask about them?"

"I've already thought about that," said Samuel. "The place to start is the priest. He knows more about the parishioners than anyone."

"That's good thinking, Samuel. You pursue that lead while I talk to the entomologist. Let's meet at Camelot on Friday."

* * *

Janak took the F line streetcar from San Francisco to Berkeley. The F line ran on its own track on the lower deck of the Bay Bridge and was the fastest way to get across the bay, as well as the most pleasant. From his seat on the tram, Janak watched the sailboats going to and fro in the water. When the car reached the East Bay, he could see the cargo being unloaded at the Oakland docks. Then the streetcar turned north, passing through Emeryville on its way to Berkeley. He got off at the Shattuck Avenue stop and walked up the hill to the Berkeley campus of the University of California, listening to the Campanile bells playing their hourly tune as he searched Wheeler Hall for the entomologist's office. He found it on the second floor of the old building and knocked on the glass pane of the door.

A scholarly looking man with a shock of white hair and rimless glasses ushered him in, introducing himself as Jonathan Higginbotham, professor of entomology. He wore a threadbare sports coat with leather patches on the elbows and looked like a disciple of Charles Darwin. Insects were scattered throughout the office, either pinned to corkboards or in jars, and reference books filled the room, half of them seemingly authored by the professor. The musty smell of the past engulfed Janak as he entered.

Janak explained the reason for his visit, giving him a short history of the crime, including where the body was found. He took photographs from his briefcase and placed them on the table, explaining that he wanted to know as much as he could about the blue insect found at the scene. There was plenty of light streaming in through the window, and the professor studied the pictures closely with a magnifying glass.

After a few minutes, he looked up at Janak. "In order to know more about this insect, I'll have to do some research and that will cost money," he said.

"If you can verify that it doesn't come from Richmond, but from somewhere else, I will need you to testify at a criminal trial."

"I see. And when might that be?"

"I'm not sure yet. I'll have to let you know."

"Where will this trial be?"

"In Martinez."

"You understand, you'll have to pay for my time, just like you're doing today," said the professor. He no longer looked like the kindly old man Janak had seen when he first arrived.

"Yes, I understand that very well."

The professor got up slowly, indicating that the meeting was over. "Lawyers always want the service, but they seldom want to pay," he said, extending his hand to Janak. "You look like an honest lad, so I'll be glad to help you. But I had to remind you of the rules."

"My clients' lives may depend on your testimony, Professor. So for me, it's not a question of money."

* * *

While Janak was meeting with Professor Higginbotham, Samuel boarded an AC Transit bus and headed across the bay to Saint Vartan's Armenian Church in Oakland. Although the bus deposited him just one short block from the church's Spring Street address, Samuel was early for his two o'clock appointment with Father Agajanian, so he walked until he found a Chinese restaurant a short distance away.

The familiar smell of fried rice wafted from the kitchen as he waited for his food. Once it arrived, Samuel wielded his chopsticks with more gusto than skill, dropping some of the greasy chow mien onto his shirt.

The large aquarium filled with golden carp near the front door reminded him of Chop Suey Louie's, a restaurant located in his old stomping ground of San Francisco's Chinatown. He thought of how much he missed his old friend Louie and how he missed the bets they made on football games, even though Samuel never won a bet in all the years they knew each other.

He felt guilty when he thought of how Louie was murdered by the Chinese thugs who were really out to kill him. Thinking about how Louie inadvertently took the bullets meant for him sent a chill up Samuel's spine. It seemed a long time had passed since then, but it was really only less than a year.

Samuel's thoughts returned to the present only when he opened the fortune cookie that came at the end of his meal. It predicted he would be rich beyond his wildest dreams. He laughed at the irony as he put the slip of paper with the message in his jacket pocket and paid the $1.75 check.

Samuel walked back to the church, taking in the 1920's-era faded-pastel clapboard buildings along the way. At the appointed hour, he knocked on the door at the back of the church as he'd been instructed in his telephone call.

The same priest who had presided over the service for Hagopian a few days before ushered him into a room lined with bookcases, all filled with titles that Samuel couldn't identify but assumed were in Armenian script. There was also a large Bible resting open on a stand.

"Good afternoon, Father Agajanian. I'm Samuel Hamilton from the morning paper. Thanks for giving me your time."

"How can I help you?" asked the priest, his eyes taking in the grease stain on his visitor's shirt.

Samuel smiled, brushing at the spot. "You'll have to excuse my table manners, Father. Stains just seem to follow me around."

"Don't worry about it, young man," the priest said.

"As a reporter, I'm thrust in the middle of many different lives and cultures and I need lots of help understanding them."

"We Armenians are not so different from others in this society," said the priest, "but for some reason we've been painted with the broad brush of the Levant. In fact, we're an Aryan race and, for immigration purposes, the federal government has classified us as white since 1923. That's why you see so many of us. Without that designation, we wouldn't have been welcomed into this country in such large numbers."

"I'm not sure I know what you mean, Father."

"The public thinks we're part of the mysterious Orient, that's all. Our official designation is 'Other.'"

"I see. I'm sure if there are any major cultural differences you'll educate me. Let's start with Mr. Hagopian. Did you know him?"

"He was a big contributor to this parish, which covers most of the Bay Area, and he was a fine man. I baptized his children personally. I saw him once or twice a month. If I needed some help on a project, I could always call on him. And not just for money. That's what I'm trying to convey. The man had a social conscience."

That's interesting, thought Samuel, a little surprised, even though it was hard to doubt the priest's sincerity. His own thoughts drifted to Janak's clients' deformed children.

"Did you know anything about his business?"

"What do you want to know?"

"He owned a very important industrial dumpsite that was widely used and immensely profitable."

"Yes, sure," said the priest.

"Did he have any enemies? You know success breeds envy among competitors, and there are people who despise anyone who gets ahead, and even plot against them."

"I personally know of no one who wished him harm. Really, he was held in high esteem, and not just in the Armenian community. On the other hand, if someone wanted to hurt him, I would be the last person they would tell."

"Yeah, I thought that was probably the case," said Samuel. "Do you know where he was the night he was killed?"

"I'm afraid I don't. You'll have to ask his family those questions."

"Do you know if he was having any family problems?"

"That's also something you would need to discuss with his family. Even if I knew something, I wouldn't be at liberty to talk to you about it."

"I'm scheduled to meet with the family tomorrow," said Samuel. "I'll ask them then. I have some photos taken on the day of his funeral, Father. Can you help me identify some of the people?"

Samuel put the photo of the suspicious-looking group of men on the table.

"These people. Do you know who they are or where they

come from?"

"I'm not sure, Mr. Hamilton. They're not from our parish and they're not from the Bay Area. I assume they came to pay their respects to the Hagopians."

"Do you know the names of any of them?"

"I do not. Perhaps Miss Candice or Mr. Hagopian's widow can give you more information."

"Do you have any idea why they would show up at Mr. Hagopian's funeral?"

"The practice is quite common among Armenians," said the priest. "If you have other photographs of the crowd, I can point out families from places like Los Angeles, and especially from Fresno, where there is a large Armenian community and many families are related to each other either by blood or marriage."

The priest's eyes shifted away from the photograph and Samuel saw his shoulders tense. When he spoke again, Samuel detected evasiveness in his tone.

"As I said, you'll have to take anything else up with the family."

"How about Mr. Hagopian's employees? Do you know anyone who worked at the dump?"

"Only his sister, Candice, and their cousin, Joseph, who was very close to Armand and his family. I understand that they came to America together. He's the only man in the photograph you have of Mr. Hagopian's wife and sister. He helped out for a while in the business, but he went back to Fresno to his farms. Besides them, I don't know anyone else who worked there."

Samuel spread the rest of the photos of the mourners on the table. The priest rattled off names and Samuel wrote their phonetic spellings and as fast as he could on the back of each photograph.

"Do any of these people have any special connection with

Hagopian?" asked Samuel.

"I don't know. I recognize them because of their relationship with the church."

When Samuel casually placed the photo of the suspicious-looking group in front of the priest for a second time, he saw that the man became nervous again, his eyes shifting to the Bible on the stand.

* * *

Samuel made arrangements for Marcel, the newspaper's photographer, to go with him to Hagopian's apartment in Pacific Heights, San Francisco's most elegant neighborhood. Ordinarily Samuel would have taken the bus, but since Marcel had a car, they cruised Broadway in his 1947 jalopy, looking for a parking place. It was four o'clock by the time they arrived.

Hagopian's ten-story building was maintained like a jewel, complete with polished bronze, well-oiled woods and impeccable marble. The walls of the foyer were covered with panels of fine wood in three tones, with designs dating from the early twentieth century, and the floors were dark green and ivory Italian marble. Light streamed in through beveled-glass windows, adding to the illumination from the three teardrop glass chandeliers.

Constructed before the First World War, the building and had been remodeled with modern baths and kitchens, new elevators and air conditioning. The architects in charge of the renovation had taken great care to preserve its sober elegance. There were no renters in the building; for the most part, the apartments belonged to members of the city's oldest and wealthiest families. The fact that Armand Hogopian, a first-generation immigrant and the owner of a chemical dump, owned one of the apartments showed he'd had good connections and a lot of money.

Samuel and Marcel rang the buzzer and were received by a doorman right out of a turn-of-the-century British novel. He was dressed impeccably in a Brooks Brothers three-piece suit that neither Samuel nor Marcel could have afforded to buy even secondhand. He was thin and solemn, with white hair that was combed straight back and a professional demeanor that made him appear intimidating. Because he held himself so erect, it was difficult to guess his exact age, but there was no doubt the man was over eighty.

"I'm Samuel Hamilton of—"

The doorman interrupted him. "You're the reporter, right? Miss Candice and Mrs. Hagopian said you would come at four-thirty. I'm afraid you've arrived a little early. Just a moment, please." He discreetly made a phone call and then told them they would be received. "Please proceed to the tenth floor."

"Thank you Mr...? I'm sorry, what is your name?" Samuel tried to ingratiate himself with the doorman, sure this wouldn't be his only visit to the Hagopians.

"Carlton's the name. Mr. Thaddeus Carlton."

"Nice to meet you, Mr. Carlton." Samuel smiled. "Here's my card. Please don't forget who I am."

"No need to worry about that, Mr. Hamilton," the doorman replied, guiding them to the elevator at the back of the foyer. "I never forget a face."

Once the elevator doors had closed, Marcel laughed. "Did you see the scornful look the doorman gave us?"

"This must be the first time a reporter has come to this building," said Samuel. "It's not every day that an occupant is hanged and castrated at a dump."

"That Thaddeus Carlton, or whatever his name is, probably has a lot of information."

"I can assure you that we won't get one word out of him," said Samuel.

King of the Bottom

The elevator opened directly on the Hagopians apartment. They exited into a small mirror-lined hall, where a maid in a black uniform and white apron greeted them.

"Miss Hagopian is expecting you," she said in a strong French accent, ushering them into a large room filled with ornate furniture, Persian rugs and folding drapes. "Would you like tea?"

"No thank you," they answered in unison.

The windows offered a spectacular view of the bay, which shone in the winter sun. Two large freighters passed one another in front of Alcatraz Island, one sailing east in the direction of the Golden Gate, the other headed for the docks south of Market Street or, perhaps, across the bay to Oakland. Looking out over the panorama, Marcel gave an admiring whistle.

Shortly after, two women entered. They were both dressed in black and were heavily made up: red lips, black eyeliner and thick, orange-tinted foundation that gave them a mask-like appearance. Despite the exaggerated picture they presented, they were attractive.

The taller and more stylish woman extended her hand.

"I'm Candice Hagopian, Armand's sister. This is his wife, Almandine."

Samuel shook their hands, overwhelmed by the women's heavy perfume. He was again surprised at how young Almandine looked. The heat was on full blast and it was insufferably hot in the apartment, but the young widow appeared dressed for snow: she wore a turtleneck cashmere sweater that came all the way up to her ears, knit stockings and boots.

"As I told you, Miss Candice, I'd like to ask both of you some questions," said Samuel. "I'd also like to get a couple of photographs, if that's okay with you."

"This has been very unpleasant for our family," said Candice. "We spent a lot of time with the police answering a myriad of questions."

"I understand what you're going through and your need for privacy." Samuel spoke as compassionately as he could. "I'm not here to interfere with your personal lives. I'd just like to know what kind of man your brother was. I'm looking for an explanation for why this happened, and hopefully it will lead us to who did it."

Candice gestured dismissively with a well-manicured hand.

"The District Attorney has assured us that some of the men who did it are in jail."

"Was that Mr. Graves?" asked Samuel as he wrote her words in his notebook.

"Yes. He said that justice would be swift."

"Did he tell you what kind of evidence he had against these men?"

"Only that their fingerprints were found at the scene and that there wasn't much doubt that they did it."

"He said that, did he? Was he talking about the workers who filed suit against the company and your brother?"

"Yes, the very ones. Ungrateful people! No one had any complaint against my brother except for those bums, who, fortunately, are now in jail."

Candice grabbed a tissue from the box on the coffee table and dabbed at her tears.

Almandine sat on the edge of the sofa, her head down, her legs and hands pressed together. She seemed oblivious to their conversation, although Candice occasionally looked over at her, as if seeking her approval.

"Can you tell me something about your family?"

"I was married, but my husband died, so I reclaimed my maiden name and came here from Paris to help my brother Armand and our cousin Joseph run the family businesses."

"You're from France? I noticed you had a slight accent."

"We're Armenian. I don't suppose you know much about

us as a people?"

"Frankly, I don't. Can you give me some background so I can tell your story? It's important to educate the public."

"Come with me. I need to show you a map."

She took them to the library, where there was a big map of the Mediterranean Middle East. She directed them to seats in front of the map. "You need to know some of what our people have been through so you can grasp the magnitude of what happened to my brother. We're a Christian people who lived in peace within the Ottoman Empire. We were persecuted late in the nineteenth century, but things had quieted down after that.

"We're a people of great enterprise and industry. We have added tremendously to every culture we've been a part of. By the early 1900's we had established a wide area of influence throughout the Middle East that stretched from Turkey and part of Syria all the way to the Black Sea, in what is now the Soviet Union."

"Why did you leave?" asked Samuel, ceasing his furious note-taking for the moment.

"Our father was a very successful businessman in Erzerum, Turkey. She pointed to the city on the map. "All the members of our family were born there—my brother Armand in 1910, Joseph, our cousin, in 1912, and me in 1915. I was born just when trouble started up again.

"The Turks chose the wrong side in the Great War. They went with the Axis powers. In 1915, they resumed a terrible genocide against our people, one that they had begun years before. In our region alone, there were over two hundred thousand Armenians. By the time the Turks and the Kurds were through with us in 1922, there were only fifteen hundred left. All this happened while an indifferent world stood by and watched.

"At first, our father thought his wealth and position would

protect us, but his naiveté cost him his fortune and his life. Luckily, he was able to funnel some of his assets out of the Armenian sector, and we escaped through the deserts of Mesopotamia with our mother, an uncle, and his son, our cousin Joseph."

She showed him their escape route down through Basra, located in modern-day Iraq, to the Persian Gulf.

"We fled on a French ship and were granted asylum in France, where we started a new life. At the end of the 1930s, however, it began all over again with the Nazi threat. My mother, Armand, our uncle and his family escaped to the United States just before the Second World War and settled in Los Angeles. I was married to a university professor by then, and we spent the war years in England, where my husband worked for British Intelligence. After the war we returned to France. When my husband died in 1950, I came to America.

"How did the rest of your family end up in Los Angeles?" asked Samuel.

"We had distant relatives there."

"How many of your people were ultimately killed?"

"By the time the Turks and the Kurds were through, they had killed more than a million and a half Armenians." Her voice broke. "They killed us because they had impunity. We were Christians; they were Moslems—we were in their tent, so to speak, so they had all the power. It was not unlike what the Nazis did to the Jews in World War II. They were jealous of us. We were successful in all facets of society that we were involved in, and their empire was a mess and they had to blame someone. We were the sacrificial lambs."

"What's the status of your people now?"

"Not good. What's left of Armenia is behind the Iron Curtain in the Soviet Union. We asked for our territory back at the Peace Conference at Versailles after the Great War, but nothing ever came of it. And the Turks have never acknowledged their brutality, let alone apologized."

"I'm very sorry," said Samuel. "Please tell me how your family got into the chemical dump business."

"We started in Los Angeles. Other immigrant groups that had come before already controlled the desirable jobs, so there wasn't much of a choice, except for the garbage and chemical dump businesses. The Armenians got a foothold where they could."

Samuel thought of Melba's description of Hagopian as "King of the Bottom."

"How did your brother end up at Point Molate?"

"Our uncle was a good man. He got the businesses functioning well in Los Angeles, and when my brother finished at university, he sent him up north to start his own dump.

"Joseph, our uncle's son, managed the Los Angeles part of the business and also began farming in Fresno in Central California."

"I think you said before that he wasn't working in Richmond any longer?"

"He's in Fresno. His children run the Los Angeles businesses."

By this time, it was clear that Candice was spent emotionally. Samuel figured that he wasn't going to get them to pose for photos.

"Does your family still have strong ties to France?"

"Yes, some of our relatives live there, and Armand's daughters go to school there. They are from his first marriage."

"And you visit them often?"

"At least once a year."

"By the way, will his daughters be coming to the United States now?"

"No. He's already been buried and everyone agreed it would be too hard on them to come now."

"Were there any conflicts between family members that

you can think of?"

"None." Candice looked over her shoulder at her sister-in-law, who was still in the adjacent room, seated on the edge of the sofa like an obedient student.

"Could I talk a little with Mrs. Hagopian?" asked Samuel, taking in Candice's glances and the widow's passive attitude.

"Almandine has been deeply affected by what happened. The doctor had to give her sleeping pills and tranquilizers. She's very young, as you can see."

"It looks as if she's twenty years younger than her husband," said Samuel.

"Twenty-four years to be exact, but she's very mature for her age. At the moment she's sedated, Mr. Hamilton. Going back to your question, I suppose that in all families there are some problems, especially ones where there are teenage daughters, but in ours there's nothing to speak of."

"Do the daughters come home for summer vacations?"

"Yes, they were usually here for a month or two. They are very busy with their studies."

"Can you tell me how many people work at the dumpsite?"

"There are three of us who work in the office, all members of our family. A cousin and a niece work for me, and we have ten workmen in the dump area. I'm in charge of the office staff and the billing. Armand was the boss."

"The workers are all Mexican?"

"We also had workers from our own region, and a couple of Americans."

"How can we get in touch with them, including your cousins?"

"I'm very sorry, Mr. Hamilton, but the District Attorney has asked us not to give anyone access to any of our employees. You'll have to go through him."

"I see," said Samuel, writing the word "Shit!" in his

notebook and underlining it.

Candice turned toward her sister-in-law and they quietly exchanged a few words.

"Would you mind if I got a photograph of your family for the paper?" Samuel asked.

"I'm sorry, but we're just not up to it," said Candice, wiping the mascara that was running beneath her swollen eyes. "And we don't want Joseph's daughters exposed to the public."

Although disappointed, Samuel decided to move on.

"I have one other matter," he said, pulling out the photos of the suspicious-looking group of men he'd shown to the priest. "Do you recognize anyone in these photographs?"

Candice and the widow studied the pictures. They glanced at one another for a moment, but then shook their heads.

Samuel was disappointed again. The women's reaction to the photos was just as strange as Father Agaganian's had been. Samuel wanted to know why. He tried to engage the widow, but Candice kept interrupting, and he couldn't complete a conversation with her. The only thing he found out was that she hadn't been married very long to Hagopian.

After they spent a few more minutes exchanging sorrowful observations about the whole affair, Samuel and the photographer left the plush apartment.

"That son of a bitch Deadeye Graves, he's put the clamp on everything!" exclaimed Samuel in the elevator. "He's trying to prevent his house of cards from collapsing."

"Candice wasn't much help either," said Marcel.

"She did give us a lot of background on the Armenian people, which is informative. But you're right; she's hiding something. She and Deadeye are making my job next to impossible."

On the ground floor they ran into the phlegmatic Thaddeus Carlton, who accompanied them to the front door in silence. He offered only the slightest bow as they exited, as if he'd decided the pair deserved nothing more.

Marcel stopped at a telephone booth on the their way back downtown so Samuel could call Janak's office. He explained to Marisol that he wasn't able to get the names of Hagopian's employees. She drafted interrogatories, asking for the names of all the workers who'd been employed at the dump for the last three years, signing Janak Marachak's name to the documents before sending them out.

* * *

The next morning Samuel was hard at work in his office, going over his notes. At about nine-thirty he took a coffee break and began reading the Associated Press copy coming in over the wire. When he saw the lead story coming in from Fresno, Samuel let out a shout that echoed throughout the newsroom. Joseph Hagopian, a well-known and respected farmer in the area, had been found murdered in his plum orchard the day before. He had been hacked to death and emasculated, his private parts stuffed in his mouth.

"This is incredible!" Samuel exclaimed, and immediately dialed Janak's number. He got Marisol on the line. "It's really important I get ahold of him," he told her, breathing heavily.

"There's not much I can do. He's at the jail, and then he's going to talk to the coroner."

The muscles in Samuel's face tensed and his grip on the phone intensified.

"There's been another murder. Someone has done in another Hagopian. And the wire report says that Miguel Ramos's fingerprints were found on the murder weapon, a machete. The Associated Press is making a big deal out of what happened up here at Point Molate, and says that the same people are being sought for the Fresno murder."

"It couldn't have been Miguel or Jose," said Marisol. "They're in Mexico, and Juan and Narcio are in jail."

"Either the cops in Fresno don't know that, or they don't believe it," said Samuel. "I need to go down there and see what I can find out. I'm leaving right now. Tell Janak what I've told you and that I'll call him this evening from Fresno if I have something new to tell him. Otherwise, I'll just see him tomorrow at Camelot."

Samuel put the receiver down, wondering if it was possible that Miguel or Jose had never actually left the country or, if they did, that they had come back across the porous border and committed the crime, only to slip back into Mexico. But if either of those far-fetched possibilities were true, what was their motive in murdering a Hagopian cousin who had very little to do with the dump?

* * *

Samuel arrived at the Fresno Airport at two in the afternoon and took a cab to the local newspaper office, where he asked to speak to the reporter in charge of the Joseph Hagopian murder case. After a short wait, a young man—tall and thin, with long blond hair—emerged from a cubicle on the newsroom floor and ambled down the aisle toward him.

"Bucky Hughes," the man said, extending his hand. His long, angular face was dotted with freckles, and he had a gap between his crooked front teeth.

Samuel took an immediate liking to him and decided to get down to business.

"I've got a problem and I need your help, Bucky. I'm investigating and writing articles about the death of Armand Hagopian in the Bay Area. Joseph was his cousin and he got it pretty much the same way Armand did with the emasculation thing. One difference, though: Armand was strangled instead of being hacked to death."

"And you say his things were cut off too? Jesus!"

"They sure were. Now here's the problem, and I'm telling you this in confidence, between newspaper reporters, so I know it won't be repeated to the cops or appear in print until I say it's okay. You understand?"

Bucky nodded in agreement. He was just as anxious as any reporter for inside information, and he wanted to hear more.

Samuel explained that some of the evidence in the Richmond case was the same as in the Fresno case, and that Miguel Ramos wasn't in the country when either of the murders was committed.

"Wait a minute," said Bucky. "Does that mean what I think it means?"

"Yeah. It means someone planted his prints."

"How would they do that?"

"We're not sure yet, but we'll find out."

"I don't think anybody would be stupid enough to leave his prints and the weapon at the scene of the crime," said Bucky.

Samuel explained what Deadeye was up to.

"I'm not sure the Fresno D. A. is any better," said Bucky.

"Can you tell me anything about this Joseph Hagopian?" asked Samuel.

"Pretty straight shooter. He was a hard-working and very wealthy man, a person of the community. No dirt so far, at least not that we know of."

"His cousin was that way, too. Was Joseph killed where they found him?"

"That's the way it looks. Why do you ask?"

Samuel explained that Armand was probably taken to the dump after he was killed, authorizing Bucky to publish that information without revealing his source.

"That's great," said Bucky, as he straightened his long frame up from against the wall. "Now, how can I help you?"

"Can you get me crime scene photos and the police and forensic reports?"

"There are ways to get those items," said Bucky. "You'll have to give me a little time, though."

"That's not a problem. Do you know of a cop with information on this case who will talk to me about all that's happened so far?"

"That's probably not a good idea. These are locals and you know how it is. They resent people coming in from the outside. But I'll be your man in Fresno. I like the idea of getting a bigger story than just the local one."

5

El Turco

WHILE SAMUEL WAS SETTING off to discover the unfolding horror story in Fresno, Janak went to Martinez to talk to the coroner. He couldn't afford to maintain a car, so he borrowed Marisol's. Before his meeting, however, he planned to visit Juan Ramos at the county jail. The three-story jail, located next to the courthouse, was a dingy-looking gray stone building that had long reached its capacity and was now bursting at the seams with inmates from the county's growing suburban population.

It wasn't yet visiting hours, so Janak headed to the courthouse's coffee shop, a windowless basement room with yellow walls and five tightly packed tables. Off to one side of the room was a noisy refrigerator with a glass door and shelves of cold drinks, a coffee maker with two pots on warmers and a wax-paper-lined tray of doughnuts and pastries . The smell of coffee and confections filled the small enclosure.

A man stood behind a cash register. He had a cartoon face—a bulbous nose, deep wrinkles and teeth that were yellow, black or even missing. Each eye was a different color— one green, the other a mottled combination of white and gray. From the distorted and vacant look on his face, it was obvious he couldn't see much, although he moved with the certainty of someone who knew his territory well. His attitude toward the customers was cheerful and accommodating.

Janak approached him, handed him a dollar and told him he had a cup of coffee and the morning paper. The man brought the bill up to his greenish eye and studied it carefully. He then put it into one of the slots in the open cash drawer and handed Janak seventy-five cents.

"Have a nice day, Counselor."

"How'd you know I'm a lawyer?" asked a surprised Janak.

"Your attitude," said the blind man, laughing. "You act like you're ready for a fight."

Janak saluted him with his free hand, although he realized it was unlikely the man could see the gesture.

"Pretty soon I'll be spending a lot of time down here with you."

"Looking forward to it," said the blind man. "What's your name?"

"Janak Marachak. What's yours?"

"Donald's my name. Nice to meet you."

Janak sat down at one of the tables, where he drank his coffee and read the paper until it was time to return to the jail.

* * *

Janak entered the jail through a tall iron door with bars on its window. He handed his card to the deputy sheriff on duty at the reception desk.

"Here to see Juan Ramos. I'm his attorney."

The deputy led him to the back of the building, where a small cell had been converted into an attorney-client visiting room. Juan Ramos sat at the lone table, facing the bars. The deputy unlocked the cell door, ushered Janak in and locked it behind him.

"Attorney visits are a half hour," the deputy said through the bars. "If ya need more time, just yell and I'll extend it. But remember, there's only one attorney room and there's a load of 'em wantin' to get in here."

"Yeah, thanks. We'll work as fast as we can."

Juan Ramos looked up at Janak, a panicked expression in his brown eyes. He had the face of a *mestizo*, a person of mixed European and Indian blood. His black hair had a hint of a curl, and there was stubble on his face from not having shaved for several days.

"I can't believe they are accusing me of this awful thing, *Licenciado*. I never done no harm to another person in all my thirty-seven years. And my family is really suffering!"

"I know this is hard on you, Juan, but we have to just get tough and get through it. I need to get as much information as you can give me about what went on at the dump."

"I will do my best, *Licenciado*. What do you want to know?"

"Some people are trying to pin the blame for this crime on you, your two nephews and on Narcio. The way I see, it they've had someone on the inside plant evidence against you. We have to figure out who that was and then get to the people behind him or her. I'm pretty sure whoever killed Mr. Hagopian didn't work at the dump. So let's get started. Tell me about your fellow workers."

"There were the Mexicans, five of us. You know who they are, 'cept maybe for Mauricio."

"He's the one they made foreman when you left?"

"That's what they told me, *Licenciado*. They also hired some new guys but I don't know them."

"Besides the Mexicans, who worked there?"

"There were two *gringos*, Bob and Johnny, and there was a guy we called *El Turco*."

"*El Turco*? You've got to be kidding! A Turk working for

an Armenian company?"

"I don't know about that, *Licenciado*. All I know is we called him *El Turco*."

"Did this guy speak Spanish?"

"Like *gringos* speak. You know, a word here and there."

"Was he more friendly to you than the two *gringos*?"

"*Sí, señor*. He was always with us, asking how to say this or that, and we ate together. He was real interested in our food and our traditions. Like I said, he asked a lot of questions, mostly by pointing and trying to say the word in Spanish after one of the boys taught him."

"What did this guy look like?"

"He was taller than any of us and weighed about 145 pounds. Black hair and dark eyes. Heavy eyebrows. And he talked some language I never heard of, but very little English."

"What was his name?"

"I already told you. *El Turco*."

"He had to have a real name."

"I don't know, *Licenciado*. We only knew him by *El Turco*."

"What about the gringos?"

"We didn't have nothing to do with them. They stuck to themselves. They drove the bulldozers, moving the piles of chemicals around."

Janak pulled several photos out of his briefcase, showing Juan the ones of Hagopian with the rope around his neck.

"One other thing, there was this strange knot tied around Hagopian's neck when they found him."

"*Madre de Dios*," exclaimed Juan, turning pale and making the sign of the cross when he saw the photo of the dead man's distorted face, a fragment of rope dangling from his neck.

"*Pobre señor*. Who would do such a thing?" He took a few seconds to calm down. "I'm sorry, *Licenciado*, what did you ask me?"

"Do you recognize the knot?"

"*Sí, señor*. That's a knot we use at home to haul the cattle in when they are out in the open. You know, you are on a horse and you throw it. It's a strong one, so they can't get away."

"You didn't tie that knot, did you?"

"*No, señor*. But I will tell you that Miguel, Jose and I taught *El Turco* how to tie this knot." Juan bowed his head, once again overwhelmed by the photo.

"Did any of you ever tie one of these knots and give it to *El Turco*?"

"I don't remember, *Licenciado*. We tied it for him lotsa times."

"Why did you do that?"

"'Cause he asked us to teach him how to round up the cattle."

"Just like that, he asked you this?"

"*No, señor*. We was talking about what kind a work we did in San Juan de los Lagos, and we told him we catched the cows, you know. So then he asked us to show him how we made the knot." Juan simulated tying the knot, pulling both ends of the imaginary rope to secure it.

Janak watched with interest. Then he showed Juan other photographs. "You see the Coke bottles? They have chemicals in them. Did either you or Miguel or Jose put anything in those bottles?"

"*No, señor*, I sure didn't. I didn't watch those boys all the time, but why would they want to do that? So…I say no, they didn't."

"You realize Miguel's and Jose's fingerprints were on those bottles?"

"We all drank Coca-Cola at work and when we was done, we put them in the boxes right outside the office."

"You mean the boxes in this photo?"

King of the Bottom

"*Sí.*"

"I bet *El Turco* drank Cokes with you, didn't he?"

"*Sí señor*. Every day."

"Do you know what kind of chemicals caused the birth defects in your nephew's children?"

"*No tengo idea, Licenciado.*"

"I didn't think so," said Janak. "Tell Narcio I'm coming to see him in a few days and fill him in on what we talked about today. But be careful not to say anything when anybody else is around. There are a lot of jailhouse snitches in here and the deputy D.A., Deadeye Graves, is a bad man. He'll try and have them get close to you to trick you into saying something that will hurt you. Do you understand? You have no friends, so just don't start talking to anyone just for the hell of it."

"I understand, *Licenciado*. We'll keep our mouth shut."

"Okay, Juan, see ya next week." Janak put the photographs back in his briefcase and whistled for the deputy to let him out of the visiting cell.

Juan turned to him just before the cell door opened. "You know *Licenciado*, I worry about my woman finding another man."

* * *

When Janak left the jail, he walked over to the coroner's office and informed the woman at the desk that he had an appointment. She looked in her book and then picked up the phone, announcing that Mr. Marachak had arrived. A tall man came out from behind a door with an opaque window on which his title was etched in block letters. His gray hair was parted to one side and he had brown eyes, black bushy eyebrows and yellowish skin that was scarred by acne.

"Hello, sir, I'm Janak Marachak."

"I know who you are. You'll have to make it snappy; I'm

very busy. Everything you need to know about Mr. Hagopian's death is in the report we wrote."

"I'm sure," Janak said, "but there are some discrepancies we need to clear up."

The coroner turned his back and began to fidget with the papers on his secretary's desk.

"Frankly, I'm not at liberty to discuss any discrepancies with you, Mr. Marachak." He spoke without turning around.

"Does that mean that Deadeye's told you not to talk to me?"

"I beg your pardon. Are you referring to Deputy District Attorney Earl Graves?"

"Yeah, that's who I'm talking about. You're a public official and I'm a citizen, just like the rest of the people who live in this state. I want to discuss some points with you that might save two men's lives. Are you against talking to me about any of them?" he asked, waving the report in the air.

"I'm not against anything. Here's the report that was prepared by my department. You are entitled to it by law. Other than that, I have nothing to say." The coroner gave Janak a condescending look and handed him a sheaf of papers.

Janak understood that the meeting was over. "So how do I consult with you on the forensic evidence in this case?"

"You get permission from the deputy district attorney handling the case. If he says I can talk to you, I will talk to you."

"But you don't work just for the D.A.," said Janak, narrowing his eyes in anger. "You work for all of us."

"I don't have anything more to say to you, Counselor," the coroner said, his acne-scarred complexion now red. He turned and walked back through the door, closing it firmly behind him.

Janak, clearly annoyed with the brush-off, pursed his lips and turned to the secretary, his face flushed. "Is he always this accommodating?" he said, stuffing the report in his briefcase.

She looked down at the papers that the coroner had been rearranging but didn't respond. Janak picked up his briefcase and walked out, slamming the door behind him. But by the time Janak had walked down the stairs and reached the exit, he had calmed down. In fact, he was no longer the least bit distressed. He knew the coroner was a political hack. That's why he'd already made arrangements to hire his own pathologist.

* * *

Before going back to his office, Janak took advantage of having Marisol's car and stopped in at the Richmond Police Station, a small yellow-stucco building with a huge radio antenna on its roof. He asked the police officer behind the counter if he could talk with Lieutenant Bernardi. After a few minutes, the stocky detective, dressed in his usual brown suit, came out into the waiting room.

"Hello, Mr. Marachak, I'm Detective Bernardi. I'm glad to meet you finally. I've heard an awful lot about you." Bernardi smiled broadly and extended his powerful hand in greeting.

"The pleasure's mine, Detective. I've heard a lot about you, too."

"Follow me," said Bernardi, motioning toward a door behind him. "We can talk in my office."

He ushered Janak into a small office crammed with files and sat down at his walnut-stained desk. Janak plopped down in one of the two chairs on the other side of the desk, placing his heavy briefcase beside him on the floor. Diffuse light coming in through the dirty, large-paned aluminum-frame windows gave the room a cheerful ambiance. On the walls were photographs of the detective as a football player and wrestler in his younger days. Bernardi pointed to a photograph on the credenza, which depicted what appeared to be an extended-family picnic.

"That's my grandfather on his hundredth birthday," he said nostalgically, indicating the elderly man seated in the center of the group. "Now ... what's on your mind, Counselor?"

Janak's face was tense.

"You know what's on my mind. I'm conducting the defense of a first-degree murder case, and the law gives me permission to collect evidence. Some of that evidence is in your hands!"

"Calm down, Mr. Marachak," said Bernardi. He picked up some papers and waved them in the air. "I'll give you a copy of this report, which I just received from the crime lab."

"What does it say?"

"I have no idea. They just gave it to me this morning and I was going to go over both it and the coroner's report together. Have you seen that one yet?"

"Yeah, I was just with him," said Janak, his face reddening with anger at the memory of his encounter with the coroner. "I have to admit that whoever is running this has sure shut down the information pipeline. But that's not going to continue because, if I have to, I'll go to court. And if that doesn't work, I'll figure something else out."

"You know I can't comment on that. But off the record?"

"Yeah, off the record," agreed Janak.

"I'm not in favor of that policy."

"Good. Tell me what you know."

"Can't do that either, not if I want to keep my job. But I can give you what you're entitled to, and maybe a little more before you leave."

"I'm not sure what you mean by 'a little more,' but okay. First, I want a list of all the employees who worked for Hagopian over the last year."

"You've come to the right guy, Counselor. Do you have a pen and paper handy?"

Janak retrieved a yellow pad from his briefcase and extracted a pen from his shirt pocket.

"Shoot."

Bernardi recited several names, addresses, and even phone numbers, and Janak took them down hurriedly.

Janak knew exactly what he was looking for. "What about this one? Nashwan Asad Aram. Does he still work there?"

"Nope, can't seem to find him at the moment."

"You mean he's disappeared?"

"Let's just say he's been misplaced. We'll find him."

"That name isn't Armenian, is it?" asked Janak.

"I don't think so. I've been told it's Kurdish."

"That explains some of the mystery," said Janak.

"Pardon?"

"Nothing. Just talking to myself. Do I get the forensic evidence report?"

"Sure, here it is." Bernardi handed a copy to Janak, who used his thumb and forefinger to flip through the document's thirty or so pages.

"Anything in particular you'd like me to focus on, Detective?"

"If there's one thing I already know about you, Mr. Marachak, it's that I'm sure you're several steps ahead of us."

Janak gave a slight smile.

"I have a question for you, Counselor," said Bernardi. "Where is your client Miguel Ramos?"

"I'm not at liberty to discuss my client's whereabouts with you."

"I figured you'd say that."

Janak put the report in his battered briefcase and stood up. "Thanks, Lieutenant. We'll see each other again."

He shook Bernardi's hand and began to walk out of the detective's office, but before he'd reached the door, the detective called out after him.

"There's something more you should know. There's been another murder. This time it was Joseph Hagopian, the cousin. He was found brutally murdered at his farm in Fresno."

"What's that got to do with my clients?" asked Janak, struggling to absorb the shock of this news.

"Miguel Ramos's fingerprints were found on the murder weapon. It was a machete."

Janak's turned white. He could feel his briefcase slipping from his grip as his palms began to sweat. "That's impossible!"

"Why do you say it's impossible, Counselor?"

"Believe me, it's impossible. They must have been planted by the same people who killed Armand Hagopian."

"I'm willing to listen to that argument," said Bernardi. "But you have to give me something to go on."

"I may do just that," said Janak. "But right now I have to know more about what you've just disclosed."

"I told you I was going to give you something you weren't entitled to, and I've done that. The rest is up to you."

Shaking his head, Janak exited the small station and got into Marisol's car. He placed the brown briefcase on the front seat beside him and stepped on the accelerator, his eyes searching the streets for a public phone. When he found one, he called his office and Marisol filled him in on what she'd heard from Samuel about the Fresno crime.

"I just heard the same thing from Bernardi." Janak sighed. "Since Samuel's on it, I'll just have to take a deep breath and wait 'til he gets back."

"Take an aspirin, boss," said Marisol.

Janak hung up the phone and returned to the car. He sat in the driver's seat with his head in his hands and closed his eyes, waiting for his thoughts to stop racing.

After a few minutes, he pulled out the forensic evidence report Bernardi had given him and began to leaf through the pages, stopping only when he came to the photograph of the partial footprint found at the edge of the raked area near the front gate of the dump. He also studied the plaster of Paris impression made of the footprint, quickly calculating that the shoe was about a size nine.

* * *

Janak went to Camelot the next evening with the idea of finding Samuel, whom he hadn't heard from for a couple of days, and telling him of the chilling evidence that was being mounted against his clients. A cold wind was whistling through the steep canyons of San Francisco's streets, but inside the bar the warm and relaxed atmosphere of a Friday prevailed. The patrons were celebrating the end of the workweek with more drinks than were probably good for them. Almost all were men in shirtsleeves, their ties loosened and their suit jackets hanging off their shoulders. No doubt some would leave Camelot late in the evening to exchange their work clothes for leather and slip off to neighborhoods south of Market, where an incipient community of gays hung out. There were also single women at Camelot—dressed in the obligatory office uniform of skirts, jackets, cotton blouses and high heels—but they could be counted on the fingers of both hands. Recently there had been several articles published about the problem of alcoholism among single women in San Francisco, and Melba and Blanche frequently had to pour one or another of their female patrons into a taxi to make sure they got home safely.

Entering the front door and looking beyond the crowd surrounding the round table, Janak saw Samuel talking to Blanche at the horseshoe bar. He frowned. He couldn't understand why Samuel acted like such a wimp. It was obvious he was crazy about Blanche. Any other guy in his shoes would have made a move on her, but all Samuel did was hang around her with his mopey, sad-dog face. Oh well, thought Janak; it wasn't his problem. Anyway, who was he to give advice? It wasn't like he'd had such great luck with women.

He elbowed his way through the crowd and tapped Samuel on the shoulder. Samuel didn't look surprised to see him; Blanche had already indicated with her eyes that Janak was approaching.

"I have bad news," Samuel blurted out.

"Hi, Blanche," said Janak, leaning over the bar to kiss her on the cheek. Then he turned to Samuel. "I also have bad news and I think it's the same. Joseph Hagopian?"

"Exactly!"

"You look like Dracula," interrupted Blanche, handing Janak a whiskey. "Let the house buy you a drink?"

"Thank you, you're an angel."

He turned back to Samuel. "Time flies," he said. "This case is a lot of work. We have to talk."

"You never offer me a drink, Blanche," said Samuel, only half-joking.

"What a bad memory. Mother doesn't charge you for half of what you consume. With more clients like you, Camelot would be broke."

"That's Melba, but you treat me like a stranger."

Blanche filled a glass with water and put it in front of him. She winked. "I suppose you want to talk in private," she said, turning serious. "My office is open."

The men walked past the hors d'oeuvre table to the back of the bar, where two polished mahogany doors faced each other. The one on the left led to the phone booth, the other to the office. Samuel opened the door on the right, which creaked under the pressure of the steel spring that snapped the door shut when it was released.

Samuel groped his way through the dark to the desk

against the back wall and turned on a small lamp. As Blanche always said, her mother couldn't be accused of good taste, and the lamp, which Melba had bought in a secondhand store and whose shade was decorated with pink ribbons, was no exception. Bad taste aside, it did its job, casting a soft light on the mess in the small room, which also contained a swivel secretarial chair in front of the desk and an ordinary kitchen chair to the side. Janak stared at the back wall; tarpaper and nails covered the space between the exposed studs. The contrast between the bare-bones office and the elegant bar was notable.

Samuel sat down in the swivel chair and indicated that Janak should take the other seat. He cleared a corner of the desk so they would have space to write. Janak, who was now sweating, placed his briefcase on the floor and unzipped his tan raincoat.

"You first," he said. "Tell me what you learned yesterday in Fresno."

Samuel told him of his encounter with Bucky Hughes.

"We need to find out if there was a machete at the Molate dumpsite," Janak said. "If not, we need to know if fingerprints can be transferred from one item to another, maybe with Scotch tape."

"I see what you mean," said Samuel. "It's all up in the air right now, at least until we get the reports from Bucky. Tell me what you found out."

Janak went over what he had learned from Juan Ramos and Bernardi, an account that Samuel summarized quickly in his notebook. In turn, Samuel described what he had gotten from the Armenian priest and the Hagopians.

"Just to be thorough in our investigation, I suppose we have to find out who the suspicious-looking people in these photos are," said Janak. "You're in charge of that, okay?"

Samuel nodded and made a note in his book.

"So far my most important discovery," Janak continued, "is about this guy Nashwan, a Kurd called *El Turco*, no less. He spent a lot of time with my clients and learned how to tie the specific knot that was found around Hagopian's neck. As far as the coroner goes, I didn't get anything from him. He wouldn't talk to me. But there is one more thing, and I think it's important: the police found a footprint at the dump, at the edge of the crime scene. Looks like it's about a size nine."

"What about the insect?"

"Right now, we have no information. The entomologist is looking into it and will get back to me for a price. What do you think of all this, Samuel?"

"Most worrisome are the fingerprints on the Fresno murder weapon. We need to find out if Miguel handled a machete in Richmond. If he did, then we're obviously dealing with a setup … Moving on to something else, Hagopian's wife is really young."

"A lot of rich men have young wives, Samuel."

"With adolescent children?"

"Put that on our list of things to look into," said Janak.

"I'm surprised that you got the Turk's name so easily," said Samuel. "Your assistant, Marisol, was going to try and get the names and addresses of all the employees, but she told me it would take awhile.

"The name's only a start," said Janak. "Now we need to find the guy."

"Hagopian's sister gave me some background on the history of the Armenians and the Turks," said Samuel. "I think it's weird that this guy Nashwan is a Kurd but they call him *El Turco*."

"I thought it was weird too, so I asked Marisol, who's Nicaraguan. She told me that all Latin Americans call Middle Eastern immigrants *Turcos*, because when they came to Latin America, they all came on Turkish passports. It doesn't make any difference what country they were originally from. Turks, Kurds, Armenians—they're all called *Turcos*."

"Isn't that insulting to them?"

"It's cultural," said Janak. "No one is offended by these things in Latin America. In any case, we have to find *El Turco's* whereabouts."

"After my talk with Candice Hagopian, I went to the university's Bancroft Library and delved further into the history of the Armenian genocide," said Samuel. "It's actually not such a shock to find a Kurd in their midst. The Turks treated the Kurds badly, and they still do. I mean, if this guy was actually a Turk and they were stupid enough to hire him, I could see him blowing up the dump or something like that.

"Let's talk about the French connection for a minute," Samuel continued. "That seems important here."

"What d'ya mean?"

"As you said before, one of us should go to France and see if we can find out anything about the Hagopians. We need to find out if there's some skeleton in their family closet that could have led to this."

"I'd love to go to Paris," said Janak wistfully. "I've got some unfinished business there. Unfortunately, I can't do it. There's just too much going on here with this case. Is there any possibility you can go, Samuel?"

"It's possible," said Samuel, obviously liking the idea. "But it'd have to be on my own dime. The paper would never spring for a trip like that. The boss would kick me out of his office if I even asked. Of course, if I find out something important that I can write about, I'll get reimbursed some day."

They both laughed.

"Tell me more about your visit with the coroner. Aren't you worried about him?"

"Sure I am," said Janak. "But evidence is evidence. If he wants to ignore the physical facts in order to make Deadeye happy, he's going to embarrass himself. I've already hired a pathologist and a criminologist who are better than he is. From the way he talked, he's probably not even an M.D." He stretched his legs, his gray socks showing beneath the pant legs, and folded his arms.

Samuel looked through the forensic evidence report, focusing on one page in particular.

"Isn't it suspicious that the chemicals in the Coke bottles are the very ones you've claimed caused the birth defects in your clients' children?"

"Yeah, and it should be obvious to any moron that your average Mexican workman wouldn't have the slightest idea what those chemicals were or what their effect would be on people. If they knew that, they wouldn't be working around them, would they? That kind of information had to come from someone much more sophisticated."

"Like?"

"Like Hagopian himself," said Janak. "Or someone who had access to the legal documents in the civil case and knows something about chemistry."

"In other words, someone could have gone to the courthouse and read the file. Is that what you mean?"

"That," said Janak, "or the defense attorney's file in the civil case."

"Does the clerk keep a record of who has access to the court file?"

"We'll find out soon enough," said Janak.

"Can I get copies of all those documents so I can study them?"

"Drop by the office Monday afternoon. They'll be ready for you. There's a lot to do, Samuel. We're going to have to split up the tasks. Let's make a plan as to who does what and how often we should get together to compare notes."

"I hate to bring it up again," said Samuel, his tone ironic.

"Because I know I'm the one who'll have to go. I'm referring to France ..." They both laughed.

* * *

Janak left to go back to his office, where he worked late into the night, and Samuel moved over to the horseshoe bar to see Blanche. Although she'd been serving clients in the hot and noisy space for many hours, she still looked fresh in her white sweats, her ponytail held neatly in place with a rubber band. She wore a trace of red lipstick and her blue eyes sparkled.

Samuel already had drunk his quota of alcohol for the day, so he ordered a mineral water; he didn't want it, but it gave him an excuse to stay a little longer at Camelot.

"You fellows were in the office for more than an hour," said Blanche. "What'd you talk about?"

"Just going over a lot of stuff about the case Janak is working on. The most interesting thing that keeps coming up is that there appears to be some kind of a connection between Hagopian and France. Janak and I agreed it needs to be looked into, and that it's going to fall on my shoulders." Samuel gave a theatrical sigh.

"Oh! Poor you! A trip to France! How awful! Is Hagopian the man who was killed at the dump?"

"The same."

"Did Janak tell you about Lucine?"

"Lucine? He's mentioned an Armenian girl that he knew in Paris. I see that Janak tells you about his private life. You two get along very well from the looks of it." As soon as he said that, Samuel realized he sounded sarcastic, even ridiculous, but Blanche didn't seem to notice.

"In this job you hear a lot of confidences, Samuel, and my mother's rule is that you shouldn't repeat anything. When men drink their liquor, they feel lonely and then they start talking. Janak is very private, but once in a while he needs a shoulder to cry on, just like everyone else."

"Tell me what you know, Blanche. This has to do with a mutual friend, so it's not the same as gossiping."

"I will, on one condition."

"What's that?"

"That if you go to France you look for Lucine."

"How do you expect me to find her? Paris isn't just a neighborhood.

"I have an address."

"You have her address? Why?"

"Because the night Janak talked to me about Lucine, he had a letter he'd written her. But the next day was Saturday and his office was closed, so I told him I would mail it for him. I guess it was easier for him to give it to me."

"Did you read it?"

"How could you think such a thing, Samuel! Of course I didn't read it. But I was moved by what he told me about the girl, so I wrote down the address."

"What did he tell you?"

"He said they met in the street, fell in love and spent several intense weeks together. But when Janak saw that the relationship was getting serious, he ran away."

"You mean he dumped her?"

"Just like that. He told me he came back to California without even giving her an explanation. Of course, he regretted his decision a few days later and called her, but he couldn't reach her. Then he started writing her, but Lucine never answered him. This was a couple of years ago, I think. Lucine must have been furious."

"With wounded pride?"

"Something like that, or it could be that she's completely forgotten him. But if there's a speck of hope, I think we should help Janak."

Samuel's face burned and he began to sweat with relief. It was evident Blanche wasn't romantically attached to Janak or she wouldn't be acting as midwife to a frustrated love affair. Even if it were just to keep Janak at a prudent distance from Blanche, he would look for that Lucine street by street in Paris.

"Give me the address and I'll look for her. And if she's Armenian, maybe she can help us find out something about the Hagopians."

"Don't tell Janak what you're doing. He would kill me for interfering in this. Promise?"

"I promise."

6

The City of Lights

SAMUEL HADN'T BEEN A great student of languages in school—
he botched up French with more boldness than dexterity—but
he had a good ear. The problem was, given his limited abilities,
it was going to be a challenge to get critical information about
Janak's case in a place like Paris.

After what seemed like an eternal journey from San
Francisco, Samuel arrived in Paris exhausted. He went directly
to the hotel, where he fell into bed and slept for twelve hours.

The next day, his first stop was La Roche et Fils, a tailor shop
on Rue St. Laurent, one of the city's most exclusive shopping
venues. Even there, as in less affluent neighborhoods, the scent
of freshly baked croissants and coffee permeated the morning
air. Samuel figured the smell came from the hotels that dotted the street. Water ran in the gutters, the flow directed by a
row of rolled-up rags, and laborers wearing blue work jackets
swept the sidewalks clean, Gauloises cigarettes hanging from
their lips.

The tailor shop was next to a store called Gucci, a name
Samuel wasn't familiar with. Nonetheless, he couldn't help
admiring the shoes in the window, even though he knew he
would never be able to afford them. Gucci and La Roche et
Fils weren't for people like him, but he entered the tailor shop

boldly and asked in English to speak to the manager.

The manager presented himself promptly. He was neatly dressed in a fashionable gray pinstriped suit, and wore a conservatively patterned blue silk tie and a matching silk handkerchief in his lapel pocket.

"May I be of service to you, *Monsieur?*" the manager asked in English, to Samuel's great relief. But he felt the man staring at his plain khaki sports coat, which needed a pressing, at the very least, even though it had no cigarette burn holes like in the old days.

"My name is Samuel Hamilton," he said, handing the man his card and showing him the coroner's photograph of the label inside of Armand Hagopian's suit jacket. "I'm from San Francisco and I work for its most important newspaper. I need information about the man you made this suit for. The number's right here." He pointed to the number 7934 stitched above the tailor's name. "It should help you identify him."

The manager took a small magnifying glass from his coat pocket and examined the label.

"Excuse me," he said. "I'll look in our records."

Once he had left the room, Samuel examined the large fabric books lying on several low tables and the double-stacked rows of men's suits in expensive garment bags against one of the walls. On another wall, women's clothing hung in transparent bags, the material protected but still visible to passing eyes. A dark green plush sofa and a carved wooden coffee table faced a large plate glass window. Clients could sit on the sofa and browse the fashion magazines or fabric books, in full view of the tourists and other shoppers wandering from shop to shop.

After twenty minutes, the man returned, a troubled look on his face.

"With regard to the account that interests you, we are unable to give you any information concerning this garment or the person who bought it."

"I know who it belonged to," said Samuel, disappointed. "It was Armand Hagopian."

"If you know who it belongs to, why are you asking these questions of me?"

"I haven't made myself clear," said Samuel, deciding that the direct approach was best under the circumstances. "This man was murdered a short time ago in California, in the San Francisco Bay Area."

"Armand Hagopian, murdered?"

"Yes, and I'm trying to find out if anyone in France had anything to do with his death."

"Let me say that, if this is true, it is quite a shock to me personally," said the man, turning pale. Samuel noted a slight tremor in the pencil he held in his right hand. "If Mr. Hagopian was killed, as you say, you should be dealing with the French police and not with me. We cannot give out information about our clients."

Turning away from Samuel, he stuffed the pencil he was fidgeting with behind the silk handkerchief in his lapel pocket and fingered the sales tags on the worktable. Samuel tried to get his attention by moving to the other side of the worktable to confront him again, but the man refused to acknowledge his presence. Their conversation was clearly over. Samuel thanked the man but, when he didn't get a reply, he left, calling out "*Au revoir, Monsieur*" on his way out the door.

Despite getting nowhere with the shop manager, Samuel wasn't discouraged. In his business, doors were frequently closed in his face.

Samuel thought about what to do next, wondering how long the time change between San Francisco and Paris would slow him down. He felt like his brain was full of cotton. He walked around the block to the park next to the Champs Elysées and sat down on an empty bench, yanking on the sleeves of his sports coat in an attempt to pull the wrinkles out. For the first time, he noticed a chill in the air.

Once his head had cleared, Samuel decided to go back to the Left Bank and have lunch in an environment more hospitable to his pocketbook. Since he had come on the Metro, he didn't know how to get back to the hotel, but from where he sat, he saw several bridges crossing the Seine River, so he figured he couldn't be too lost. He approached a policeman and, in the best French he could muster, asked for directions to the Left Bank. The officer directed him to cross the river at the Pont Neuf, which was the oldest standing bridge in Paris.

The winter sky was overcast, and Samuel began to worry that it might begin to rain or snow. He hadn't brought an overcoat to Paris; all he had was his khaki sports jacket and a scarf. As he crossed the Tuileries Garden, its plane trees bereft of leaves, Samuel rubbed his hands together to keep them warm.

Once on the other side of the bridge, he dashed into Le Marinier, the first restaurant he came across. The interior was dark, and the only decorations were models of sailing ships hanging from the ceiling. He negotiated a place by the window, which offered a view of the quick-flowing Seine beyond the stone wall on the opposite side of the narrow street. The river was quiet, devoid of all activity. Just as the sidewalk tables —so ubiquitous throughout Paris in warmer weather—had disappeared with the cold, so, too, had the boat traffic.

As its name implied, Le Marinier was a fish restaurant, but since Samuel wanted something that would stick to his ribs, he asked the Brazilian waiter to bring him steak and pommes frites with a half bottle of red wine. Ordering was done more with his hands than with words, since each party spoke very different versions of the same language.

Janak had told him it was impossible to have a bad meal in Paris and Samuel soon understood that his friend was right, that even simple meals were well served and reasonably priced. He left the young man an extra large tip and, still suffering the effects of the time change, hurried back to his hotel to take a nap.

He awoke an hour later, splashed cold water on his face and took a crumpled piece of paper out of his wallet, studying the address Blanche had given him for Lucine. At the reception desk, he showed the clerk the address and asked for directions. The man consulted a street guide and showed him how to get there.

Samuel went back to his room and tied his red wool scarf around his neck to ward off the chill. Then he marched off to the Metro, heading for the stop at Chausee d'Antin.

From what Janak had told Blanche, he knew that Lucine lived in an attractive building in a comfortable part of the city near the Galeries Lafayette Department Store. He found the building—located at 12, rue de Provence—and climbed the staircase to the second floor, where he knocked on the only door. A young woman in her early twenties answered. Samuel explained that he was looking for Lucine Clarke. She shook her head and told Samuel in rapid French that she had lived in the apartment for more than a year and there was no Lucine there.

Tired of struggling with his poor French, Samuel tried English.

"Do you think that someone in the building knows where she has gone?"

"Let me think," she answered in English. "It is possible one of the girls who has lived here a longer than I have knows of her. Come with me, *Monsieur*." They descended to the first floor and the girl knocked on the door. After some delay, a striking woman with black hair and blue eyes appeared at the door.

"Oh, it's you," she said, smiling cautiously. "I was expecting

Renée. Who is your friend?"

"This American is looking for Lucine Clarke."

"Lucine Clarke … *Mon Dieu*, she hasn't lived here for about two years," the woman answered, looking Samuel over suspiciously. "What does he want with her?"

"I assure you I only bring good news from America," Samuel said in his meager French, smiling at her reassuringly.

"You know the American who was her lover? Is that it?"

"I bring news from him, *Mademoiselle*."

"I'm not so sure Lucine is anxious to hear of him," she scoffed.

"I was asked to deliver a message to her."

"Yes, yes," she said, laughing. "They all come back, one way or another—some on their knees, begging for forgiveness, others triumphantly, eager to show off their wealth and position. Into which category does your friend fall?"

"Do you know where I can find her?" asked Samuel, sensing he had come to the right door.

She thought for a moment, looking at Samuel with renewed interest. "You will have to come back later. I will make some inquiries."

"I understand," said Samuel. "I'll be back tomorrow morning. How about ten?"

"*No, no, Monsieur.* That is too early for a Sunday. Let's say one o'clock. *Au revoir.*" She slammed the door.

Samuel thanked the young woman who had helped him and left the apartment house with a sense of hope.

* * *

At the appointed time the next day Samuel rapped at the door of the first floor apartment. The same striking woman opened it.

"I see you Americans are very punctual."

"It's just that I have important business with Lucine."

"Yes, I am sure," she said in a sarcastic tone. "She will see you. However, I said nothing of your mission. I just told her someone was looking for her, and she gave me her new address."

"Excuse me, *Mademoiselle*, but I didn't tell you what my mission was."

"You don't have to. What you want to do is put her in contact with her long-lost lover. Isn't that true?"

"Is that what you think, *Mademoiselle*?"

"Is that the truth or not?" she asked defiantly, her hands on her hips.

"It has to do with some letters from America. Since Lucine moved, I don't think she received them." Samuel improvised, feeling like an idiot and greatly affected by the rare beauty and insight of the young lady.

"I don't know how the mail is in America, but here it is very efficient," she said.

"Is there a phone number?" asked Samuel.

"Yes, of course. How else would I have called her? But she said to give you her address. Here it is." She handed him a piece of paper.

"How do I get to this number 20, rue de La Victoire?" asked Samuel, studying the paper.

"You can walk, it's close by. *Au revoir*." She began to shut the door, but Samuel put his hand out to stop her.

"Thank you for helping me, *Mademoiselle*. I will tell Lucine of your kindness." Samuel gave her his best smile, eager to extend the visit for a little while. It was difficult to say goodbye to such a pretty girl. As she closed the door, she gave him a look of confusion. And this time she didn't slam it.

Samuel sat down on the front steps of the building and took out his pocketbook map of Paris. He studied it and discovered that the street Lucine lived on was, in fact, close by.

King of the Bottom

When he found the building, he took a deep breath before entering. What would he say to a woman he didn't know?

His rapped on the door. After a minute it opened and he found himself face to face with a very attractive, slender young woman with big brown eyes, an angular face, and black hair that fell loosely about her shoulders. She radiated elegance and calm. Samuel was surprised; somehow he didn't expect Janak to have such good taste. He gave her his business card and introduced himself as a friend of Janak Marachak.

Her face reddened and her eyes narrowed.

"Janak Marachak, you say?" Though visibly angry, she had the presence of mind to respond in English. "Is this about him?"

"I'm sorry to bother you, *Mademoiselle*. It is about Janak, but he doesn't know I'm here."

"I don't understand."

Searching for a way to appease her and to keep the dialogue going without doing more harm to his friend, Samuel tried again. "As I told you, I'm a friend of Janak's. I know that he thinks about you all the time, with affection and a bit of confusion, because he's lost contact with you."

Lucine straightened, her eyes narrowed again and her color increased. Samuel thought it was all over; he expected to have the door shut in his face, but apparently she was searching for the right words.

"Janak abandoned me, Mr. Hamilton. So it is almost impossible for me to believe that he remembers me at all."

"I'm serious. He really does, *Mademoiselle*. He gave me an address for you," Samuel lied. "But you don't live there anymore. He said he wrote you many times but got no answer."

"Yes, I know exactly how many times he wrote me, Mr. Hamilton." Lucine, regaining her composure, wiped her hands on the apron she was wearing and opened the door. "Please come in. It is very rude of me to keep you on the doorstep."

Samuel entered the apartment, which was filled with the faint aroma of spices, and found himself in a simple living room. It was full of light— through the window he saw the barren branches of the trees—and the ambiance was cozy and cheerful. The living room motif was vaguely Middle Eastern, but he wasn't sophisticated enough to tell where each piece of furniture was from. A bronze brazier in the middle of the room acted as a coffee table and was surrounded by low-slung chairs and colorful silk pillows. If the woven tapestries on two of the walls were as old as they looked, Samuel imagined they were quite expensive.

"Janak said you were a banker." Samuel lied again to break the ice.

"Yes, that is my work," said Lucine.

Samuel was momentarily stumped. What did one talk to a banker about? He searched his memory, trying to remember what Blanche had told him about this woman. Once she invited him to come in, however, Lucine's attitude changed. She directed him to a sofa, which was covered in crude, colored linen, and had two hand-knit cushions at each end. He was relieved that she didn't offer him one of the low-slung seats, where his knees would have been at the same level as his ears. She sat down beside him.

"What brings you to Paris, Mr. Hamilton?" she asked, observing him attentively. "I assume you didn't come solely to give me a message from Janak?"

"I'm actually doing a job for him." Samuel explained the details of the crime and his need to get information about Hagopian.

"It is very generous of you to come to France to help your friend," she said, smoothing the fabric of the dark skirt she was wearing. "Why are you doing it?"

"Fair question," said Samuel admiringly. "The main thing is to save some poor workers he represents in a legal case from the gas chamber. At the same time, I have to admit that I'll get the exclusive story for my paper."

"Did you know that I was Armenian?"

"Yes, I learned that from Janak. But your last name is Clarke, isn't it?"

"Yes, my father was English, which is why I speak the language. But he also spoke French very well so my mother never needed to learn English. Unfortunately, he's no longer with us."

"You do speak English very well," said Samuel. "This is quite a relief for me because, as you can tell, my French is not so good. I'm sorry about your father."

Samuel guessed that in spite of her earlier reaction, Lucine was warming up. Maybe it was because she was curious about the case he described. He explained that Janak, as a civil trial lawyer, usually only got involved in cases where chemicals caused injuries to consumers or workers.

"If he's not a criminal lawyer, why did he take this case?"

"Because the accused are already his clients in a civil suit against the man who was killed. Janak and I are convinced they are innocent. Besides, they are poor and they can't pay a lawyer to represent them."

"Janak won't charge them?"

"Janak works on contingency. He charges a percentage of what he gets for his clients in the civil case."

"And the criminal case?"

"Since they don't have any money, they wouldn't be able to find a lawyer to represent them. But Janak said he would. Frankly, I don't think he's thought about money."

"I understand," said Lucine, pensively. "Would you like some tea?"

"Thank you, I would," said Samuel, relieved to see that the young woman was starting to relax.

Lucine disappeared through one of the side doors. When

she returned, she was carrying a tray filled with a teapot and two teacups, a small cream pitcher, almond and honey pastries, and a dish of lemon slices. She also brought white linen napkins with colorful wildflowers embroidered around the edges, which impressed Samuel, who was more used to the paper napkins at Camelot and the Chinese restaurants he frequented. Lucine poured Samuel a cup of tea and offered him a pastry.

"The victim was Armenian, as I explained, and he had ties to Paris. But so far I haven't had any luck with inquiries." He told her about the label in Hagopian's clothes and his encounter with the owner of La Roche et Fils.

Lucine laughed. "The French are very reserved. In order to find out things in this society, you have to know someone. For that reason you've come to the right place. We call it destiny, but I think you Americans call it luck."

"What do you mean by that, *Mademoiselle?*"

"You may call me Lucine. My mother's family came here because of the genocide. Are you familiar with the history of the Armenians?"

"Yes. I've studied it, so I have a general idea of what happened and the effect it had on the survivors."

Lucine nodded. "My mother knows a lot about the families who survived and came to Paris. She may be able to give you information about some of them."

She poured Samuel another cup of tea, left the room and, after a few minutes, returned with an older woman dressed in a red dress with an apron over it. Lucine introduced her as Sasiska and explained to her in French what Samuel wanted.

When they were done talking, Lucine turned back to Samuel. "Tell me again the name of the family you are inquiring about."

"Armand Hagopian. His sister's name is Candice, and the cousin's name is Joseph Hagopian."

Sasiska didn't understand English well, but when she heard the names, her eyes lit up and she spoke to Lucine in rapid French.

"My mother says she recognizes those names."

"Will you ask her if she can give me some background on the family?"

Samuel strained to catch any of what was said, but the two women spoke too quickly for him to follow.

"She says she remembers from the early days, when her family and theirs became refugees after the massacre at Erzerum."

"Yes, that's the place they're from," said Samuel excitedly.

"My mother went to school with Armand, his sister and Joseph. They all lived in the Armenian section of Paris."

"Does that section still exist?" he asked, incredulous in the face of such luck. He stood up and took a deep breath, wishing he had a cigarette to calm his nerves.

After a lengthy discussion with Sasiska, Lucine translated for Samuel.

"Yes, there are actually two Armenian sections. The 9th arrondissement, where we live, and which is known as the Diamond district, and the Belleville district, which is in the 20th arrondissement. You can imagine, from the names, that the families that are better off live in the Diamond district and the more modest ones live in the Belleville."

"I assume that the Hagopians lived in the Diamond district?"

"Of course," said Lucine.

"Ask her if the family had any enemies."

Lucine consulted her mother again. "She doesn't remember anything like that. But if you have some time, she can make inquiries."

"I'm grateful for any help I can get. Does she think anyone at La Roche et Fils might have any information that could help us?"

"She will inquire and let you know. She invites you to tea in two days."

"Merci beaucoup, Madame," Samuel said to Sasiska before turning back to Lucine. "I have another question for her. Can she find out anything about a Kurdish man by the name of Nashwan Asad Aram." Samuel knew this was a long shot; it would be just too much of a coincidence.

"Was this man somehow connected to Mr. Hagopian?" asked Lucine.

"He worked for him, but it's possible he wasn't a friend. That's why I'm asking."

"I see. I will try and explain that to her."

* * *

Walking to the Metro on his way back to his hotel, Samuel reflected on his good fortune. Not only had he found Lucine, he also had stumbled upon an entrée to the Armenian community. He was taken with Lucine and wondered how Janak could leave a woman like that. His friend must have been out of his mind.

When he got back to the hotel, he made another of his lists, this time of things he hoped to learn from Sasiska about the Armenians. His notebook was full of lists. He couldn't do his work without them.

1. Was there anyone in the Armenian community who wanted to harm the Hagopians?

2. If so, I need the names of the people or groups and the reasons.

3. Did anyone Sasiska spoke to already know about the Hagopian deaths in California before she talked to them?

4. If there was a person or group of people who wanted to hurt the Hagopians, did they have any U.S. connections? Did

they have the muscle to carry out the murders? And if they did, where should he look in the U.S. for more information?

5. Was there a connection between the Kurd and the Hagopian family?

After reading over the list a couple of times more, Samuel added one more question:

6. How can I put Janak in contact with Lucine without getting caught up in a mess?

* * *

Two days later, Samuel showed up at four o'clock for tea with Lucine and her mother. Sasiska was dressed more formally than the last time, and looked as if she'd made a recent visit to the hairdresser. That touch of coquetry on a woman old enough to be his mother touched Samuel. Lucine, on the other hand, wore the same clothes she had on the first time he saw her.

After tea and pastries, they talked a long time—with Lucine acting as interpreter—until, suddenly, Samuel noted that it was dark outside. He looked at his watch, realizing he'd monopolized the mother and daughter for over four hours. Although he still wanted to pursue something the mother had said about a Hagopian family servant, he thought better of it, at least for the time being.

"I apologize for taking up so much of your time," he said. "Please allow me to take you to dinner."

"No, no," said Lucine. "Instead you will join us for an Armenian supper. We thought this conversation would last a long time, so my mother prepared something to eat. You cannot say no, because then she will be offended. She's a very good cook."

Sasiska, sure he would stay, had already left for the kitchen.

"I'd like that very much. Thank you."

Lucine opened a bottle of Chablis and brought two crystal glasses from the china cabinet. They toasted his good fortune, and then she began to explain the many details of Armenian food.

"We call dinner *josh*," she said. "It's always served after five o'clock." It was now after eight.

She ushered him into the dining room, where Sasiska was waiting for them. In addition to the many different aromas coming from the food on the table, Samuel also detected the smell of roasting meat wafting in from the kitchen. As Lucine poured a glass of wine for her mother, she spoke softy to her and then left the room, leaving Samuel alone in the dining room with Sasiska. Neither spoke the other's language and Samuel didn't attempt to speak French. But after four hours together, he felt comfortable with her, so he didn't hesitate to ask her the names of the various dishes by pointing to the plates in front of him.

"*Ensalade de lolik, varung, giazar, sokh avec panir,*" she explained, pointing out the tomatoes, cucumbers, carrots, onions and cheese in what she called the salad. She pointed to the bowls of black olives on the table. "*Zertun,*" she announced.

Then, signaling to three bowls of yogurt: "*Mitzun.*" She smiled, showing her beautiful teeth, which were only slightly yellowed by age.

Samuel ate the salad with pieces of bread.

"*Hots,*" she said, taking a piece from the basket, which was within easy reach.

Seeing that he eyed a bowl of soup, she quickly added a new word to the conversation: "*Spas.*"

"What's in it?" asked Samuel, admiring its deep red color. "*Borsch.*"

Samuel recognized the name. The Armenians must have gotten their soup from the Russians, he thought. Just then Lucine returned.

"I see you are already enjoying the food. As you can tell, Armenians are serious eaters, but don't be fooled by what you see in front of you. There is still the main course. The salad and the soup are always at the table, so the visitors will be attracted, like flies to honey. Most guests who have never dealt with Armenians overdo it—especially when they see their hosts eating so much bread. We do like our *hots*."

"I have an important question," said Samuel. "Am I at liberty to tell Janak that I've found you?"

Lucine blushed. "You are capturing my thoughts, Samuel. I don't know you very well, so I can't ask you to do this for me with any certainty that you will do it, but I will ask anyway. I would prefer if you just told Janak that you found me. You may give him my current address but no more. I have my reasons. For a long time, I haven't wanted to hear from him. Before I begin any kind of dialogue with him, I need to make sure that's what I want."

"You've been a great help to me, Lucine, and also to him. And believe me, I am a man of my word. I will do exactly as you wish. But I need to share the information that Sasiska has gathered for me."

"I understand that. Perhaps one day I will be able to explain my reasons."

"You don't have to explain them to me, Lucine," said Samuel kindly. He dabbed his chin with the white napkin and took a drink of his wine. "Sasiska never mentioned the Kurd or even how to find out anything about him. Is he a lost cause?"

"'Lost cause'?" Lucine repeated, confused. "I don't know that word in English."

"It means dead end. No information available."

"She wasn't able to find out anything, but I will talk with you about him tomorrow. I have some ideas. I have helped the bank locate many people over the years, so let me contact my sources to see if we can learn something about this man."

Sasiska brought the main course in from the kitchen and the three of them toasted the dish, which was fragrant roast pork surrounded by grilled eggplant, potatoes, onions and a variety of peppers.

"It is called *khorovatz*," said Lucine. "The meat has been marinating in a special sauce since yesterday. Do you see how many different colored peppers there are?"

"It's a good thing you warned me that there was another plate or I would have filled up on bread, salad and soup." Samuel devoured the pork roast, enjoying each and every bite. He took sips of Chablis when he needed to wash down the meat.

"Ever since Sasiska mentioned him yesterday, I've been thinking about this Hector Somolian, the Hagopians' servant when they lived in Erzerum. Do you think we could talk with him tomorrow?"

Lucine consulted briefly with Sasiska. "We will both have to go with you because he doesn't speak French very well. Somolian probably isn't his real name. Most likely it's one he adopted for protection."

"I understand," said Samuel. "Do you think we'll find him at home?"

"Oh, yes, he is an invalid. He has been one since Erzerum. He lives in a small hotel room in Belleville with several of his relatives. They make shoes, so he is always there. In fact, he and his family have made shoes for us for many years."

After they had agreed to meet at ten the next morning, Samuel got up to leave, but Lucine stopped him with a gesture. He hadn't yet tried her mother's *torte*. Sasiska brought a pastry from the kitchen and cut a slice for Samuel. It was laden with walnuts and fruit, covered with chocolate and piled high with mounds of vanilla icing. Lucine presented the bombe with pride.

"My mother is the reigning champion of *tortes*. No one in Paris makes them any better."

Samuel couldn't argue. It was delicious. When he finished, he was tempted to ask for another slice, but knew better. Any more food and he'd likely get sick.

"Excuse my curiosity, Lucine. Now that I've met you, I can't imagine what happened between you and Janak to bring about so much resentment. I've known Janak for a few years now and I admire him. He's a man of integrity. He has an unyielding sense of justice, and is always willing to defend the underdog against all odds. What'd he do to disappoint you so much?"

"It was more than that, Samuel." she replied, turning away so that he couldn't see her tears. "But that is all in the past."

Samuel realized that he'd gone too far. On an impulse, he went to her, put an arm around her shoulders and gave her a brief hug.

* * *

After Samuel left, Lucine poured another glass of Chablis and stared blankly out the window, overwhelmed by her memories. Janak had more than disappointed her; he had betrayed her. She met him a few years ago when she was a student at the Sorbonne. He was an American tourist who asked for directions. Attracted by the contrast between his rough and weathered looks and the soft expression in his eyes, she decided to accompany him to his destination. It took only four blocks of walking and an afternoon talking at a coffee shop for both to realize that they were smitten. A few days later they knew they'd fallen in love. At least, she had. It was a trite story, Lucine thought. A girl falls in love with a stranger, gets pregnant in spite of precautions, and her life changes forever.

It was an accident. It happens sometimes. It can happen to anyone, she'd said to Janak, feeling stupid and guilty.

I didn't know you were willing to do this, Lucine. I certainly am not. Don't you realize that we can't even consider having a baby?

She'd begun to cry softly. He took her in his arms and explained to her once again that he was just beginning his career and didn't have his feet planted yet; he couldn't support a family. Of course, he added, he would take care of the problem financially—it was the only reasonable thing to do.

She replied that abortion was illegal in France and that she was not sure that she was in favor of it anyway.

You can't ruin your life by becoming a single mother, Lucine, he'd said firmly. It was then she understood that Janak was not the man she thought he was. He wouldn't even take responsibility for his part in it. In his eyes, it was her problem only.

A few days later, a taxi took them to an address in the Marais Lucine had gotten from a friend. They located the stairs in the rear and climbed them slowly. Each step increased the girl's terror. Janak knocked on a door with iron bars and the *faiseuse d'ange*—"the angel maker," as she was crudely known—opened the door. She took Lucine by the arm and ushered her into a pale green room with one fluorescent light in the middle of the ceiling. A buzzing fan moved from side to side and a scratchy-sounding radio played Edith Piaf songs, which were occasionally interrupted by commercials.

A middle-aged woman with tired eyes and streaks of gray in her hair greeted them with a comforting smile. She wore a wrinkled nurse's uniform in need of washing and sat behind what looked like an old teacher's desk, which had probably been picked up at a rummage sale.

Bonjour, ma cherie, she said, setting her Gauloise in the ashtray. Although she looked at Lucine kindly, she never once acknowledged Janak's presence. *Don't worry, it will soon be over. Just put your five hundred francs on the desk.*

Janak put the money down. The nurse counted out the combination of tens and twenties he'd laid on the table.

King of the Bottom

Tout est prêt, she said, winking at the girl. *Follow me.*

She led Lucine into an adjacent room, also painted the same pale green. It had a table with straps and stirrups, and one bright fluorescent light shone directly above. Janak cringed and Lucine, terrified, began to shake.

You wait outside, Monsieur," said the nurse. *"This is woman's work."* She closed the door in his face.

Lucine disrobed and put on the white gown the woman handed her. As she climbed onto the table, she made the sign of the cross. *May God forgive me,* she mumbled.

Relax, girl, the nurse assured her. *You're doing the right thing, and you won't even know it happened.*

The nurse washed her hands, inserted an IV and told Lucine to start counting.

The next thing Lucine knew, Janak was helping her off the table. She was very groggy and he had to put her dress on for her.

What time is it? she asked.

A quarter past nine.

Morning or night?

Morning. You've only been here a short while.

The nurse, clearing her throat to gain their attention, fitted Lucine with a sanitary napkin. She then handed her a package of more napkins, along with some antibiotic pills.

If the bleeding doesn't stop within two days, see a doctor. Take the antibiotics twice a day, starting this evening. We have already given you a dose in the IV, which should last you all day. Take it easy for a while and no sex for six weeks. Let me tell you, chérie, you will forget this very soon. Adieu et bonne chance.

Merci, Madame, Lucine managed to say, nauseated by the Gauloise the nurse had just lit.

After Janak took her home, she never saw him again.

* * *

The next morning, Samuel picked up Lucine and Sasiska at their home and they walked the short distance to the Metro. Sasiska wore a bright green silk dress and a white scarf on her head. Lucine looked as if she'd had a rough night; she had bags under her eyes and a tired look on her face. But Samuel sensed that this was not the time to pry.

They walked down the stairs at the Metro station and Samuel bought three round-trip tickets to the Belleville district. They entered the bowels of the underground with the rest of the crowd and the *poinçonneur* punched their tickets. Stopping in front of a map fastened to the tiled wall, Lucine pointed to the stops they would have to make to get where they were going. They followed the sign toward Porte de Mairie de Montreuil. On their way to the platform, Samuel saw a poster of a man dressed in work clothes. He had a red nose and an enormous belly that was held up by a wheelbarrow.

"Does that mean what I think it means?" asked Samuel.

"Probably. We have a problem with people who drink too much wine," said Lucine. "It's a national disgrace."

"Interesting," said Samuel. "I thought France exported all its wine."

"What? Don't be silly! The best wines stay in France."

They boarded a wooden car with huge rubber tires and sat down.

"You didn't seem very happy when we met this morning," said Samuel, finally overcome by his curiosity.

"You coming to see us brought back many memories."

"About Janak?"

"About the time we spent together in Paris. It wasn't all bad, you know…But this is something I'd rather not talk about."

By then they'd arrived at the République station, where they transferred to the 11 line, and in no time found themselves at the Jourdain Metro station, with its typical vaulted tile design. They climbed the stairs to the Rue de Belleville, which was crowded with a colorful array of people dressed in ethnic clothing.

"Where are all these people from?" asked Samuel.

Lucine laughed. "From everywhere. They're Greeks, Poles, Jews and of course Armenians."

"How about Turks?"

"Not in this neighborhood. They wouldn't be welcome. In fact, it would be dangerous for them, and not just because of the Armenians. You know they also have big problems with the Greeks."

"What's that across the street?" asked Samuel, pointing.

"That is the *shuka*," answered Lucine. "The market."

Open stalls faced the sidewalk and extended at least three hundred feet, with aisles every few feet leading into the interior of the market. The stalls he could see were filled with a great variety of fresh vegetables and fruits, even though it was the dead of winter. There were also vendors hawking fresh meat and dry goods, and several kebab stalls.

"Where does all this fresh produce come from?" asked Samuel.

"From their farms or from their countries. It comes by truck, train and ship, and some of it even comes by plane. People will pay extra to buy food from their own country."

"What's in back of the food stalls?" asked Samuel.

"Clothing, bedding, furniture, spices—everything imaginable. The meat salesmen have their main shops on the inside of the market. They stand outside to get the people's attention. Would you like to stop and have some tea or Armenian coffee?"

"No thanks. I want to talk to Hector Somolian, or whatever his name is."

Once past the *shuka*, Samuel took note of the buildings, which were old and weathered. Their wooden and stone façades had long ago been painted a variety of colors—white, yellow, green and brown—and were in need of fresh coats of paint. The faded and flaking fronts gave the buildings the appearance of being abandoned, but they clearly weren't, since people streamed in and out.

Samuel, Lucine and Sasiska continued their walk up the Rue de Belleville until they reached Rue des Fêtes. Sasiska guided them to the left, and they soon came to a black iron sign above a stone arch that read "Hotel." The black wooden entry door that filled the arch had so many coats of paint on it that the surface was uneven. Sasiska pointed to a large metal latch and Samuel stepped forward to haul the door open.

Once inside, they found themselves in a gloomy entranceway. Feeble light from the few remaining bulbs in the dusty chandelier—most of the bulbs were either burned-out or missing entirely—did little to illuminate the space, which had the appearance of a dimly lit cavern.

"This place is spooky," said Samuel.

"The people who live here are poor, so it isn't so well taken care of," said Lucine. "We are almost there."

They proceeded down the corridor past the hotel reception counter, a large dark mahogany rectangle with a dull, battered top. It was covered with knife carvings of many peoples' initials. On top of the counter was an old black phone and hanging from the wall directly behind it was a cabinet of sorts, with several pigeonholes. At one time they had held the mail and the keys to the rooms; now they were empty and gathering dust.

Sasiska took them further down the dark hallway until they came to the third door on the left, where she stopped and listened before knocking gently. The door opened a crack and a Middle Eastern-looking woman with a scarf around her head peered out. When she saw Sasiska, she unlatched the chain and opened the door. The women embraced and spoke rapidly in what Samuel thought had to be Armenian,.

An odor of food, glue and leather wafted through the open door. Looking through the opening, Samuel saw seven people sitting at makeshift workbenches making shoes. Sasiska and the woman with the scarf walked hand-in-hand to a small, one-legged man seated at an industrial sewing machine, bent over a shoe. His white hair reached to his shoulders and his wrinkled, bronze face showed his advanced age. A pair of crutches leaned against the work platform beside him.

Sasiska touched his shoulder. Recognizing her, he gave a toothless smile and turned the machine off. Placing his one leg on the floor, he lifted himself to a standing position, hopping in a semi-circle to face her before lowering himself back down.

While Sasiska and the man exchanged greetings, Samuel looked around. "As you said, it's a shoe factory," he whispered to Lucine.

"It is during the day. All these people belong to the same family. This is where they live and work. At the end of the day, they bring down the beds and then they cook their meals in that corner over there," She pointed to a pot simmering on the small stove.

"What about bathrooms?"

"They are at the end of the hallway. All the tenants on a floor have to share them and keep them clean. Many old buildings are like that, Samuel. Private bathrooms are a modern luxury."

"I assume this is Hector Somolian? Do you think he will talk to me?"

"Yes, that is why we brought you here."

"Ask him how well he knew the Hagopian family."

Lucine asked Sasiska, and she in turn asked the little man, who became very animated and talked to her in a frail voice for several minutes. Sasiska, speaking French, translated for

Lucine, none of which Samuel was able to understand.

"He says that when he was young he was one of the Hagopians' servants. When things got really bad in Erzerum, just before the Turks went house to house killing everyone, the Hagopian family left in a hurry, in the dead of night. He saw the man who led them away and he says he wasn't an Armenian. He was a Turk—a high-ranking military officer. At first Hector thought his master's family had been betrayed and that they were being taken away for execution. Before he left, Mr. Hagopian told the servants to take anything they wanted from the house. The servants thought it was safer to stay there than hide somewhere else, so they turned out the lights and hid in the cellar for several days until they were found and attacked."

"The Turks finally got them, huh?"

"No. It was other Armenians. They came and killed all the servants except for Hector. They hacked him with a sword, they cut his off his leg and…" She hesitated. "They also cut off his private parts, stuffed them in his mouth and left him for dead."

Samuel was horrified. "Why would the Armenians do that to the servants?"

"No one knows. Hector obviously didn't die, as you can see. His family came to the Hagopian compound and carted him off and hid him in a cave outside Erzerum until he was able to travel. They then escaped through Bulgaria and ended up here in Paris. The family changed their name to Somolian to protect themselves from whoever was trying to kill them."

"Were they ever able to figure out who that was?"

"No, and they finally decided it was safer not to inquire. If they investigated more, the people responsible might find out Hector was alive and come after him and his family."

The little man sat comfortably in his chair, sipping a cup of tea. He had a calm and soft look on his deeply wrinkled face, which made it clear that he was at peace with himself and very grateful he'd survived and lived so long.

"Will he give me his real name?" asked Samuel.

When asked, Samuel saw fear in the man's face for the first time. His family members all began speaking at once.

"No one wants anybody else to know that he or any member of his family is alive and safe in Paris. Besides, they don't know who you are, Samuel."

"Tell them I'm a newspaper reporter trying to find out who killed Armand and Joseph Hagopian," said Samuel. "I won't tell anyone where Hector or any member of his family is."

There was a gasp from the entire family when Sasiska translated the news that Armand and Joseph were dead. The women turned pale.

"They want to know if you are talking about the two young Hagopian boys," asked Lucine.

"Yes, but please remind them that they weren't the young boys this family probably remembers. They were mature men and they were both murdered."

The fact that Samuel was a newspaper reporter and that the boys were murdered did not sit well with the family. They explained that they were better off staying anonymous. Hector lowered his head and began to turn his seat back around. The three women waved their arms, all talking to Sasiska at once. Lucine interrupted, trying to calm them down. Then she turned and spoke again to Samuel.

"Don't worry. I will come back and visit Hector. I hope he will relax and maybe even provide more information. I will assure him that everything he tells me will be confidential, but I suppose it will take a little time."

"You seem very sure of yourself," said Samuel. "Like you've done this kind of work before." He was trying to measure the tension among the family that his words had precipitated.

"As I said, I make unusual inquiries for the bank all the time. We will get you what you want. But you need to protect them, understand?"

"Yes. As long as I know what I am protecting them from."

"The family is getting ready for a meal of *spas and hots*," said Sasiska in French. "They invite us to join them."

Lucine and Samuel looked at each other. It was obviously important to the Somolian family that the visitors accept their hospitality. They stayed and dined on a simple meal of bread and soup. Sasiska slurped her soup and chatted happily in her native tongue, while Samuel admired the way three generations of Armenians huddled together in that small room, united in spite of everything.

* * *

After visiting the Somolians, Samuel prepared to leave Paris. He'd made good use of his time there, developing his story as well as helping Janak with the defense of his case. Lucine agreed to meet him at a café near the Bucci market the day before his scheduled flight back to San Francisco to tie up any loose ends.

Samuel wore his still-wrinkled khaki sports coat and a madras shirt, the red wool scarf wrapped around his neck, since he was still ill equipped for the chilly climate in Paris. Miraculously, he hadn't caught a cold, and was sure he owed it all to the mysterious Chinese herbs that Mr. Song sold him, which he took without asking questions, since he wouldn't have gotten any answers from the albino sage anyway.

When Lucine entered the Café Palate, Samuel was seated at a stained walnut table near the front window, sipping his *café americaine* and reading the *International Herald Tribune*. She took off her dark wool coat with its white fur-lined hood and put her leather gloves in her coat pocket. Samuel indicated the other seat near the window and called for the waiter.

After a long delay, a young man with a vacant stare appeared. Lucine ordered an espresso and a croissant. Samuel thought the boy's face lit up when he realized he no longer had to deal with the pale tourist who butchered the most beautiful language in the world. He soon appeared with her order, taking half the time to serve Lucine as he had Samuel. Lucine dissolved a sugar cube in her cup and delicately tore off a small piece of the croissant.

"I want to thank you for all your help, Lucine," said Samuel. "It's almost unbelievable how much you've done for me and Janak."

"You are most welcome. But we are not done yet. I need your address so I can send you more information."

He scribbled his address and phone number on a page of his notebook, ripped it out and handed it to her.

"I will first look for the Kurd's birth certificate. If he was born in France, it will be recorded at the office of the Registrar of Births here in Paris."

"If you do find it, can you get me an official copy with a government seal on it?" Samuel realized he was demanding a lot of her.

"Of course," said Lucine. "I assume that such a document may be important in a legal proceeding."

"Do you really think you can get Hector to tell you his real name?"

"I think so. I'm sure I can convince him, after all these years, that no one is looking for him. But it is important to keep his location a secret. If you just use his name, no one will know whether he is alive or dead. Considering the way they left him, I am sure no one would think that he lived to tell about what happened to him."

"Someone caused that man's injuries and hurt others.

If you find out anything more about the Hagopian family's friends or enemies, I'd appreciate it if you'd let me know immediately."

They sat in silence for a while, savoring their coffee and thinking about how, in just a few short days, they'd established a friendship.

"Do we need to discuss any further what you will tell Janak about me?" Lucine's eyes searched Samuel's.

"I think not. As I told you when we first talked about this, I'm a man of my word. Janak gets your new address and permission to write you, but no details about your private life. I'll say it any way you want me to. I won't even tell him that, if you prefer. Without you, Lucine, we wouldn't have learned anything. Of course, if you send me something new, I'll have to tell him where I got the information."

"I am not concerned with that. I just don't want Janak to know much about me. I'm not sure what my sentiments are about him. For a time I thought I hated him, but now I'm not so sure. I still can't talk about that, Samuel."

"Frankly, Lucine, I can assure you that Janak is a different man than the one you imagine. I know that he thinks of you constantly."

"We shall see about that, Samuel," she said, a certain hardness in her brown eyes.

7

Nibbling Around the Edges

WHILE SAMUEL WAS IN PARIS, Janak was preparing for trial. He spent long days in the law office library with Bartholomew Asquith, going over photographs of the crime scene, reading newspaper articles about the case, and reviewing the reports from the autopsy, police, coroner and the crime lab. Janak could see that Deadeye Graves was using the media to make damaging claims against his clients, with no opportunity on their part for rebuttal.

Janak realized he had to do something about the venom that was poisoning the community or he wouldn't be able to empanel an impartial jury. He went to court and asked for an order to prevent the leaks, but the judge, unconvinced they were coming from the D.A.'s office, denied the motion. Janak understood that in order to halt the flow of one-sided disclosures he had to employ other tactics.

Before he left for Paris, Samuel had made sure that the forensic and police reports about the Joseph Hagopian murder case would be forwarded to Janak when they arrived from Bucky Hughes' office in Fresno. Once they had, Janak and Asquith removed important pages from the various reports and Scotch-taped them to the books on the library shelves, so they could be easily accessed. Asquith was working overtime, but he looked more composed than usual. He'd forgotten, at least for the time being, his morbid fear of appearing in court. Relieved of the effects of his phobia, his enthusiasm was contagious. His colleagues gave a collective sigh of relief and gratitude.

Janak faced a difficult decision. Because he knew the trial was going to be expensive and that he would be unable to rely on his erratic cash flow to fund the case, he asked his mother to pledge some of her stock, her only asset aside from the house his grandparents left her. With that stock he was able to borrow five thousand dollars from the Hibernia Bank at a reasonable rate of interest. This allowed Janak to guarantee payment for the testimony of the experts he would need at trial and to hire an investigator to stand by for last-minute inquiries, subpoena witnesses and follow up on anything unexpected.

Since every criminal defendant was entitled by law to a jury trial, he didn't have to worry about jury fees. However, daily court reporter transcripts were the responsibility of the litigants unless the court ordered them. Janak would request the court to do so in the hopes that the financial burden would be lifted from his shoulders.

His biggest problem, at least financially, was that hiring an investigator to run down Deadeye's leaks would consume the entire trial fund. Instead, he needed to come up with a creative solution.

It was Thursday. The trial was scheduled to start in about three weeks, and Samuel was due to return the next day and to meet with Janak and Asquith on Sunday. In the meantime, Janak and Asquith were trying to figure out who Deadeye's witnesses would be, the order they would be called and what each was expected to say.

Asquith was also working on several motions *in limine* to prevent prejudicial evidence about their clients from being mentioned in the proceedings. They would present the motions to the trial judge to be heard before the jury was chosen or before opening statements were given. The motions were particularly important because Janak didn't want any evidence introduced that would incriminate either Jose or Miguel Ramos, who were absent. He also didn't want the prosecutor trying to submit evidence that suggested complicity between them and his clients, Juan Ramos and Narcio Padia. And he certainly didn't want any mention of the Fresno murder or the fact that Miguel's fingerprints were found on the weapon used to murder Joseph Hagopian. The admission of any such evidence would be prejudicial to his clients, who were literally on trial for their lives.

It all depended on which of two judges was assigned to try the case. Judge Lawrence Pluplot was the best qualified, and Janak and Asquith both hoped he would be chosen. The other possibility was Alfred Pickering, a highly conservative jurist who had handled mostly probate cases and who wasn't very knowledgeable about criminal law. Janak thought that even the D.A. might challenge Pickering, given the possibility of the mistakes he could make on the introduction of evidence or instructing the jury. Should the State win, mistakes would make the case vulnerable on appeal. However, Janak knew that with Deadeye Graves representing the People, anything could happen.

* * *

Samuel wasted no time. Even though plagued by jetlag, he was in Janak's office the afternoon of his arrival in San Francisco. Ignoring Asquith, who sat at the end of the table next to a pile of open law books, the first thing he did was hand Janak Lucine's address.

"How did you find her?" asked Janak once he had overcome his surprise. "This is a different address than the one I had."

"Aren't I your detective?" responded Samuel, smiling mischievously.

"Did you find out if she ever got my letters?"

"Don't ask me, man. Talk to her." Samuel refused to say more as per his promise to Lucine. "I'll tell you how I tracked her down later. Let's deal with what else I found out."

He explained what happened to the Hagopians' servant after the family escaped from Erzerum, adding that they probably didn't even know about it.

"The man wouldn't give me his real name, but my contacts in Paris think that they can find out what it is. He calls himself Hector Somolian."

"What do you mean, 'your contacts'?" asked Asquith.

"Just what I said. I've got contacts working on getting more information."

"We should find out who attacked Somolian," said Janak. "That could be important."

"That's the first thing I asked," said Samuel. "But he couldn't or wouldn't tell me because those people tried to kill him and he thinks that they still can. We have to be patient. First, let's get his identity, and then we'll ask him questions."

"We don't have a lot of time," said Janak, who was concentrating on taking notes at the table in front of Samuel.

"It doesn't depend on us. Like I said, they're working on it in Paris. Also, they're trying to find out about the Kurd's past.

"What are you talking about?" said Janak. "The guy's a Kurd, not French."

"I have a hunch," said Samuel. "I'd like to know if he has connections with France or with the Armenians in Paris. It's part of the investigation; something might come of it."

"Take a look at this," said Janak, handing a newspaper article to Samuel, who quickly skimmed the piece.

"Jesus Christ! This is slanderous, downright dirty yellow journalism," he said. "The author has tarred and feathered your clients. Where did this information come from?"

"It could only have come from the D.A.'s office," said Janak. "And that's not the worst of it. Every person who's read it now knows that Miguel's fingerprints were not only on a murder weapon that's not even a part of this case, but that they were also on the Coke bottles found on Armand Hagopian's body. Even though Miguel won't be in court, his co-workers will be, and there's always guilt by association. Pretty well thought out, don't you think?

"Then the defendants are blasted for coming across the border illegally and taking American workers' jobs," he continued. "The suggestion is that if Americans were working for Hagopian, this terrible crime would never have been committed."

Samuel handed the article back to Janak. "What are you going to do about it?"

"We need some help from you, Samuel."

The three men huddled together for the better part of an hour discussing strategy. Samuel was too tired to think through how to achieve any of the ideas suggested that day; moreover, he didn't have a clue where to start. After leaving Janak's office, he walked down Market Street to the cable car hub at Powell Street, where he caught the next car and rode up to Camelot to say hello to Blanche. He gave her a short report on Lucine, asking her to keep it confidential, and then went back to his apartment to wrestle with exhaustion before finally falling asleep.

After Samuel and Asquith had gone, Janak sat alone in the library, the paper with Lucine's address on it held tight in his hands. He smiled and touched the scar on his cheek, which she had kissed more than once in the brief time they shared together. It had been more than a couple of years, he thought. He was happy to realize he hadn't given up hope. He wanted to write a letter to her that very moment, but realized that wouldn't be enough. He owed her an explanation, face to face.

* * *

The next day, Samuel was up at the crack of dawn. He unpacked the wrinkled clothes he'd worn on his Paris trip and outfitted himself with a pair of freshly laundered khaki pants and a new button-down blue shirt. He shined his brown penny loafers with Shinola, removing the scuffmarks they'd picked up from roughing it on the streets of Paris. When he looked in the mirror, he smiled. He looked pretty good for someone who'd just returned from his first trip to the other side of the world.

Since it was so early, he walked from his apartment at the edge of Chinatown to North Beach and installed himself at one of Café Trieste's indoor tables. It had a more European atmosphere than his usual stomping grounds. Samuel also liked the stronger coffee he'd gotten used to in Paris. He ordered a cappuccino and a croissant, neither of which compared to the ones he'd had the week before, though he liked them just the same, and read the morning paper cover to cover, trying to catch up on what his fellow reporters had been up to in his absence.

Just before ten, he headed back to Chinatown, stopping before a nondescript doorway beneath a sign reading MR. SONG'S MANY CHINESE HERBS. The shop, located on Pacific Street, between Kearny and Stockton, was just opening. Samuel entered, triggering the entrance bell. Once across the threshold, a Chinese man dressed in a blue jacket and pants greeted him with a toothless smile.

Samuel looked around the shop, noting that nothing had changed since his last visit. Stacks of earthen-colored jars lined the east and west walls. Behind the black lacquer counter, which featured elaborate Chinese scenes painted on its front panels, wooden boxes were stacked all the way to the twenty-foot ceiling. He recognized the pungent odor of the herbs hanging from the many wires stretched across the room.

"Is Mr. Song here?"

The man put up his hand, indicating that Samuel should wait, and he disappeared behind the blue beaded curtain. Soon the beads parted and Mr. Song appeared. As always, Samuel was shocked by the strange appearance of the albino herbalist. Mr. Song's black silk jacket, which was subtly decorated with woven mountain designs and had a Mandarin collar, stood in sharp contrast to his white skin. He wore his usual black skullcap and eyeglasses that magnified his pink eyes. He did not seem surprised to see Samuel. It was as if he had known that, sooner or later his client would return for another consult. Mr. Song smiled and nodded his head slightly.

"I need to talk with you," said Samuel.

Mr. Song put up his hand and called for his assistant. He muttered something and the man rushed out the front door, the bell tingling after him.

"No smoke?" he asked, fixing his penetrating stare at Samuel.

"No. Almost a year now, thanks to you and your hypnosis, Mr. Song. Well, the truth is I've had a few accidents. Why should I lie to you?"

The wise man pointed a long white finger that looked like a candle. "No smoke!" he ordered.

That was the end of their conversation until Mr. Song's bucktoothed niece—wearing a plaid skirt and a starched white shirt featuring the pagoda logo of the a nearby Baptist school on its front pocket—popped in through the door.

"Hello, Mr. Hamilton," she said. "We haven't seen you for a while. But rumor has it that you're a successful reporter now."

"Is that what they're saying?" asked Samuel, blushing.

"Oh, yes. Everyone reads your articles. They're translated into Chinese and published in our press here in Chinatown. People are really interested, especially when you write about crime."

"I've heard that Chinese people are interested in crime stories. In fact, the reason I'm here is to ask for your uncle's help on a case that I'm working on in Martinez."

"Is that the one about the Armenian man?" she asked.

"You know about that?"

"I told you we like mystery stories, Mr. Hamilton."

"I'll be dammed. Okay. Will you ask Mr. Song if I can talk frankly with him about the case?"

She chatted briefly with Mr. Song

"Mr. Song says you kept your word to him and stopped those awful men from coming around to his shop, so he will listen to you. After he hears what you have to say, he'll decide if he can help you."

"I'm working on a story your niece knows about," said Samuel, putting his elbows on the black lacquer counter and cupping his chin in both hands as he leaned forward to talk to Mr. Song. "My friend Janak Marachak is an attorney representing two Mexican workers who are accused of murdering a prominent Armenian businessman. The assistant district attorney, who is a really bad person, has been getting stories published in the Contra Costa County newspapers that are hurting Mr. Marachak's clients. We need to stop him."

The niece translated what Samuel said, her arms waving dramatically. Mr. Song didn't say anything, but Samuel could tell he was listening very carefully; he nodded from time to time as she talked to him.

"My honorable uncle says that it's very interesting that you would ask for his help in a matter that's not related to anything that has to do with Chinatown, or even San Francisco.

Why do you think he can help you with something that happened in a place so far away?"

"Tell him I know he has influence all over the Bay Area.
That's why I came to him."

"He, like me, knows of your case. He also knows about the
articles that have appeared in Contra Costa County."

"How did he find out about the case?"

"The same way I did, Mr. Hamilton. He read about it in
the Chinese press."

"Does he know someone in Contra Costa County who
can help us put an end to the bad publicity?"

"He says he does. In fact, he knows what you should do
about it."

"He's kidding."

"No, Mr. Hamilton. My honorable uncle never jokes. He
is a very serious wise man."

Mr. Song disappeared behind the blue beaded curtain,
leaving Samuel alone with the niece. Several minutes passed,
which seemed like an eternity to Samuel. When the old man
finally returned, his hands tucked inside his tunic, he wore the
same inscrutable expression.

Buckteeth translated his instructions. "He has a plan you
can use to discredit your enemy from the District Attorney's
office, and he's already called someone in Martinez that you
should contact. She will be waiting for you."

"Your uncle always surprises me," said Samuel, amazed.

"Mr. Song knows many things. He says that the person
who is waiting for you will tell you the plan. So long, Mr.
Hamilton."

"How much do I owe your uncle?"

"No, no. He says you are his client only for the herbs. Information is free. Also, he is grateful that you have kept that
evil Mr. Perkins and his nasty men away from this place."

The reporter hadn't imagined that the presence of Perkins,

the assistant U.S. attorney who had intervened in the Chinatown murders that Samuel had reported on the previous year in a series of articles entitled "The Chinese Jars," had had such an effect on Mr. Song. Perkins had confiscated various jars from the albino's shop, which Mr. Song considered a personal insult, since his actions could have cost Mr. Song the confidence of his clients. In addition to being an herb shop, Mr. Song's establishment acted as a bank; his Chinatown clients deposited their most valuable possessions in the store's clay jars. Mr. Song's reputation would have been endangered, and possibly even ruined, if people saw the sacred jars being removed.

Samuel took down the name and address of the person Mr. Song indicated, said his goodbyes and walked out of the herb shop. He smiled as he walked down the street. I have the instinct of a bloodhound, he thought to himself, thinking of the detective novels he'd read in his early twenties. He'd only gone to Mr. Song's shop on a hunch but the result couldn't have been better. Or was it just on a hunch? Perhaps Mr. Song had called him telepathically. Anything was possible with that man.

* * *

Samuel picked up some newspaper clippings and went to Martinez with Marcel. The address Mr. Song had given him was just off Main Street, only three blocks from the courthouse. They pulled up to an unpainted and dilapidated wood-frame building, complete with a covering that reached out over the sidewalk; it looked like something you'd see in a deserted Wild West town. The building had two plate-glass windows, one on each side of the front door, which was also see-through glass. The window to the left read MING'S LAUNDRY in large blue letters outlined in white. The one to the right listed prices in the same, though smaller, lettering.

Samuel laughed.

"What's so funny?" asked Marcel

"I finally understand," he said.

"You finally understand what?"

"What Mr. Song used to say to me last year: *no ticky, no laundry.*"

"What the hell are you talking about?"

"Never mind, it's a private joke. I'll call you when it's time to take the photographs."

Samuel went into the laundry, where a Chinese girl stood behind the counter.

"Excuse me, do you speak English?" he asked.

"Of course," she said, examining him from head to toe. "How can I help you?"

"I was sent here by Mr. Song to speak with Mae Ming."

"Are you Mr. Hamilton?"

"Yes," said Samuel, surprised.

"Miss Ming is expecting you." She lifted the center portion of the counter and motioned for Samuel to follow her through a door directly behind her. Samuel found himself in a large room with several Chinese workers who were sorting piles of clothing on a counter against the wall; other workers then put the clothes in industrial-size washing machines located in a row along the opposite wall. Samuel followed the girl through a makeshift aisle to the rear of building. She knocked on a door next to a large glass window through which Samuel could see a gray-haired Chinese woman sitting at a desk, concentrating on her work. The girl opened the door.

"This is Mr. Hamilton," she said.

The woman stood up, and Samuel saw that she was almost six feet tall. Her hair was short and she wore horn-rimmed glasses that rested on her high cheekbones. He thought she looked more like a professor than a person in charge of a laundry service. She extended her hand and smiled.

"I'm Mae Ming. I understand you have a problem in Contra Costa County and would like some advice—maybe even some help."

"Yes," said Samuel, impressed by the woman's perfect diction and poise. He looked over her shoulder, eyeing the bookshelf that covered the wall behind her desk. It was crowded with novels, books of poetry, several scientific journals and various notebooks. Some were in English, others had Chinese writing on the spines. Curious, he looked around more closely. Taking in the framed diplomas on the wall, he was surprised to discover that Mae Ming had been awarded a Ph.D. in biological sciences from the University of California at Berkeley in June 1950.

"Is that you?" he asked.

"I'm afraid so. In a Chinese family sometimes one has to choose between parents and career. My family is very traditional. There came a time about eight years ago when, because of my father's failing health, my honorable parents could no longer manage the business they'd built up, so I came back to stabilize it. After that, things just got out of hand. The county began to prosper and, as a consequence, business kept growing. By the time I'd caught my breath, I'd been away from my discipline for so long I couldn't find a job. It was harder than it should have been, given that I'm Chinese and a woman, with what is more typically a man's degree. But that's enough about me. Let's talk about your problem."

Samuel was transfixed and had to shake his head in order to recall the reason for his visit.

"I'm not sure where to begin."

"I know the background of your case, and I know Earl Graves," she said with a perceptive nod.

"Then you know he's been planting those atrocious stories about Mr. Marachak's clients in the local press."

"Yes, I've read some of them. Even though I knew what he was up to, I wondered how long he could get away with it. So, in that sense, I'm glad you're here."

Samuel pulled the articles Janak had given him from his briefcase and spread them out on Mae's desk. He spoke of the significance of each one and how Deadeye had twisted the evidence or made information public when otherwise he wouldn't have been able to use it. As he talked, Mae scanned the articles she hadn't seen before.

"Do you know any of the reporters who wrote these?" Samuel asked.

"Yes, I know them all. Some are customers of ours, as is Mr. Graves. They all bring their laundry here."

Samuel and Mae went over the articles, one by one. It took the better part of an hour.

"Mr. Song said you would know what to do about all this. Is that true?"

"I suggest you come back here this evening about ten. Do you have a flash camera at your disposal?"

"I certainly do. Is that all I need?"

"That will be more than enough."

Mae sat back in her chair, took off her heavy glasses and rubbed the bridge of her nose. It was then that Samuel noticed that she had the most perfectly shaped black eyebrows he'd ever seen.

* * *

As directed, Samuel and Marcel were at the rear door of the laundry at ten o'clock. Mae took them into her office. She'd exchanged her white work coat for a tailored red jacket and black slacks. She explained where they would find Deadeye Graves, what he looked like, what time he usually arrived, and what to expect. Samuel already knew what Deadeye looked like. That wasn't his concern here.

"How do you know all this?" he asked.

"I'll fill you in later. Please pay attention to what I'm telling you and don't get there before eleven.

Samuel and Marcel went back to the car and waited for another half hour to pass. Marcel lit a cigarette. Samuel wanted to ask for one; instead he rolled down the window, even though it was cold outside. The smell of the smoke in the car was too tempting for a former heavy smoker like him.

"That's a shitty habit you have," said Samuel, breathing in with pleasure what was left of the smoke. "Why don't you visit Mr. Song and try to stop?"

"No thanks, I like it."

"Yeah, I can tell," said Samuel. "I'd ask you to do it outside 'cept it's your car." They both laughed.

Marcel took out the map Samuel had drawn in Mae's office and, using a lighted match, they oriented themselves to it one last time. When it was time to go, they took off toward the waterfront and soon found a building with a three-foot-high green neon sign near the top that read "Bar." The sign's lights were sputtering, barely functional. Below was a dark, one-story edifice with no windows that were visible from the street.

"This place looks like a real dump," said Samuel.

"I hope Mae's right," said Marcel.

"I have no doubt Miss Ming knows what she's talking about," said Samuel. "Do you have film and flashbulbs?"

"Don't ask silly questions. That's my job, man."

"Before we go in, let's see if there's another exit."

They searched both sides of the building, eventually finding a side door on the left.

"I hope it isn't locked," said Marcel.

"There should be an emergency exit that's kept open during business hours," said Samuel. "That's the way it is at Camelot. When we go in, you stay near the door. You'll recognize Graves from the funeral. If I want him photographed, I'll point at him. And you know what to do if we get a shot, right?"

"Just like you taught me, boss," said Marcel.

They approached the bar's double front doors, which were illuminated from above by a dim recessed light. Samuel tried one of the two doors, but it was locked. When they opened the other door they found themselves in a large, smoke-filled enclosure with many tables, most of which were occupied. With a pretext of using the bathroom, Samuel walked to the other end of the establishment, along the way estimating that it held about fifty people. He passed the exit door they'd seen from outside, a small dance floor, and an instrument-filled stage. Close to the facilities, he saw a bar with several people standing with their backs to him. Two bartenders manned the bar. One was to Samuel's right, at the end of the bar, pouring drinks for the cocktail waitresses; the other, stationed in the middle, took care of the standing customers, who shouted out their orders. As in most bars, there was a large, dirty mirror directly behind the bartenders, bottles of liquor crowding the shelves that fronted it.

His reconnaissance mission complete, Samuel sat with Marcel at a small table next to the front door. He waved his hand in front of his face in a feeble attempt to ward off the smoke and scanned the bar patrons, focusing in on a tall man he'd seen on the way to the bathroom. The man, who was standing between two women, had gray hair and was dressed in a dark suit and cowboy boots. He was laughing and he had his hands on the women's butts. Samuel had no doubt the man was Deadeye Graves, and that he'd had too much to drink.

It would be a big scoop if he got a photograph of a deputy district attorney grabbing two women's asses, but Deadeye wasn't facing the camera, so he'd be able to deny it was him. And Marcel would only be able to get one shot before all hell broke loose.

Just then the cocktail waitress approached them. She looked like a tired housewife in dire need of the extra money she got from moonlighting at a busy nightspot, where no doubt the tips were good. She raised her eyebrows at the two men huddled at the small circular table. They looked out of place, especially given Marcel's bulky camera, which sat on top of the table.

"Scotch on the rocks for me," said Samuel.

"I'll have a beer," said Marcel. "Make it a Grace Brothers."

"What time does the band start?" Samuel asked.

"Should be any second now. They've been off more than fifteen minutes."

That was good news. If he could get Deadeye to turn around, they just might get what they were after.

True to the waitress's word, the band members began filtering back to the bandstand, and within a couple of minutes, they were playing dance music. Deadeye turned, the two women turning with him. He put an arm around each and the three of them moved toward the dance floor.

"Get a picture of that son of a bitch and then get the hell out of here!" Samuel spoke in a hoarse whisper.

Marcel focused his camera and pushed the shutter-release button. In the dimness of the bar, the resulting flash had the effect of a cannon shot. Its blue light gave the bar an unreal quality, Samuel thought, like a film noir, complete with all the important elements: the smoke, the pale clients, the worn-out waitresses, the villain with the prostitutes, the reporter with his photographer. He only had a moment to reflect on that image before Deadeye, recovering from his surprise, realized what had happened and rushed after Marcel, who had run out the front door. As he darted past, Samuel stuck out his leg. Deadeye tripped, landing in a heap on the floor in front of the table.

"I'm terribly sorry," said Samuel, pretending to help Dead-eye up but holding on to his suit jacket to prevent him from going anywhere. Deadeye, furious, pushed the smaller man to the side and ran out the door just in time to see Marcel's car peel out from the curb and screech around the corner. Given the distance and darkness, it was impossible for him to see the license plate number. Deadeye hurried back inside to confront Samuel. By then, however, he had disappeared out the side door. Samuel ran like a rabbit to meet Marcel, who was waiting for him around the corner, the motor running.

* * *

The photograph, which was ready the next morning, was sensational. Not only did Deadeye look drunk, the two women with him appeared hard and trashy. Samuel rushed over to Janak's office with ten copies. At first, they sat in the library laughing; then they pondered just what do with them.

Samuel called Mae as she'd requested.

"Okay, Miss Ming, I have the print. He was right where you said he'd be. I don't know how to thank you for this help; it's more than we could have dreamed possible. I assure you that Graves won't be happy to have the public know about this. Now, how can we get this photograph published in all the Contra Costa County newspapers?"

"I need to see the photograph before you do anything with it," she said.

"Okay, I'll get it to you. Let's say around noon, unless you hear from me before then." He hung up the phone.

"Marisol, can we use your car?" yelled Janak.

"Why do you even ask me, boss?" she called out from her cubicle at the other end of the office. "You use it more than I do. In any case, it needs gas."

"Do you want me to go with you?" Janak asked Samuel.

"I don't think that's necessary," said Samuel. "But she said you could use her car, not me."

"Marisol, is it okay if Samuel drives your baby?"

"What choice do I have?" she yelled, laughing.

Samuel made the quick trip over to Martinez and knocked at the back door of the laundry. Mae was waiting for him, dressed in her white work coat. They sat at her desk to examine the photograph.

"Very good job, Mr. Hamilton."

"How did you know he would be there with those women?"

"Those aren't women," answered Mae. "That's why I wanted to see the picture. They're men."

"Men?" exclaimed Samuel, busting into laughter. "You mean transvestites? Can I use your phone?"

He called Janak and explained what he'd just discovered.

"What's next?" asked Janak, choking with laughter.

"I haven't gotten that far. I'll let you know."

"Remember," said Janak before hanging up. "We need maximum exposure!"

Samuel turned back to Mae. "I need to know a couple of things before we try and take this public, Miss Ming," said Samuel. "First, how did you know Graves would be at the bar?"

"Ordinarily, I wouldn't tell you. But since Mr. Song sent you and I understand what you're trying to accomplish, I'll explain. The first part is simple. Mr. Graves is one of our laundry clients. My workers found a matchbook from the bar in one of his pockets. They also found lipstick on the fly of two different pairs of his trousers, so I sent a spy to the bar to see what was going on. The spy went there several times and saw Mr. Graves keeping company with Mimi and Max, who are really men dressed up as women. You happened to come to see me on the day of the week when Mr. Graves regularly gets together with them."

"Now, here's the question," said Samuel. "As my friend Janak would say, how do we get the most publicity out of our find ?"

"I already thought of that," she answered. "I have prepared a list of the editors of the most influential papers in Contra Costa County. Every one of them printed stories prejudicial to Mr. Marachak's clients. Go and talk with them. Tell them who you are, show them the picture and I guarantee they'll publish your story and the photograph."

"Do you think they'll print it by tomorrow?"

"They're all small and hungry for this type of news. Mr. Graves has been asking for it for some time. I would be surprised if they turned you down."

"Can I use your name if I run into problems?"

"Certainly not," she said. "The reason I can provide you with so much information is that no one knows I have it. You see those notebooks behind my desk, the ones with the Chinese writing on the spines? They're filled with information on most of the big shots in this county. As a biologist, I'm conscious of the importance of details. I suppose I miss my microscope and this is my way of compensating."

"For what purpose do you collect this information, Miss Ming?"

"One never knows. In this case, I was able to return a favor to Mr. Song and, coincidentally, get even for the discourteous way Mr. Graves treats my employees." Mae smiled.

"Is your laundry the only thing those people have in common?" asked Samuel, pointing to the notebooks.

"This is the oldest and the best laundry in the county, Mr. Hamilton. Those people made the mistake of not removing the evidence from their clothes before sending us their dirty laundry."

* * *

Samuel worked the phone from Mae's office and arranged for five papers to run his story and the photograph in their Friday editions. The only condition was that he had to deliver them by four in the afternoon. He borrowed Mae's Remington typewriter and whipped out the story of the delinquent Mr. Graves and the two transvestites. When he was through typing, he wiped the carbon smudges off the sleeves of his khaki sports coat and dashed off to deliver the story and photo to the newspapers that had agreed to print it. He then rushed them across the bay to his own paper's deadline editor.

The exposé hit like a bomb. The District Attorney's office was inundated with phone calls and had to shut down its switchboard Friday afternoon. Deadeye vanished for the weekend, no doubt to lick his wounds and evaluate the damage done to his career.

The next morning Samuel, Janak and Asquith met at Janak's office to go over the published articles.

"I don't know whether to be happy or angry," said Janak.

"What do you mean?" said Samuel.

"What Deadeye did to my clients was terrible, so I'm glad we got him. But at the same time, I'm pissed off that he still got away with it. The damage to our case is already done."

"Let's just say it was a defensive move that was necessary for us to stay alive," answered Samuel. "The kind of publicity he'll get from that photo can't be good for him or his image as a deputy D.A. Don't you think it can give us an advantage in the lawsuit?"

"Depends on what the jury we get thinks about it," said Janak.

As they spoke, Asquith was busy researching whether Deadeye could be disqualified from trying the State's case because of moral turpitude.

"Don't waste too much time looking into that," suggested Janak. "He hasn't been convicted of anything, and unless the D.A. decides that the case will be hurt by him representing the People, nothing will happen."

"I think we've achieved our purpose," said Samuel. "Deadeye's not stupid and he understands the message. We have him checked. Now we wait and see if he has any other dirty tricks up his sleeve."

"In other words, we haven't checkmated him," said Janak.

"I know nothing about chess," said Samuel.

"No, but you have the nose of a hunting dog," laughed Janak.

"That's exactly what I think," laughed Samuel.

* * *

Samuel wasn't wrong about Graves. Shortly before noon the phone rang at Janak's office.

"Mr. Marachak, this is Earl Graves, the deputy district attorney from Contra Costa County."

"Yes, I know who you are." Janak used his most professional tone. "What can I do for you?"

"I propose a gentleman's agreement. You know how indiscreet the press can be..."

"Are you referring to the dirt that's been published about my clients' involvement in the Hagopian case?"

"Well, about that, and also about the scandal concerning me."

"Yes, we all saw that in the press. That's all people are talking about, Mr. Graves. I feel very sorry for you."

"I'm not an imbecile, Mr. Marachak. I can imagine perfectly how the press got hold of that photograph."

"You have a good imagination, Mr. Graves. I suppose you can also imagine how the press got all the dirt that has been published about my clients over the last three weeks."

"We both need a truce, Mr. Marachak."

"Without a doubt, it's better to play it straight, Mr. Graves."

"It's a deal then," said Deadeye, working to hide the fear and anger in his voice.

When Janak repeated the conversation to Samuel and the rest of his office staff, everyone applauded.

"A small victory in a vicious battle," said Samuel.

"I think it's more than that," said Janak. "This just means that Deadeye has plenty more to hide. It also signifies that he thinks we know a hell of a lot more about him than we actually do, and he's afraid we'll let it out."

"You're probably right, Janak," said Samuel. "I'll get together with Mae and find out what else she knows about him."

"We don't have to find out anything else. He's already wounded. We'll just keep quiet and let him fester. It'll make him much less effective at the trial."

"Do you really expect that he's not going to try another fast one in this case?" asked Samuel.

"For now, no, but I expect him to try every trick he has up his sleeve at the trial. But I'm prepared for that. It was all this marginal stuff that I wasn't able to deal with."

"It won't hurt to get some more dirt on him," said Samuel.

"Go ahead, get what you can, but I don't want him off the case," said Janak. "It reminds me of the story I once heard about a five-term governor of my home state of Ohio whose high-level associate kept getting in trouble because of nefarious deals in which he was involved. The governor stood by the rascal and kept getting reelected. When asked why he didn't fire his embattled aide, his only comment was 'Would you take the punching bag out of the gym?' Deadeye will be my punching bag.

"We only have a week to go before the trial starts. I need to know we have everything in order for our defense. So we have to go over the evidence and make sure we've correctly anticipated which witnesses the prosecution will call and what they'll say.

"I've hired several experts. Whether I use them or not will depend on what evidence Deadeye gets to introduce."

8

The Trial

CALIFORNIA PENAL CODE §§187 and 188 read, in part, as follows:

> 187. (a) Murder is the unlawful killing of a human being with malice aforethought.
>
> 188. Such malice may be express or implied. It is express when there is manifested a deliberate intention unlawfully to take away the life of a fellow creature. It is implied, when no considerable provocation appears, or when the circumstances attending the killing show an abandoned and malignant heart.
>
> When it is shown that the killing resulted from the intentional doing of an act with express or implied malice as defined above, no other mental state need be shown to establish the mental state of malice aforethought. Neither an awareness of the obligation to act within the general body of laws regulating society nor acting despite such awareness is included within the definition of malice.

The District Attorney of Contra Costa County charged Narcio Padia and Juan Ramos with murder in the first degree with malice aforethought and was seeking the death penalty for both of them. His intentions were well known in the community and there was a lot of publicity around the trial, which was to commence the following Monday morning.

Janak didn't sleep well the night before. He had his usual pretrial jitters, but this time they were much worse because, for the first time in his career, he was tasked with saving the lives of human beings.

In the middle of the night, he decided he wanted to drive to the Contra Costa Courthouse via Marin County, so he could stop by San Quentin State Prison before going to Martinez. He wanted to see where his clients might end up if he wasn't successful in court.

He got up early and called Samuel, inviting the reporter to join him and Asquith on the ride to the courthouse. The private investigator Janak had hired to help with the case drove them to the foot of the Richmond-San Rafael Bridge, where the state prison was located. Janak asked the driver to stop.

"Take a walk with me, Samuel."

They wandered down the narrow road that led to the prison. As they rounded the turn toward the west, the pumpkin-colored colossus stared them in the face. They sat down on a bench at what looked like a bus stop.

"This bench, or one like it, must have been used by thousands of visitors who came to see inmates over the hundred-year life of this place," said Janak. "In the beginning they must have come by horse and buggy or by water; later by bus or taxi."

"I think I know what's bothering you," said Samuel, "and I wish there was something I could do to make what you are doing easier. But this is one of those times when most of the weight is on your shoulders."

"That's why I asked you to come with me. I knew you would understand. If I lose this case both of my clients will be executed right here at this prison, and if that happens I'm not sure I could live with myself. I've handled a lot of complex cases involving the misuse of chemicals, but never anything like this."

"You're smart and you're honest, you've shown me that,"

said Samuel. "Everybody has to go through some dark periods in life. Some time I'll tell you some of my hell. It just got dumped on me, and I wasn't prepared for it. That's not what happened with you. You put yourself right in the middle of this even though you didn't have to. So this puts you above the fray. It gives you some distance from the terrible things that have happened in this case. Just don't let the ugliness get you down. If you get in a tight spot, reach out. I'll be there."

"Thank you Samuel. I think I know how to fight for these men's lives, and it means a lot to me that you'll be there to help."

Wrapped in his overcoat, his unruly hair blowing in the breeze, Janak took a deep breath and considered Samuel's words. The reporter, covered only by his khaki sports coat, watched him in silence.

"I know my motives are pure," said Janak.

"Hell yes! You've done the right thing. It's about representing innocent men who can't afford to pay for a criminal lawyer. If someone incompetent represented them, they'd most likely be convicted and would face execution. If that happened it would be almost impossible to reverse the process. And I'll say it again. I'm here to help you any way that I can."

* * *

On an ordinary Monday morning, the court's business was handled casually, but because of the intense interest the Hagopian case had stirred, the crowd couldn't fit into Department One, where the presiding judge assigned cases for trial. Fortunately for the defendants, their case was assigned to Lawrence Pluplot. This was a relief for Janak, as Judge Pluplot was the seasoned criminal trial judge their team was hoping for. Having him preside would prevent a lot of Deadeye's shenanigans.

The lawyers presented themselves in Judge Pluplot's chambers shortly after ten. The judge lectured them on the rules he wanted followed during the course of the trial, and instructed them that all motions would be heard that afternoon. Asquith handed the clerk the several-page document he'd prepared and gave a copy to Deadeye. The prosecution had no motions to present. The judge handed both sides a list of potential jurors and advised them that jury selection would begin the next morning. He also noted that, barring anything unforeseen, the motions would be disposed of that afternoon.

Janak, Asquith and Samuel retired to the coffee shop in the basement of the courthouse to look over the jury list, while the private investigator went to serve papers in the county.

"Hi, Donald," said Janak to the blind man behind the register. "As promised, I finally made it back for the big one."

"Hello, Mr. Janak."

"Jesus! I can't believe you recognize my voice. I've only been here once."

"Even though I'm blind, I have very good hearing and a good memory," answered the man, showing his decayed teeth as he smiled. "Besides, I knew you'd be here today,"

The two deputy sheriffs occupying one of the five otherwise empty tables finished their coffee, said goodbye to Donald and left. Janak and his companions served themselves coffee and sat down at one of the tables.

"Jury pickin' starts tomorrow," said Donald.

"Sure does," said Janak. "Any suggestions?"

"Depends on who you get to pick from."

Janak, Samuel and Asquith looked at one another, each wondering if a blind man could help with jury selection.

"Do you hear things about who's coming for jury duty?" Janak asked.

"I hear all sorts of things, Counselor. That's why I said it depends on who you get to pick from."

"If I mention a name or two," said Janak, "can you give me the lowdown on them just from your experience down here?"

"I can. I remember the names of all the jurors that come down this way. They're here for coffee, for lunch, and sometimes for afternoon snacks. I hear stuff about them, mostly from other people on the same jury. And then there are the repeaters. Some of them have sat on five or six juries over the last ten years."

"Let me run some names by you," said Janak, reading off six of them.

"Those are all God-fearin' folks, except for number four. I wouldn't let that guy use my outhouse."

Asquith crossed the name off the list and wrote an "okay" by the others. Janak repeated the process and Donald gave him positive information on most of the people on the list. He had reservations about a few others and suggested that Janak needed to find out more about three who had never served on a jury in that county before. Samuel said he would see what he could find out that afternoon while the attorneys were arguing the motions.

"What about Earl Graves?" asked Janak. "Does he ever set foot in here?"

"Not once since he's been a deputy district attorney. He don't care how the other half lives. But I'll tell you this much. He's not much liked by most of the people 'round here. That doesn't mean that the bailiffs and the clerks don't take the law-and-order side. You remember that—very few of them are with you. But he's known as a ruthless bastard. And that little exposé on him didn't help his reputation much."

"What did they say around here about that?"

"Graves almost got canned, but the old man didn't have no one else free to try the case. That's the only reason he's still around."

"I'm relieved Deadeye didn't lose his job," said Janak.

"At least I know who I'm dealing with. I bet the boss really clamped down on him, didn't he?"

"Yes, sir. He said one more false move and he was out and the D.A. would go into court and ask you to ask for a mistrial."

"Do you think the judge would consider it under those circumstances?" asked Janak. "I mean, depending on what it is he's likely to pull, I'd resist it unless getting it favored my clients."

"Hard to say. They're old friends, the D.A. and the judge, but maybe not. You know, Pluplot is a serious man and he'll apply the letter of the law. But you be careful. You got a devil by the tail."

"I never underestimate an opponent, Donald."

"You can expect the worst from Deadeye."

Janak leaned over and whispered in Asquith's ear. "Can you find out what the protocol is for getting a mistrial in a criminal case?"

Customers started coming in, purchasing a variety of items, and the three watched the blind man deal with the paper money he was handed. Samuel noted that the cash drawer remained wide open as each transaction was conducted. Although Janak, Samuel and Asquith were waiting until the patrons filed out with their purchases so they could continue their conversation with Donald, it soon became apparent that further conferencing was out of the question; too many jurors from the various courtrooms were coming in to grab a sandwich or a drink.

It was a little past noon, so the three men decided to walk down the street to a small restaurant. After lunch, Janak and Asquith returned to the courthouse to present their motions and Samuel went to Mae Ming's with the jury list. To avoid being noticed, he went around to the back door. She greeted him with a friendly smile and waved one of her long, slender hands, its fingertips bright with red polish.

Samuel showed her the names of the people they didn't know anything about. She took one of her notebooks off the shelf and shuffled through the pages.

She pointed to the first name.

"This one's all right. He likes animals and has a big heart."

She turned a few more pages, then stopped and frowned.

"This second person belongs to a very reactionary political organization. I doubt that he would give any consideration to someone who was foreign-born."

She thumbed through a few more pages.

"I have absolutely nothing on this woman," she said of the third name on the list. "What does she do for a living?"

"If she's chosen, I'll find out," said Samuel scribbling in his notebook. "Thanks, Miss Ming, you've been a great help."

"You'll need to come back and see me every day during the trial," she said. "There are a lot of rednecks in this town and they have nothing against hanging a man if he's the wrong color."

"You can bet I will, Miss Ming. I'll see you tomorrow. I'll bring Janak by so you can meet him."

"I'd like that," she said. "I want to meet the champion of the little people."

Samuel noted the irony in her tone.

* * *

Samuel arrived at the courtroom just as the lawyers were finishing arguing the motions to prevent prejudicial evidence from being submitted in court. He waited until Janak put the papers in his briefcase and headed for the exit before going over to him.

"How'd you do?" Samuel asked, unable to tell from Janak's

expression what had happened.

"We won some and lost some," Janak said, his face flushed.

"Tell me the bad news first."

"I couldn't get the judge to agree with me on a dress code. It doesn't do my clients any good to have the jury see them dressed in jailhouse garb and chains."

"Is that legal?" asked Samuel.

"So far it is," said Janak. "But I'd hate to lose the case because of it and have it be the only issue I'd have on appeal."

"Any other bad news?" asked Samuel.

"As if that wasn't enough," smirked Janak. "The rest of the stuff went my way. Deadeye can't bring in evidence of the Fresno murder or that Miguel's fingerprints were found on the murder weapon. You mark my words, though; Deadeye will try and get that evidence before the jury."

"Did he have to give you a list of witnesses?"

"Yeah, we got that."

"Well, don't keep me in suspense. Who are they going to call?"

"The detective, the tech guy called Mac, and the pathologist from the coroner's office who did the autopsy. Interestingly enough, he won't call the coroner himself. The last witness he named was the Kurdish guy."

"Is that it?" asked Samuel, looking at him in disbelief.

"Yup, except for the family members."

"Does that surprise you?"

"Yeah, it does. It means that Deadeye thinks this is an open-and-shut case."

* * *

Early Tuesday morning Deadeye sat in his office, his feet up on the desk as he studied his trial prep. He'd moved the

Louis L'Amour books to the side to accommodate his cowboy boots.

Deadeye considered his situation. Up until the photographs of him with the transvestites showed up in the papers, he'd had a pretty good couple of months. He'd done a good job of leaking detrimental information about the suspects to the press, and thus to the potential jury pool.

Thinking again about the incriminating pictures, Deadeye slapped his forehead with the palm of his hand, embarrassed. How could he have been so imprudent? His career had been moving right along, but it would be a miracle if he could save it now. Still, the public had a short memory, so maybe things weren't hopeless. The only remaining issue was how to get the tainted evidence before the jury so he could fry the Mexican bastards. He didn't know where the line was, but he didn't give a shit so long as the jury heard the evidence and he didn't provoke a mistrial. What was the old saying? Once you ring the bell, it can't be unrung.

He looked across the office to another of his favorite paintings, this one of a cowboy in leather chaps standing over a lassoed longhorn he'd pulled to the ground with his rope, the other end of which was tied to his Appaloosa pony's saddle horn. Deadeye took his feet off the desk and stood up. Placing one boot on his office chair, he copied the cowboy's pose. Deadeye smiled. He figured he had 'em where he wanted 'em—grounded and hogtied.

* * *

Janak and Asquith entered Judge Lawrence Pluplot's courtroom, which was crowded with potential jurors. They walked down the aisle, passed through the thirty-inch swinging doors that separated the viewing and working sections of the court, and sat at the defendants' counsel table on the left-hand side of the room. Deadeye Graves was already seated at the prosecutor's table to their right, next to the jury box. The clerk sat below the elevated dais, where the judge would oversee the proceedings. Janak and Asquith unloaded notebooks from their briefcases and stacked them on the counsel table. Deadeye, in contrast, had just a single notebook, which he thumbed through while awaiting the judge's arrival.

At five minutes to ten, one of the back doors opened and two bailiffs ushered in the defendants, both wearing orange county jail jumpsuits. They wore ankle shackles and were handcuffed to a chain tied around their waists, which prevented them from lifting their arms any higher than their belts. After delivering their charges to the defense table, one of the bailiffs took up position by the swinging gate, while the other moved to the courtroom entrance—just in case either defendant got any smart ideas.

Juan Ramos presented a neat appearance. He was clean-shaven and had combed his hair straight back. Compared to forty-five-year-old Juan, twenty-one-year-old Narcio Padia looked like an adolescent. He was thin and wiry, and had no facial hair—a testament to his mostly Indian heritage. Both men were nervous and frightened, fully conscious that they were being accused of murder.

Janak stood up and made room for them at the far end of the counsel table, patting them on the back as they passed. He wanted them as far from the jury as possible and had instructed them to remain seated during the proceedings to minimize drawing attention to their prison attire.

The attorneys stood when the back door opened at ten sharp and a black-robed judge carrying a bulging file strode in to the courtroom.

"Hear ye, hear ye," called the bailiff. "Department Twelve of the Superior Court of the County of Contra Costa is now in session, the Honorable Lawrence Pluplot presiding."

The judge climbed the steps to the dais and sat in the swivel chair. He had a medium build and a full head of brown hair, which was parted down the middle. His expression was intense, even earnest. Placing a pair of rimless spectacles on the bridge of his aquiline nose, he studied the participants and the jury pool. He then looked down to his left to make sure the court reporter was in her proper place next to the witness box, in front of the jury. Satisfied, he had the clerk call the case.

"People of the State of California versus Narcio Padia and Juan Ramos, case number C-607532, and C-607533 violations of California Penal Code section 187. Murder in the first degree. Counsel, can we have your appearances, please."

Deadeye stood up. He wore his standard courtroom attire: black suit, the bolo tie with its chunk of turquoise and silver-tipped black cowboy boots.

"Earl Graves representing the People of the State of California," he said in his affected soft Southwestern drawl. He sat down only after giving the jury pool an ingratiating smile.

Janak stood up next. His husky frame barely fit in the gray suit he was wearing, but his unruly brown hair was, for once, combed, and his eyes gleamed with anticipation.

"Janak Marachak and Bartholomew Asquith appearing for the defendants, Narcio Padia and Juan Ramos."

The judge gave the prospective jurors a canned speech about their responsibilities. He explained that twelve of them at a time would be seated in the jury box to be subjected to *voir dire*, or questioning by the attorneys. He further explained that since the pending case was a possible death penalty case—should either of the defendants be found guilty—he was required to ask if any of the potential jurors was against the death penalty as a matter of principle. Five raised their hands. The court called a recess and those five accompanied the lawyers and judge into the judge's chambers in order to assure all involved in the case that their position was one of conscience rather than a desire to avoid their obligation to serve as jurors. This process took the better part of an hour.

When the court session reconvened, twelve potential jurors were seated in the jury box. The judge then explained to the jury pool that there were two sides to the lawsuit and that each side had the right to excuse up to eight potential jurors for any or no reason at all. He also explained that an attorney could request that someone seated in the box be excused for "cause." Only he, the judge, could decide if the claim of cause was justified. Judge Pluplot urged the jurors not to take offense if either of those two scenarios happened to them, reminding the group that each side had an obligation to seat the most impartial jury it could empanel.

With *voir dire* set to begin, the judge noticed that it was a quarter to twelve, so he called a recess until two o'clock. Before releasing the court, however, he instructed the jury pool that they were not to discuss any aspect of the case among themselves or with any other person during the recess or at any other time during the trial, until he released them or gave them final instructions at the end of the trial.

The battle to seat an impartial jury went on for two and a half days. Not surprisingly, the biggest fight was over excluding those who had read the various articles Deadeye had planted. Twelve people were excused for cause, since they professed to believe every word they had read. In addition, Janak used twenty-nine of his thirty preemptory challenges based on information his team was getting on a daily basis from Mae Ming and Donald. It was clear these were jurors Deadeye knew he would have in his back pocket, since up to that point he'd only used twenty-two of his challenges, which meant that he still had eight.

At a quarter to five on Thursday, Janak was considering one final juror he felt uncomfortable with. He realized, however, he couldn't exercise his last challenge; that was exactly what Deadeye was waiting for.

"The defendants are satisfied with this jury, Your Honor," said Janak.

"May the People have a moment, Your Honor?" asked Deadeye. He went over the list of the remaining jurors, checking his notes against the ones already chosen. He realized he couldn't take too long to respond—that would give the impression he didn't like the jurors already in the box—so he hurried his perusal of the pages in front of him. Although his outward appearance was calm and self-assured, inside he was fuming. Deadeye knew he'd been outsmarted. He'd been waiting for Janak to make his final challenge before checking to see if he had any ringers to put on the jury, but now it was too late. He couldn't take the chance. Deadeye stood up.

"The People are also satisfied with this jury, Your Honor."

Janak and Asquith smiled at each other. They figured this round had gone to them.

The judge had the clerk swear in the jury and called the attorneys to the bar.

"Do we need alternates, gentlemen?"

"We probably should have at least two," said Janak.

"It doesn't matter to me," said Deadeye, biting his lip and staring at the wall, visibly annoyed.

They proceeded to choose two alternate jurors, who were quickly sworn in, and by a quarter past five the fourteen jurors filed out of the courtroom.

Janak and Asquith packed up and exited the courtroom, where they found Samuel waiting for them in the hallway.

"Congratulations," Samuel said. "Deadeye was chewing out some young attorney all the way down the hall. I overheard him say he was really pissed because he felt that you must have gotten inside information on the jurors. He was lying in wait for you, ready to wipe out all your gains, but you didn't use your last challenge, so he was stuck. He kept asking how you did it. His assistant told him he didn't know."

"Our system worked well," said Janak.

"Yeah," said Asquith, smiling. "A total of two observant citizens, Mae Ming and Donald, were all we needed."

"I can't use any of this in my article," said Samuel. "I'll just say that the jury was chosen and the case will go forward on Monday."

"Now comes the difficult part," said Janak. "This guy is going to be hard to handle."

"It's doubtful he'll be any harder to handle than he's already been," said Asquith, proud that he'd lasted the week without suffering a panic attack. "Let's just get prepared for his witnesses."

* * *

The following Monday Janak looked around the courtroom, which wasn't so different from the many others he'd seen in his years as a lawyer. The benches and wall panels were crafted of walnut-stained wood. Dirty globe light fixtures hung from the ceiling. Two faded flags—the U.S. and the State of California—stood near the judge's dais.

For weeks he'd slept badly and had had a metallic taste in his mouth. Janak had never been so nervous before a trial, but this morning he felt calm. He'd prepared as well as he could and he had confidence in his team and in his instincts.

The judge entered and seated himself on the bench. Janak could feel the jury's anticipation, as well as the terrible anxiety of his clients, seated next to Asquith and him at the counsel table.

Deadeye, dressed in his Texas best, black suit and boots polished to a high luster, stood up and presented his opening statement to the jury. Ripping right into the defendants as malicious murderers, he went over the evidence that tied them to the crime scene, explaining that their motive was revenge based on their erroneous perception that Mr. Hagopian had caused harm to their families. He carefully detailed the connection between the rope that was found around the victim's neck and Juan Ramos, explaining that he would prove that Juan Ramos tied the knot. He assured the jury that the defendants had first tried to kill Hagopian with the very same chemicals they claimed had poisoned their children. Finally, Deadeye reminded the jury that all the evidence he would produce showed that the defendants were guilty of murder in the first degree with malice aforethought, and that conviction justified the imposition of the death penalty. His opening took less than an hour.

When he'd finished, Janak stood up. The contrast between his rough appearance and Deadeye's carefully groomed one couldn't have been greater. He looked intently at the individual jurors, so that each believed he was talking to him or her directly. He wanted them to know that before they could convict a defendant, all twelve had to unanimously agree that he was guilty. Not only that, they had to be convinced beyond a reasonable doubt that he'd committed the crime, and Janak assured them there was no proof in this case that rose to that level. He then warned them that each defendant was presumed innocent and that if they found that there was any reasonable doubt as to his guilt, they were obligated to acquit him. He concluded by telling the jurors that he wasn't going to discuss the evidence, because at this stage in the proceedings, his clients didn't have to prove anything.

Janak's opening statement, his first in a criminal case, lasted just twenty minutes.

Deadeye's first witness was Phillip Macintosh, from the Richmond Police Department crime laboratory, who was one of the first to arrive at the crime scene. He was in his late thirties and stood over six feet tall. He had thick, dishwater-blond hair, wore spectacles and had the look of an absent-minded professor. Deadeye qualified him as an expert in scientific investigation by showing that he'd attended the University of California at Berkeley, where he received a master's degree in biology in 1949. He'd worked for the Richmond Police Department since graduation and had examined evidence in over five hundred criminal cases. Deadeye pointed out that his testimony had never been questioned on appeal.

Macintosh explained that he'd accompanied Lieutenant Bruno Bernardi of the homicide squad to the scene of the crime at the chemical dump at Point Molate in early December of the previous year. He also testified as to what they'd found there.

"Tell us, Mr. Macintosh," said Deadeye. "Whose fingerprints did you find on the Coke bottles?"

"Objection, Your Honor," barked Janak. "May we approach the bench?" The lawyers gathered on the far side of the dais with the judge and the court reporter.

"Mr. Graves knows that the only fingerprints on the bottles are those of Miguel Ramos and Jose Ramos, who are not on trial in this action. It's therefore extremely prejudicial to my clients to have him try and link others in Mr. Juan Ramos's family to the crime scene. It's obvious that he's trying to insinuate guilt by association. I remind the Court that Mr. Graves is prevented from bringing up any evidence tying Miguel Ramos to the murder of Joseph Hagopian in Fresno."

"He's stretching your ruling, Judge," Deadeye countered. "It was simply that I couldn't mention Miguel Ramos's fingerprints on the Fresno murder weapon, not that I couldn't talk about fingerprints found on the Coke bottles at Point Molate."

"He's right, Mr. Marachak," said the judge. "The ruling wasn't as broad as you're trying to make it. Overruled. You may inquire, Mr. Graves."

Deadeye walked back to his table triumphantly and repeated the question. "Tell us, Mr. Macintosh, whose fingerprints did you find on the Coke bottles?"

"The fingerprints of Miguel Ramos and Jose Ramos, former dumpsite employees of Mr. Hagopian."

"Whose fingerprints on which bottles?"

"The fingerprints on the two bottles found in the inside pockets of the suit were from Miguel Ramos and the fingerprints on the two bottles in the outside pockets belonged to Jose Ramos."

"What was in the Coke bottles, Mr. Macintosh?"

"The two that had Mr. Miguel Ramos's fingerprints on them contained the chemicals he claimed in his civil complaint had caused birth defects in his child, as well as his own sterility. The other two, which had Mr. Jose Ramos's fingerprints on them, contained the two chemicals that he claimed caused his child's injuries and his own sterility."

"Explain to the jury what civil complaint you are talking about, Mr. Macintosh."

"The employees, Miguel Ramos, Jose Ramos and Mr. Narcio Padia, the smaller of the two gentlemen sitting at the table over there, all filed a civil suit against the dump, Mr. Hagopian, and several chemical companies, alleging that the entities had contributed to birth defects in their children and to their own sterility after the birth of their children. In their complaint they named certain chemicals. Some of those chemicals were found in the bottles in the decedent's jacket."

"The very same chemicals?" Deadeye smirked.

"The very same."

"Did you find the fingerprints of anyone else at the scene?"

"Yes, sir. We found the fingerprints of Narcio Padia on the rake that was used to smooth out the ground beneath the gate."

"The rake that's shown here in this photograph?" asked Deadeye.

"Yes, sir."

"What was the rake used for?"

"It was used to rake the ground underneath the hanged body of Mr. Hagopian after it was hung from the gate arch."

"By the way," asked Deadeye, pacing back and forth before the jury, "do you know what happened to the defendants sitting here, as well to Miguel Ramos and Jose Ramos, after their civil suit was filed?"

"Objection, Your Honor," yelled Janak. "That calls for hearsay."

"I'll allow it," said the judge.

"Yes, sir," said Macintosh. "They were all fired."

"They were what?" Deadeye with feigned surprise as he looked over at the jury.

"They were fired."

"When did that occur?"

"Several months before the murder."

"Thank you, Mr. Macintosh. That's all the questions I have at this time." Deadeye smiled as he sat down, very pleased with his performance. "Your witness, Mr. Marachak."

Janak stood up. "Excuse me, Your Honor, may I use a podium? It's easier for me to converse with the witness that way."

The judge nodded yes, and the bailiff put a podium in front of the jury box.

"Good morning, Mr. Macintosh. How many cases have you handled that were murder cases?"

"I'd say around fifty."

"All fifty cases involved some kind of forensic evidence that you had to evaluate, is that correct?"

"Yes, sir."

"Have you ever seen a case like this one, Mr. Macintosh?"

"I'm not sure I know what you mean, Counselor."

"Have you ever seen a case in which incriminating evidence appeared so straightforward?"

"You'll have to be more specific, Counsel."

"For instance, when someone leaves a fingerprint, it's not usually in a place that's so open and obvious as a Coke bottle that's left on a decedent's body, is it?"

"You never know where you're going to find incriminating evidence. But it is true that finding a fingerprint in such an obvious place is a little surprising."

"So, in that sense, finding the prints that you did where you found them was a little unusual, wasn't it?"

Deadeye jumped up from his seated position at the table. "Objection, misstates his testimony."

"Overruled, this is cross-examination."

"Yes, it was unusual, in that sense," said Macintosh.

"Isn't it true that no fingerprints from either one of the defendants sitting here in court was found on those Coke bottles."

"That's true."

"Do you know where those Coke bottles came from?"

"No, sir, I don't."

Janak pulled some photographs out of the stack by the podium. "May I have these marked as defendants' exhibits, Your Honor?" He handed them to the clerk, who marked them for identification as the judge indicated.

"May I approach the witness, Your Honor?"

"Of course."

Janak handed the photographs to Macintosh.

"You see those boxes of Coca-Cola stacked next to the trailer? First of all, you recognize the trailer, don't you?"

"Yes, sir, it's the office at the dump."

"And you learned that the employees put all their empty bottles there?"

"Yes, sir."

"And there are four bottles missing from those boxes, aren't there?"

"Yes, sir."

"And the bottles that we see in the photos had the fingerprints of almost every employee who worked at the dump, including Mr. Hagopian, didn't they?"

"Yes, sir. They did."

"But prints belonging to Miguel Ramos and Jose Ramos were not found on any of the bottles in the boxes we see in these photos, were they?"

"No, sir."

"The pattern of the prints are configured the way you'd expect they'd be if someone were holding the bottle to drink from it, right?"

"Yes, sir."

"As opposed to the way someone would hold the bottle when filling it up?"

"I wouldn't go that far. You could fill it by holding it the way the prints are configured."

"But that wouldn't be the normal way to hold a bottle if you were filling it with some substance, right?"

"I wouldn't hold a bottle that way, for sure."

"Your Honor, I'd like the photographs of the Coke machine and the stacks of boxes of Coke bottles marked as the defendants' next exhibit."

"They will be so marked."

"Now I want to talk about the rope that was found around Mr. Hagopian's neck. That's not a hangman's noose, is it?"

"No, sir."

"Ever seen one like it used to kill a man?"

"No, sir. Other than in this case."

Macintosh showed him the photo of the rope around the decedent's neck. "Are you saying that this rope was used to kill him?"

"No, sir. I misspoke. It was the rope from which he was hanging from the gate. I'm not qualified to say if it killed him or not."

"You didn't find either of my clients' fingerprints on that rope, did you?"

"No, sir."

"Let me show you another photograph that the clerk has marked." Janak handed him the photograph of a footprint in plaster of Paris. "You found this partial print at the edge of the area that was raked directly underneath the body, correct?"

"Yes, sir."

"It's from a size nine shoe, isn't it?"

"Yes, sir."

"Neither of my clients wears a size nine shoe, do they?"

"No, sir."

"Let's talk about the Coke bottles. How did you identify the chemicals that were in the bottles?"

"I did sophisticated tests on them."

"In other words, without those tests, you wouldn't have had the slightest idea what any of the chemicals were?"

"That's correct."

"Do you have any information whatsoever that any of the ordinary workmen at the dump, including my clients, had any training in identifying chemicals?"

"No, sir. But they could probably identify some of them by smell after awhile."

"Now you're guessing, aren't you?"

"Yes, sir, it's speculation."

"Do you have any information that either of my clients reads or writes English?"

"No, sir."

"Or have ever read the complaint in the civil suit, or even know that it was filed in some courthouse somewhere?"

"No, sir."

"You testified on direct examination that the ground underneath the body had been raked and there was a rake left just adjacent to the area. Is this photo, marked number three, a picture of that rake?"

"Yes, sir."

"And that's exactly where you found it, as it's depicted in the photo?"

"Yes, sir.

"And the rake had fingerprints on it?"

"Yes, sir."

"Whose fingerprints?"

"Mr. Narcio Padia's."

"What was Mr. Padia's job at the dump?"

"He was a maintenance man."

"In other words, his job was cleaning up, including raking, sweeping and shoveling, correct?"

"Yes, sir.

"Did you check the brooms and shovels at the dump to see if his prints were on them, too?"

"No, sir."

"There's one more piece of evidence I'd like to ask you about, Mr. Macintosh. You see this photo of the blue insect on Mr. Hagopian's trouser leg?"

"Yes, sir."

"Did you find out where it came from?"

"No, sir."

"Why not?"

"I was told not to bother."

"Who told you that?"

"Mr. Graves."

"So you don't have the foggiest idea where it comes from, is that correct?"

"Yes, sir. That's correct."

"Can you tell me if Mr. Hagopian died where his body was found, hanging from the gate?"

"No, sir, I can't. That's really outside my area of expertise."

"Okay, but you can confirm for me that you didn't find any of his private body parts on any of the dump property, correct?"

"Yes, sir. Nothing like that was found."

"And you do know they were missing from his body?"

"Yes, sir."

"One more question. You found mud on one of Mr. Hagopian's shoes, didn't you?"

"Yes, sir."

"But that mud wasn't from the dumpsite, was it?"

"No, sir."

"Do you know where it came from?"

"We weren't able to tell without a reference."

"What does that mean?"

"It means that we would have to have a place to examine to determine if the soil matched. Otherwise, we'd be running around in circles."

"I have no further questions of this witness at this time," said Janak. "I may have to recall him, however, so I'm asking the court not to excuse him."

"I have a few questions on redirect examination, Your Honor," said Deadeye.

"Proceed, assuming you won't take too long."

Deadeye moseyed up to the podium, a big smile on his face, aware that his position placed him directly in front of the jury. "Mr. Macintosh, you've examined ropes for fingerprints in the past, haven't you?"

"Yes, sir."

"Ever find someone's fingerprints on a rope in all the ten years you've been investigating?"

"Once in a while, sir."

"Is there a reason it's only once in a while?"

"Yes, sir. A rope is porous, so it doesn't take prints very well. We always check, though, 'cause sometimes people have grease or ink on their hands and then we get lucky."

"And you checked this rope, did you not?" Deadeye showed him a photo of the rope around Hagopian's neck.

"Yes, sir."

"Let's talk about the insect. You couldn't identify that insect, could you?"

"No, sir. It required investigation by someone with a background in entomology."

"That's a person who specializes in insects?"

"Yes, sir. But that's not me."

"Thank you, Mr. Macintosh," said Deadeye.

"Very well," said the judge. "Mr. Macintosh, please give the clerk a number where you can be reached in case you're needed again.

"It's time for our noon recess. Remember, ladies and gentlemen of the jury, do not discuss this case with each other or anyone else. Counsel, how about a stipulation that I no longer need to give this admonition every time the jury leaves?"

"So stipulated," answered both attorneys.

* * *

"What did you think of the testimony, Samuel?" Janak asked as they walked down the street on their way to a restaurant.

"You made the points. Deadeye is ignoring the evidence. The question is: is the jury listening?"

Asquith intervened. "In the long run, you're getting them to tell the truth, no matter what that bastard tries to do, and that will matter."

"I don't give a shit about the long run," said Janak. "I

want these guys to get off now, not in twenty-five years. I have a bad feeling."

"Calm down, man," said Samuel. "Keep going, step by step. I'll make sure it's reported in the press."

"I think you're both wrong," said Janak. "This case is going to come down to Deadeye making another mistake. If he doesn't, we lose."

"Why do you say that?" asked Ascuith.

"Because that's the way it is in Contra Costa County in 1962."

* * *

When court reconvened at two o'clock, Deadeye called Dr. Jerome Bancroft. The witness approached the bench holding a small manila file and an envelope stamped "Official Coroner Photographs." He was of medium height and had a fringe of gray hair around his bald pate. His lips were thin and he wore glasses and a contemptuous expression. In truth, Bancroft looked like someone who spent most of his time with corpses and not so much with the living.

Deadeye had no trouble qualifying Bancroft as an expert. He'd graduated from medical school at the University of Indiana in 1940. After completing his internship, he joined the military, where he spent the four years of the war working as a pathologist. After the war, Bancroft migrated to California with millions of others and started a practice in Walnut Creek. He eventually contracted with the County of Contra Costa to perform post mortems on an as-needed basis, and was the pathologist hired to conduct the autopsy on Armand Hagopian.

"I'd like to ask you some specific questions, Dr. Bancroft," said Deadeye. "You have the autopsy protocol with you, and you're welcome to refer to it if you need to refresh your recollection. You performed the autopsy, did you not?"

"Yes, sir."

"When did that take place?"

"It was at the county morgue on December 7, 1961, at 8 a.m."

"Did you have an assistant?"

"Yes, sir. A technician helped me."

"On whom did you perform the autopsy?"

"According to the record, which was verified by the decedent's fingerprints, the person was Armand Hagopian. He was a white male, fifty-one years of age."

"Did you determine the cause of his death?"

"Yes, sir. The cause of death was asphyxiation. That means his breath was cut off."

"How did you determine that?"

"There were several ways. The neck muscles were crushed around the larynx—that's the Adam's apple—the trachea was torn and there was evidence of hemorrhage in the blood vessels of the whites of his eyes. These symptoms are classic signs of that kind of death."

"Did you find anything else that could have led to his death?"

"There were toxic chemicals found in his mouth that had seeped into his upper air passages, but it's my opinion that they were inserted after his death and that they didn't cause it."

"You mean that someone poured the same chemicals that were found in the Coke bottles down his throat?"

"All four of them, but it was too late."

"You say asphyxiation. Is that the same as hanging?"

"In this case, it's my opinion that the man was hanged. We took a rope from around his neck and he had the kind of bruises that are consistent with being hanged. Plus, eyewitness accounts confirm that he was found hanging from the gate of his establishment by the same rope."

"There was something else done to him, wasn't there?"

"Yes, sir. He was emasculated while he was still alive."

"How do you know that?"

"You see the photographs of the blood stains on his pant legs? The body bleeds while the heart is pumping."

"Do you have an estimate of the time of death, Doctor?"

"I can't tell. It depends on how much rigor mortis was present when the coroner examined him on December 6."

"So you don't know, is that your testimony?"

"Yes, sir."

"What is rigor mortis, Doctor?"

"It's the temporary post mortem condition of the body becoming stiff. It usually starts to set in three to four hours after death, and it lasts for about twelve hours."

"Thank you, Doctor," said Deadeye. "I have no further questions."

"Do you wish to cross-examine, Mr. Marachak?"

"Yes, Your Honor, thank you," said Janak, moving to the podium.

"Good afternoon, Doctor. You have the complete coroner's report, the police report, the toxicology report and all the photographs taken at the dump, as well as the autopsy report, correct?"

"I don't have all those items up here, but I have them in my briefcase."

"Would you mind getting them? I want to ask you some questions and you may have to refer to some of them."

The doctor looked to Deadeye for help. But Deadeye, not wanting to be included in any suggestion that evidence was being kept from the jury, avoided his gaze. The doctor then turned to the judge, who nodded his approval for him to leave the witness chair and retrieve his briefcase.

When he was seated again, Janak resumed his questioning. "You said rigor mortis begins to set in between three and four hours after death?"

"Yes, sir."

"But you weren't able to tell the court about the degree of stiffness in the body when the coroner examined it on December 6?"

"That's correct."

"Will you please turn to Page 1 of the coroner's notes? They're part of the file you now have in front of you."

Dr. Bancroft complied. "I have them. What is it you'd like to pursue?"

"Read them to the jury."

"The notes say: 'The body is in the beginning stages of rigor mortis. I bent the extremities and the digits of the hands, but the body was becoming increasingly stiff.'"

"He's at the scene, cutting the body down, right?"

"Yes, sir."

"Let's apply your rule, Doctor. Rigor mortis starts to set in three to four hours after death. The coroner sees him—at what time does the note say?"

"Eight a.m."

"And it's a cold December day. Does that make any difference?"

"Yes, sir. The process is slowed in colder weather."

"The police report says that his body was discovered by an anonymous truck driver at around 6 a.m. So the man died somewhere between midnight and three in the morning, right?"

"If the coroner's notes are correct, I would say yes. That's a pretty good guess."

"Do you have information suggesting that the notes may not be correct?"

"No, sir."

"Then it's more than a guess. It's your professional opinion based on the evidence, isn't it?"

"Yes, sir," said the doctor, whose lips had now become stuck over his large teeth, giving his face the appearance of a cadaver trying to wiggle out of a grin.

"Let's talk about the cause of death. You said it was asphyxiation? Caused by hanging?"

"It could have been hanging. Something was put around his neck and squeezed so that he suffocated."

"Maybe I misunderstood your testimony," said Janak tersely, annoyed by the witness's evasiveness. "Didn't you tell Mr. Graves that Mr. Hagopian was hanged?"

"Could have been hanged."

"*Could have* is a lot different than *was*, isn't it?"

"Yes, sir.

"But you agreed with Mr. Graves that he was hanged, didn't you?"

"Could have been."

Janak handed him a photograph. "You see the photograph of Mr. Hagopian with the rope around his neck?"

"Yes, sir. I've seen this photo. When I started the autopsy, he had the same rope around his neck. I cut it off and Mr. Graves introduced it into evidence."

Janak walked over to the clerk's desk. She handed him the envelope with the piece of rope in it. He took it out and held it up in front of the doctor.

"This is the end of the rope that he was hanging from when the coroner cut him down. But what you're telling us now is that you can't say with any degree of medical certainty that this was the rope that killed him, can you?"

"It could have killed him. I'm not sure."

"Let's look at the photo of Mr. Hagopian's neck. There's a rope burn on it, right there. See the indentation?"

"Yes, sir."

"But that burn isn't from the same kind of rope as the one around Mr. Hagopian's neck that was placed in evidence, is it?"

"No, sir."

"How do you know that?"

"You can see the marks on his skin. They show a completely different pattern from the rope that was found around his neck."

"So it's fair to say that when he was strung up at the gate, he was already dead."

"I'm not sure."

"If he were still alive, there'd be rope burns from the rope you have in your hand, wouldn't there?"

"Yes, sir. Probably."

"You also know he was alive when he was emasculated because of the amount of blood on his pant legs."

"Yes, sir."

"You've looked at all the evidence in this case, haven't you, Dr. Bancroft?"

"Yes, sir. All the evidence that has to do with his death."

"You never saw his private parts, or even a photograph of them, did you?"

"No, sir."

"Let me show you some photographs of the raked area underneath his body. You don't see any blood there, do you?"

"No, sir."

"And no one has ever told you there was any blood found in that area, have they?"

"No, sir."

"So given that there was no blood from the amputation of his private parts on the raked portion of the ground underneath the body, that means he was already dead when he was strung up."

"You could argue that."

"I'm not asking for an argument. I'm asking for your professional opinion based on the evidence."

Deadeye bolted out of his chair, his cheeks flushed. He'd

lost his cool-Texan composure.

"Objection. He's arguing with the witness."

"Overruled, Counsel. He can answer."

"The blood could have been raked up."

"I repeat my question. Did anyone or any report state that blood was found on the raked area beneath where the body was hanging?"

"No, sir."

"You spent some time with Mr. Graves before your testimony here today, didn't you?"

"Yes, sir."

"How much time?"

"We spent three hours together."

"What'd you talk about?"

"The autopsy, and what we found as a result of it."

"That was it?"

"Yes, sir."

"You mean you were with him for three hours and didn't go over the evidence you and I have discussed, or even that part of the coroner's report that I showed you today?" Janak gave the jury with an ironic smile.

"No, sir."

"Okay, Dr. Bancroft, you're free to go. You can crawl off the stand now. Your Honor, I won't need this witness anymore,."

Deadeye was on his feet again. "I object to this attorney harassing this witness, Your Honor."

"I withdraw the comment, Your Honor," said Janak, bobbing his head at the jury, his eyebrows arched.

"Counsel, you wish to redirect?" asked the judge, looking at Mr. Graves.

"No, Your Honor."

"You are released, Dr. Bancroft. Thank you for your testimony. Ladies and gentlemen of the jury, you are free to go. See you tomorrow at 10 a.m. Remember the admonition."

King of the Bottom

* * *

Early the next morning, Deadeye was pacing back and forth in his office with a copy of the San Francisco morning paper rolled up in his fist. He was slapping it against the arm of the leather chair his assistant was sitting in and yelling over the young man's head.

"That bastard Hamilton is out to get us. Did you read what he said about the pathologist's testimony yesterday?"

"I…I…" The young man tried to answer, but couldn't form the words.

"Shut the fuck up. Listen to this: 'The witness was obviously coached and was probably stretching the truth.' Don't you think the jurors read what that asshole Hamilton has to say?" Again, he whacked the newspaper, this time on the desk. "He's cut off. No more information from our office. Understand? Now get out of here! I have to prepare my witness for today. Tell him to come in and put the 'Do Not Disturb Sign' on my door."

* * *

"Call your next witness, Mr. Graves," the judge announced when the proceedings started that morning.

"The People call Mr. Nashwan Asad Aram."

The bailiff escorted in a young man of a little more than medium height. He was dressed in an expensive Italian suit and a mauve silk shirt. The clerk swore him in and he took the witness stand.

Deadeye got up from his place next to the jury and approached Janak's podium with casual poise.

After the usual preliminaries, he stuck his left hand in his black trouser pocket and began his questioning. "Where do you presently reside?"

"I live in Paris, France," said Aram, speaking English with only a slight accent. "I was born there on November 19, 1932.

How long have you lived in Paris?"

"Most of my life, except when I came to the U.S. to attend university and when I worked for Mr. Hagopian."

The jury took in his brown eyes, thick black hair and the suggestion of a five o'clock shadow on his swarthy complexion, which was softened by talcum powder. He was an attractive man.

"Let's talk about 1961. You were an employee of Mr. Armand Hagopian at the Molate dumpsite?"

"Yes, sir. I was working as a management trainee."

"How long did you work there?"

"For a year."

"You see Mr. Ramos and Mr. Padia sitting over there in the corner, don't you?"

"Yes, sir. I worked with them for almost six months, until they were fired."

"Fired, you say. Why was that?"

"Mr. Padia filed a lawsuit against Mr. Hagopian. Mr. Ramos's nephews, Miguel and Jose Ramos, also filed suit against him. They too were fired, along with Mr. Juan Ramos."

"Did you get to know these men during the six months you worked with them?"

"Yes, sir. I was learning the job from the ground up, so I worked with them daily, doing what they did."

"Was there ever a time when they made threats against Mr. Hagopian?"

Janak jumped up. "Objection, overly broad and irrelevant, incompetent and immaterial."

"Sustained. Rephrase your question."

"You had numerous conversations with both these defendants during those six months that you worked with them, didn't you?"

"Yes, sir."

"In what language were these conversations?"

"They both spoke enough English for us to understand each other."

"Do you speak Spanish?"

"Pidgin Spanish. I speak only enough to ask for food or say hello. They volunteered to teach me words. However, our talks were mostly in English."

"Tell me, what did they say to you about Mr. Hagopian."

"Mr. Padia was very upset that his child was born deformed and that he, himself, had become sterile. He was angry he couldn't have any more boys. He said it was Mr. Hagopian's fault, so he had to pay for it."

"Was he talking about Mr. Hagopian paying him money?"

"No, sir. He said that where he was from money wouldn't fix things. It was a matter of honor, and Mr. Hagopian had dishonored him and his family, so he would have to pay the ultimate price."

"Did he say what he meant by the ultimate price?"

"He said he would have to pay with his life."

"Did you tell Mr. Hagopian what he had said?"

"Yes, sir."

"Did Mr. Ramos say anything against Mr. Hagopian?"

"He was beside himself because his nephews had children with birth defects and, according to him, both of his nephews had become sterile. He said as a family they would stick together and make Mr. Hagopian pay."

"Was he talking about making him pay money through the lawsuit?"

"No, sir. He showed me a rope and he tied a knot in it and said it was for Hagopian and that he would hang from the end of it to pay for his crimes."

"Did you tell Mr. Hagopian about these conversations?"

"Yes, sir."

"What did he say?"

"He said he thought they were just blowing off steam, but that he would keep an eye on them."

Deadeye rummaged through the evidence until he found what he was looking for. "You see the knot at the end of this piece of rope?"

"Yes, sir. That's the kind of knot Mr. Ramos tied and talked about."

"Why are you so sure?"

"Because he went through the same routine every day. He would tie the knot and then slide it down the rope and say that this was what was going to happen to Hagopian."

"Thank you, Mr. Aram," said Deadeye, smiling as he took his seat. "I don't have any further questions."

Janak got up and slowly walked to the podium, where he stood looking at the witness for a long time. He took so long that even the judge peered over his glasses at the silence in the courtroom.

Samuel noticed that Nashwan Asad Aram had on a pair of highly polished black Gucci loafers, complete with a distinctive strip of red-and-green striped cloth. He recognized the logo from the shoes he'd seen in the window of the shop next to La Roche et Fils in Paris. He also recalled how much shoes like that cost. Samuel felt profound antipathy for the man and hoped that the jury would feel the same.

"Are you Armenian, Mr. Asad?"

"No, sir. I'm Kurdish."

"Why were you born in Paris?"

"My parents were refugees. They escaped from the Turks. The Kurds were persecuted by the Turks during the Great War just like the Armenians were, and they had to flee our homeland. My parents ended up in Paris."

"Why did you come to the United States?"

"I came to study."

"Really? What?"

"I got a degree in chemical engineering."

"Where?"

"At the University of Pittsburgh."

"Why did you come to California?"

"After graduating I needed practical experience. I learned that Hagopian Enterprises was involved in the disposal of chemical waste. I negotiated a job with them as an apprentice."

"Who was your contact person in California?"

"Mr. Hagopian himself. He was generous to me. As I said, our families shared some of the same hardships caused by the Turks."

"What size shoe do you wear, Mr. Aram?"

"I beg your pardon?"

"I want to know what size shoe you wear."

The witness looked startled. "Thirty-four, I believe."

"You're measuring centimeters. How does that translate to U.S. standards?"

"I have no idea," said the witness, annoyed.

"Your Honor, may I have the witness take off his right shoe?"

Deadeye was immediately at the podium, standing next to Janak. "Objection. This witness is not on trial."

"Gentlemen, please approach the bench," said the judge, motioning with a finger. Once there, Janak explained his request.

"He can't give us an American shoe size, Judge. I need to compare his foot size with the footprint evidence left at the dump. He's already admitted he worked there."

"This is a desperate attempt by Mr. Marachak to try and shift blame," said Deadeye, visibly flushed.

"I will allow it," said the judge.

Janak took the plaster footprint from the evidence table in front of the clerk. The judge ordered the witness to remove his right shoe and Janak placed it in the mold. The shoe fit perfectly. Janak made sure the jury saw it.

"Where were you on the night of December 5 of last year, Mr. Aram."

"I was at my apartment in Oakland."

"Not at the dumpsite at Point Molate?"

"No, sir."

"Can anyone back that up?"

"Objection," yelled Deadeye, waving his arms. "This man's not on trial."

"Overruled," said the judge.

"I was alone, since I lived alone," said Aram.

Janak showed the witness a photo of the Coke boxes. "You recognize where this photograph was taken, don't you?"

"Yes, sir."

"You'd drink Cokes with the other workers right in that area, wouldn't you?"

"Yes, sir."

"And when you'd finish, you'd put the empties in those boxes right next to the machine, correct?"

"Yes, sir."

"And you would do that every day?"

"Maybe not every day, but several times a week."

"You'd drink with Jose and Miguel Ramos, right?"

"Yes, sir. We all drank and we all put our bottles back in the boxes."

"You watched where they put their bottles and you took Coke bottles with their fingerprints on them right out of those boxes, didn't you?"

The witness shifted in his seat. "I certainly did not."

"Once the men were fired, you never drank another Coke. Right?"

"I already told you we drank Cokes several times a week."

Janak pulled out an invoice and had it marked for identification. He showed it to Deadeye and then to the witness. "What's the date on that invoice, Mr. Aram?"

"May 12, 1961."

"Then you changed the delivery schedule, didn't you? You realize that was the last pick-up of the Coke empties that year, whereas in the previous six months it was done every month?"

"I have no way of knowing that."

"Those workers were fired in early July and that's when you removed all the bottles with their fingerprints on them."

"No, sir, not me," said the witness, again shifting in his seat.

"Well, those are your initials, N. A., and that's your handwriting. 'Stop pick up,' isn't it?"

"Objection," yelled Deadeye. "Assumes facts not in evidence."

"Overruled," said the judge, chidingly. "This is cross-examination, Mr. Graves."

"I don't know whose handwriting that is," Nashwan answered.

"It was you who got Juan Ramos to tie the knot in the rope, wasn't it?"

"No, sir, it was the other way around. He said he was going to use it on Hagopian."

"You helped hang Hagopian from the gate, didn't you?"

"No, sir."

"Your Honor," interrupted Deadeye.

"You have an objection, Mr. Graves?"

"Withdrawn."

"That's your footprint in the plaster of Paris, isn't it?" asked Janak.

"No, sir."

"We know that Mr. Padia's duties at the dump included shoveling and raking. You confiscated the rake after you saw him use it, didn't you?"

"No, sir.

"Let's talk about your education. You are a chemical engineer. That means you've studied a lot of chemistry, doesn't it?

"Yes, sir."

"You were one of the few people on Hagopian's staff who knew the properties of the chemicals these men were complaining about in their lawsuit?"

"Yes sir. I knew what chemicals they claimed did them damage because I helped Mr. Hagopian analyze the claims made in the lawsuit."

"It was more than that. You knew what kind of chemicals were involved and you knew where to get them and how to handle them, didn't you?"

"I knew what they were."

"And where to get them?"

"Yes, sir."

"Isn't it true," Janak shouted, "that you're the one who put those chemicals in the bottles and then put them on Mr. Hagopian's body?"

"Objection!"

But before Deadeye could continue, the judge interrupted him. "Overruled, he can answer."

"Tell us!" Janak spoke with such passion that the scar on his cheek turned purple. "It was you who planted the bottles, wasn't it?"

"No, sir." Aram was sweating. "Judge, can I have a glass of water?"

"Before your water, one more question, Mr. Aram. You helped kill Mr. Hagopian somewhere in the Central Valley, didn't you?"

"Of course not!" rasped the witness, looking more and

more uncomfortable.

"I'm through with him, Judge," said Janak, suddenly exhausted.

Deadeye solicitously brought the witness a cup of water. "I just have a few more questions, Your Honor."

"Your witness, Counselor," responded the judge.

"When did you leave the Bay Area?" Deadeye asked.

"I showed up for work early in the morning, but there was a crowd of people and I heard that someone had killed the boss. I panicked and left."

"Thank you, Mr. Aram."

Janak stepped into the breach. "You never identified yourself to the police that morning, did you?"

"No, sir."

"And the reason you didn't was because you didn't want to be questioned. Or was it that your clothes were covered with blood?"

"No, that's not true."

"Yeah, sure. You wouldn't be so clumsy so as to show up at the scene with blood on your clothes or mud on your shoes."

Deadeye was on his feet. "Objection!"

The witness addressed the court. "Your Honor, I need protection from this attorney's accusations."

The judge took his glasses off and looked at the witness. "This is a trial, Mr. Aram, and it's your job to answer the questions put to you. I'll decide when and if the attorneys have gone too far." He then put his glasses back on and turned to Janak.

"Do you have any further questions, Mr. Marachak?"

"Yes, Your Honor, one more.

"On which airline did you travel, Mr. Aram?"

"Air France."

"When did you make the reservation?"

"The morning I found out Mr. Hagopian was dead."

"I'm through with this witness for now," said Janak, "but I may need him to come back. Can we get an address and phone number for him?"

"I'm scheduled to leave the country tomorrow, Judge," said Aram. He was clearly agitated.

"You'll just have to wait until you're released."

The judge then turned to the jury. "We'll take our morning recess, ladies and gentlemen. Please return to the courtroom in twenty minutes."

Deadeye walked out of the courtroom, his arm on Nashwan Aram's shoulder, faking a calmness he was far from feeling. For what he was trying to accomplish, the witness was no longer necessary, but he was worried that Marachak might recall him. How much damage had the questioning done? His rival hadn't been able to prove anything; he'd only raised suspicions. On the other hand, the first part of Aram's testimony had been devastating to the defendants. Deadeye had experience with juries and he knew that a young, attractive, educated and well-dressed man like Aram made a very good impression. His instinct told him that Aram had gone over well with the jurors, especially the women, and that Marachak's unfounded accusations would be ignored, but he couldn't be absolutely sure. He turned, head down, and walked toward his office. Aram went downstairs to the coffee shop to get a pastry and a cup of coffee.

Janak and Asquith huddled together in the back of the courtroom with the investigator, trying to figure out their next move. Samuel sat apart from them, deep in thought. He realized that Nashwan Aram's testimony had been prejudicial to the defendants. According to Janak, he was the only witness who had direct contact with the workers and who'd gotten information from them.

Samuel knew that he had to be careful. His job was to present the facts in an impartial manner. His version of how the murder occurred had changed upon hearing Aram—now he wasn't sure of anything. Putting aside the antipathy for the man and his Gucci shoes, Samuel thought the Kurd's testimony was believable.

*   *   *

When court resumed after the recess, Earl Graves rested his case. This took Janak by surprise since there had been no testimony from the wife, sister or any other member of the Hagopian family, even though Deadeye had named all of them on the list of witnesses he was going to call. Janak had to ask the Court for a delay before beginning the defense because he didn't have any witnesses present for the remainder of the morning session.

When court resumed that afternoon, Janak called the entomologist, Dr. Jonathan Higginbotham. The professor was dressed much the same way as when Janak had visited him in his office a few weeks earlier. If anything, his sports jacket with the leather patches on the elbows looked more worn, his pants more wrinkled and his shoes even dirtier.

Janak led the entomologist through a litany of questions regarding his qualifications and background, prodding him to list the many books he had written on insects throughout his forty-year career. After establishing the professor's credentials, he began his questioning.

"What's your present position?"

"I'm a full professor of entomology at the University of California at Berkeley. The university has employed me for the past forty years. I started out as a teaching assistant, then became a lecturer and, eventually, began climbing the academic ladder until reaching this level, where I have been for the past fifteen years."

"Please tell the jury what an entomologist does."

"An entomologist is basically a bug doctor," he said. The

jury members laughed. It was obvious that they liked him and his relaxed manner.

"In other words, Doctor, you're paid to know the difference between one bug and another, correct?"

"That's one of our jobs. But we start out by trying to find out where a particular insect comes from. That helps us determine if it is carrying a disease that could contaminate our population or if it has some predatory characteristic that could jeopardize some part of our food chain."

"Doctor, I've shown you what remained of the crushed blue insect that was found on the pant leg of the decedent in this case. I've also shown you several photographs of it, have I not?"

"Yes, sir, you have."

"Were you able to identify that insect, Doctor?"

"Yes, sir, I was," the professor answered. But before he could elaborate, Deadeye was on his feet.

"Objection, no foundation."

"Your Honor, we've more than established this man's qualifications," said Janak.

"Overruled," said the judge. "You may answer."

"The insect in this photograph is a Chitosi beetle. Its country of origin is Japan."

"You mean it's not native to Northern California?"

"No, sir. It probably migrated here on one of the sailing ships that came from Japan during the last century. No doubt while one of them was making its way up the Carquinez Straits to Stockton and Sacramento, the insect jumped ship."

"You mention Stockton and Sacramento. Is there any evidence that any of those Chitosi beetles disembarked in Richmond."

"Even if it had gotten off at Richmond it wouldn't have stayed there. The climate is too temperate for that critter."

Deadeye squirmed in his seat. This witness troubled him.

The jury liked him too much.

"Even if it were comfortable in Richmond, could it have survived at Point Molate?"

"Objection," yelled Deadeye, on his feet once more. "No foundation."

"I'll qualify, Your Honor," said Janak.

"Very well," said the judge.

"You went to Point Molate at my request, did you not?"

"Yes, sir."

"Did you find any evidence of insect life in or around the Hagopian dumpsite?"

"Objection," yelled Deadeye again. "No foundation."

"Overruled," said the judge. "You may answer."

"No, sir, none."

"So it couldn't survive there, correct?"

"Yes, that's correct."

"Your Honor, I ask that this man's testimony about the beetle not being able to survive be stricken," said Deadeye. "He's not a toxicologist."

"He can ask him questions on cross-examination, Judge," countered Janak. "Right now the professor is my witness."

"Motion denied, Mr. Graves," said the judge. "You can take that up on cross."

"Where does this Chitosi beetle make its home in Northern California?" Janak asked.

"Up until you asked me to investigate its habitat, I hadn't seen it in the Bay Area for several years, other than in the Stockton area. I checked again after your inquiry several weeks ago and, sure enough, that's still the only place it seems able to survive."

"Why there and nowhere else, Doctor?"

"Insects choose climates that they are comfortable with and will search out environments that are similar to where they come from, especially if they inadvertently get waylaid from one place to another as this one did."

"Do you have an opinion, Doctor, about which geographical area the insect we're talking about attached itself to Mr. Hagopian's pant leg.

"Objection," yelled Deadeye, without even bothering to get up. "No foundation and calls for speculation, Your Honor."

"Overruled," said the judge. "Take it up on cross."

"My first opinion is that it did not attach to his pant leg at Point Molate simply because that's not where it's from."

"You have more opinions, I'm sure. Please explain, Doctor."

"So it either attached to Mr. Hagopian's pant leg in the Stockton area, where it definitively thrives, or his body was wrapped in something that came from there."

"How can you be so sure, Doctor?"

"If you look at the beetle closely, you can see it has no blood from the victim on it, yet the victim's pant leg is soaked in blood. Furthermore, the beetle has been crushed. You can see some of its remains on Mr. Hagopian's pant leg. So that means it attached to his pant leg after he was dead and the blood was dry. It probably got trapped while he was being wrapped for transport."

"Thank you, Doctor," said Janak, smiling as he took his seat.

Deadeye understood that he had to be careful. The jury liked the professor, and he couldn't risk alienating any of them by going on the attack. Instead, he decided to ask some perfunctory questions in the hope that the jurors would think that the doctor was agreeing with him. Carrying a sheaf of notes, he approached the podium.

"Doctor, your Ph.D. is in entomology, right?"

"That's correct."

"And you have never studied toxicology, is that right?"

"That's right."

"And you have no idea where the beetle attached to Mr. Hagopian's pant leg, do you?"

"No, sir. Other than it wasn't at Point Molate."

"Thank you. I have no further questions."

The witness gathered his notes and put them in his briefcase. He then returned the photos he had examined while on the witness stand and left the courtroom.

Next, Janak put a pathologist on the witness stand. The pathologist explained that the rope burns on Hagopian's neck couldn't have come from the Mexican knot. They had come from a more substantial rope, he said, leaving deep impressions that could only have been sustained while the victim was still alive. The pathologist also testified that the large amount of blood on Hagopian's pant legs confirmed that the emasculation took place while the man's heart was still pumping. Showing the jury photographs of the crime scene, he noted that there was no blood on the ground, proof that the mutilation couldn't have taken place at the dump.

Next, Janak called the Armenian priest to take the stand. The cleric refused to testify, requesting that he be granted priest-penitent privilege. Deadeye didn't even bother to argue. However, it was obvious he knew what was going on. He understood that Janak was hoping the priest's refusal to testify would leave the jury with the impression he had something to hide. The court heard a brief argument on the matter, after which it sustained the priest's refusal, noting that although the penitent in question was dead, the priest also shared the clergy privilege, and thus was not required to disclose information shared in confidence.

Following Nashwan's testimony, Janak had subpoenaed his travel itinerary from Air France. Due to red tape, however, he was told it would not be available for thirty days. Janak asked the judge for a postponement of the trial until then, but the request was denied.

* * *

It was the end of another trial day. Janak and his team agreed there was a lot to do before court the next day. Samuel offered that since he knew where Candice and Mrs. Hagopian lived, he would try and serve a subpoena on them for the following morning.

Marcel took Samuel to a costume shop near the Opera House in San Francisco, where he rented a nice three-piece suit and a natural-looking black wig. He didn't want Thaddeus Carlton, the doorman, to recognize him. He figured that if he looked important enough, Carlton would let him go up to the apartment. Dressed in the outfit, he went to a flower shop and bought a bouquet of roses.

"You look like a million bucks, Samuel," said Marcel as he straightened his friend's ascot tie and wig. "You should dress up like this more often."

Samuel rang the bell. Thaddeus came to the door and looked through the wrought iron bars. After examining him for a moment, he opened the door. "Hello, Mr. Hamilton, nice to see you again."

Samuel blushed. "I have some flowers here for Mrs. Hagopian. Can I run them upstairs?" His head itched underneath dammed wig.

"Sorry, Mr. Hamilton." The doorman smiled, his posture erect. "I'll make sure they're delivered, but this is as far as anyone goes without authorization."

"Can I just have a moment with her?"

"No, sir. Out of the question. I'll give her the flowers, if you wish. Otherwise, come back some time when you're invited." The doorman walked toward Samuel, causing him to back up until he was at the door, with no choice but to leave.

Samuel returned to the car. "Marcel, I need some help.

King of the Bottom

Can you hold this subpoena and watch the apartment to see if Mrs. Hagopian comes out? And if she does, will you serve it on her? In the meantime, I'll go downtown and write my story. I'll be back as soon as I'm done."

"Okay. Bring me back a sandwich, will you?"

"Sure thing. What do you want?"

"Salami on a French roll. And a Grace Brothers beer."

"Beer during working hours?"

"Are you my mother or something?"

"Okay, see you later," said Samuel as he ran to the bus stop.

* * *

Samuel returned around nine, but Marcel hadn't seen anyone come out of the building. He handed Marcel his sandwich and his beer, then drank his coffee, which by then was cold. They waited in the car until well after midnight. Finally, they gave up and went home to get some sleep so they would be able to function the next day.

Samuel reported to Janak early in the morning. Janak thanked him and admitted that he didn't think there was much hope of finding the widow or the sister, so he'd made plans to proceed without them.

Later, when court started, Janak called the two American workers at the dump. They testified that they'd seen Nashwan prancing in front of the trailers while Juan Ramos threw a lasso around him as if he were a stray calf. They also said that they saw Juan showing him how to tie a knot on several different occasions.

Janak asked that Nashwan be recalled to testify, but he'd disappeared. Deadeye argued that the only appropriate remedy would be a mistrial, but when the judge asked him if he was proposing such a strong remedy, his response was vague. Janak, sensing that Deadeye had something to do with Nashwan's disappearance, decided to follow his instincts. Instead of asking for a mistrial, he asked that the judge instruct the jury that Nashwan had defied the court's order to be on standby. As a result, he argued, the Kurd's testimony should be disregarded. Although the Judge chastised the absent witness in front of the jury, he stopped short of striking his testimony.

In the end, even though Janak was uneasy, he couldn't produce any further witnesses. He rested his case.

It was Deadeye's turn for rebuttal. He called a homicide detective from Fresno, a fat man with a red face who was sweating so profusely that he looked as if he were on the verge of having a stroke. He landed in the witness chair like a sack of rocks, the seat groaning under his weight. Deadeye wasted ten minutes proving the qualifications of the witness before beginning his questioning in his smoothest velvet accent.

"You investigated the murder of Joseph Hagopian, did you not?"

Janak rushed to the podium, elbowing Deadeye out of the way. "Your Honor, this questioning is way out of line. And before it goes any further, may I remind the court of your order that anything that happened in Fresno was not to be mentioned."

"Exactly what is your point in examining this witness, Mr. Graves?" asked the judge, almost as upset as Janak.

"To show the jury that the same people were involved in both crimes, Your Honor." Deadeye spoke defiantly.

"I've heard enough, Mr. Graves. The jury is excused. Counsel report to my chambers with the court reporter."

As the jury filed out of its box, Janak told Graves he was a son of a bitch, and he would pay for what he'd tried to do. A few of the jurors heard him. Deadeye, trying to ingratiate himself, smiled mischievously at them. Then he gathered a few papers from his desk and walked quickly to the back door of the courtroom toward the judge's chambers.

"There has to be a good reason why he tried that. I'm sure it wasn't a mistake," Janak said to Asquith. "He knows something we don't and he's trying to provoke us into asking for a mistrial."

"I'm sure it has something to do with Nashwan," said Samuel, approaching the table where the two lawyers were sitting.

"Deadeye's already suggested that Nashwan's failure to appear was grounds for a mistrial," said Asquith.

"It hasn't gone so great for us, and under ordinary circumstances I would be grateful for a mistrial," answered Janak, scratching his scar. "But when the prosecutor wants one that bad, I have to think twice. I just wonder what the hell happened?"

The bailiff opened the door next to the dais and motioned for Janak to join the others in the judge's chamber. The judge was furious. He read the riot act to Deadeye, threatening to grant a mistrial.

"It's up to you, Mr. Janak," he grumbled. "Mr. Graves has violated the court order by even bringing up the Fresno matter. If you want a mistrial, it's yours."

"I've considered my options, Judge, and I don't want a mistrial. But I do want a strong condemnation of Mr. Grave's action in front of the jury. After that, I'll take my chances."

"Very well, I'll make sure they know they're not to consider that evidence. Mr. Graves, you report to my courtroom next Friday and show cause why you shouldn't be held in contempt."

On the way out of the judge's chamber's Janak patted Asquith on the back. "Good thing you looked up the issue of the mistrial. It was nice to know that only if the prosecution is granted a mistrial does double jeopardy attach. If we accepted the mistrial our clients would be subject to a retrial."

When court reconvened, the judge delivered a strong instruction to the jury that it should disregard any testimony about Fresno. He also advised them that attorney Graves had been reprimanded for attempting to open that line of questioning when it wasn't a part of the case. He then sent the jurors home and advised them that argument and deliberations would commence the next day. He asked the attorneys to stay so they could go over instructions.

Deadeye sat down, satisfied that he'd put as much of the tainted evidence as he could before the jury. He would have preferred a mistrial requested by the defense, but he hadn't been able blurt out any more information quickly enough before Janak stopped him with his objection. Nonetheless, he'd planted enough with the jury, and nothing the judge said could erase it. Still, he had to hand it to Janak; he was sharper than he thought.

Samuel went downstairs to get a cup of coffee and shoot the breeze with Donald. What he heard from the blind man left him dumbfounded. Samuel immediately sat down at one of the tables to write an article he thought would do justice to the story he'd just heard, but had second thoughts. He decided to wait until Janak got out of court and discuss it with him first. In the meantime, Samuel checked with the sheriff's office and confirmed the story the blind man had told him, although the deputy he spoke to was reluctant to give him all the details.

* * *

Samuel ran back to the courtroom and waited anxiously for Janak and Asquith to appear, so he could tell them what he'd learned in the coffee shop.

"Is this just my idea or is this important?" he asked after filling them in on the details.

"That must be why Graves tried to get us to request a mistrial," said Janak. "He was afraid that the jury would find out."

"I thought you were going to ask for a mistrial if he brought up the Fresno case," said Samuel.

"That was my intention, but there was no way, knowing what Asquith found out about double jeopardy. It only works as a bar to future prosecution if the prosecutor asks for it," said Janak.

"I hope you're right," said Samuel, "because I'm worried. I admit that after Aram's testimony I had doubts about the defendants' innocence, and I assume the jury felt the same way."

"Maybe Donald's story can help us," said Asquith.

"We can't argue that something has happened that may damage the prosecution's case, when we don't know if there are any witnesses who can testify about it."

The two lawyers laughed. "I guess I won't get much sleep tonight," said Janak. "My hunch is to just argue the case the way I see it and let the chips fall where they may."

"I'd like to put this twist in my article if it will help you," said Samuel, showing his handwritten notes to Janak.

"You can't disclose what you just learned until after the trial," said Janak. "If you do it now, it may hurt my case and then Deadeye will be off the hook. As I said before, the outcome of this case really does depend on what the jury knows about the character of the prosecution's witnesses. I'm going to present the case as if they're all exaggerating. If they believe me, we win."

Although Samuel wanted to rush to the paper with the story, he knew had to wait until the jury came in with its verdict. In any case, it wasn't much of a dilemma for him. He knew he'd still have an exclusive story, since no other reporter covering the case had a clue as to what he'd learned in the cafeteria.

* * *

Closing arguments started the next day at ten o'clock. Deadeye was smooth and articulate as he went through the evidence that connected the defendants to the crime scene. He spoke for an hour and a half, concluding his arguments by reminding the jury that Narcio Padia and Juan Ramos would be a menace to the community if they were allowed to go free in Contra Costa County.

Once Deadeye had finished, the judge dismissed the jurors early for lunch rather than risk interrupting the defense's closing argument. When Janak finally rose to speak in the early afternoon, his voice was heavy and he appeared sluggish. Samuel and Asquith were worried; Janak didn't seem full of conviction that his clients were innocent. As he went on, however, he picked up steam, pointing out the flimsiness of the evidence against them and hammering home the exaggerations and inconsistencies in the witnesses' testimony. Then something strange happened. The afternoon sun broke through the clouds that had hung around for several days and shone through the courtroom window, illuminating Janak as he stood in front of the podium questioning the veracity of Nashwan's testimony. It was a startling moment and served to accentuate the defense lawyer's words. Just as suddenly as it had broken through, the sun disappeared behind the clouds again and the courtroom returned to its usual muted ambiance.

Deadeye was perfunctory in his rebuttal. He felt he'd gained the advantage in his opening and saw no need to rehash the hard evidence of the fingerprints and the knot, both of which tied the defendants to the crime scene.

When the arguments were completed, the judge took over. "Ladies and gentlemen of the jury, it is now my duty to instruct you on the law. I want to remind you that in order to reach a verdict, all twelve of you have to agree.

"I'm also sure you are cognizant that this is a death penalty case, and that if you reach a verdict of guilty, you have to be convinced beyond a reasonable doubt that the defendant has committed the crime of which he is accused."

Janak had argued forcefully for a manslaughter instruction but the court turned him down. There was no basis for it. The crime was too brutal and either these defendants committed murder or they didn't.

The judge then read the lengthy instructions, finishing up at four o'clock. He asked the jury if they wanted to start their deliberations right away, in order to move the case along. They nodded their approval and he sent them to a jury room, reminding the attorneys to advise the clerk of their whereabouts. They needed to be close by in case he wanted them called back to court on short notice.

Deadeye headed to his office. Janak and Asquith went downstairs to the coffee shop with Samuel.

Once they had arrived, Donald repeated for Janak what he had told Samuel earlier. "I wonder how anybody could be so stupid," said Janak. "There had to be witnesses. I wonder who they were."

"There were people here," said Donald. "The sheriff knows who they are. I guess whoever that person was thought that because I was blind, I wouldn't notice." The men laughed.

"This is the worst time for me," said Janak. "All this waiting for the jury." He strode back and forth across the cramped floor of the coffee shop, fingering the scar on his cheek. "All the uncertainty. Plus, I remember all the things I wanted to say but forgot to. Now it's too late."

"Relax, Janak," said Samuel. "You did the best you could."

"Doing my best isn't enough. The only result that is worth anything is a verdict of innocent."

After an hour, which seemed like an eternity, a deputy

came to the door to announce that the jury had returned with a verdict.

Janak's cheeks reddened, his hands began to sweat and his heart galloped in his chest. "That's the fastest verdict I've ever been involved in!" he exclaimed to Asquith and Samuel.

In a matter of minutes, the lawyers were in their seats and the judge motioned for the bailiff to bring in the jury. As they filed in, Janak saw that the person holding the verdict forms was the most conservative member of all those chosen. Janak would have gotten rid of him except he couldn't exercise his last challenge for fear that Deadeye would retaliate by striking all the moderate selections he'd made. He and Asquith looked at each other. Samuel saw the worry on their faces. They all hoped Mae Ming was right about the juror.

When the members of the jury were seated in the jury box, the judge faced them. "Has the jury reached a verdict?"

"Yes, we have, Your Honor," answered the foreman.

"Will you please hand it to the clerk."

The juror handed a piece of paper to the clerk, who walked to the dais and gave it to the judge. He read it silently and returned it to the clerk.

"Will the defendants please rise," ordered the judge.

Janak motioned to them to stand up. Both were pale and Padia's teeth were chattering. The clerk read the verdict in a clear and precise voice.

"We the jury in the case of the People of the State of California vs. Narcio Padia find the defendant not guilty of all charges.

"We the jury in the case of the People of the State of California vs. Juan Ramos find the defendant not guilty of all charges."

Janak, incredulous and wild with enthusiasm, turned to his clients and hugged them, saying in his pidgin Spanish, *"non cupable, non cupable."* Both defendants started crying when Janak explained that they were free to go and would never be bothered by these charges again in their lives.

Deadeye buried his head in his hands, then silently slipped out of the courtroom before any of the reporters could find him to ask the obvious question: What happened?

As soon as the verdicts were announced, Samuel rushed out of the courtroom ahead of the throng of reporters, running for the nearest pay phone to call in the story.

Judge Pluplot pounded his gavel, calling for order. When he had the commotion under control, he thanked the jury and excused them. He also reminded them he was up for re-election the following year and advised them that they were now free to talk about their experiences if they wished.

The foreman made a beeline for Janak. "You were right about that Kurd, Nashwan. He's a terrible person and you really exposed him for what he is. Several of us jurors were in the coffee shop and saw him steal money from the blind man's cash register. We figured if he were capable of that, he was capable of sending a pair of innocents to their death. A liar and a thief, that's what that man is."

"I'll be damned," said Janak "It's a good thing I followed my hunch. Otherwise, we'd have had to go through this all over again."

He thanked the rest of the jurors and went down the hall to tell Samuel and Asquith that the verdict hadn't been based on his skill as a lawyer, as he would have liked, but on a stroke of luck—some of the jurors had seen Nashwan steal Donald's money and he'd lost all credibility.

"It was Deadeye's mistake that had caused him to lose the case," said Asquith. "He relied on a dishonest witness."

"I think it was more than just one dishonest witness," said Samuel.

But he wasn't through with the story. It bothered him too much. After the others left the courthouse, he went back to the sheriff's office and talked to the deputy in charge of the investigation. Rather than discussing it with Samuel in detail, the deputy allowed him—off the record—to read the incident report. Samuel learned that there had been four jurors seated at the tables in the coffee shop when Nashwan came in. Ordinarily, the jurors would not have paid much attention to him, but he had just testified in their courtroom and they all recognized him.

The foreman, in particular, noticed the expensive clothes he was wearing, so he kept an eye on him as Nashwan waited for the other customers to pay for their purchases and leave.

When the rush was over, Donald left his cash register to restock the shelves, leaving the drawer open as usual. That's when Nashwan went over and began stuffing its contents into his trouser pockets. The jury foreman yelled and rose to intercept him. As soon as he did, Nashwan bolted from the room, ran down the hallway with the foreman in pursuit, and fled the building. The foreman reported what he'd seen to the sheriff's office and gave the names of all the other jurors who were present. Each was interviewed as a part of the investigation.

After reading the report, Samuel wrote a scathing article for the morning paper, naming reliable sources, and then relayed what he had learned to Janak.

"This was one of those lucky breaks that almost never happens," said Janak.

"Yeah Janak, but I think you'll admit, it couldn't have happened at a better time."

9

So Now What?

DEPRESSED AND EXHAUSTED, Deadeye hid in his office after his defeat. He didn't want to see anybody, reporters least of all, but he couldn't stop his boss, the District Attorney, from descending on him like a hurricane. The D.A. stormed into the room, his hair mussed and a menacing look on his face.

"What happened Graves? How could you lose this case with all the evidence you had against those defendants?"

"I'm sorry, sir. Some of the jurors saw my key witness stealing money from the coffee shop."

"Stealing from the blind man?"

"Yes, sir."

"That was the only error in this case, Graves?"

"No, sir. The Mexican guys were probably set up by persons unknown and my key witness was probably lying."

"For God's sake!" the D.A. yelled, slamming his fist down on the subordinate's desk. "What are you saying, man?"

"I doubt if the Mexicans did it."

"And you're just telling me now?"

"They looked guilty because we had hard evidence and the corroboration of what looked like a solid witness," said Deadeye, scratching his head. "Now our case has fallen apart. We're screwed."

"What's the next step then?"

Deadeye took a pen from the inside of his black suit jacket. He pulled a yellow pad from one side of his desk and proceeded to draw something.

"What's that?"

"An olive branch," answered Deadeye.

"Are you making fun of me, Graves?"

"That never occurred to me, sir. I'm simply suggesting a truce until we get more evidence."

"All right, but keep me posted. I want all the details. Get in touch with Bernardi immediately and tell him to reopen the investigation." He left the office, slamming the door behind him.

Deadeye waited for him to disappear before flipping him the bird. He hated that man but he wouldn't have to put up with him for much longer because he was going to quit. He could make more money as a top-notch criminal defense lawyer. He wondered if he could replace him...That would be more difficult now that the matter of the transvestites had come out, but there wasn't a better candidate than he, and Deadeye hoped the public would soon forget about that pathetic episode.

He cursed Janak Marachak. That son of a bitch hadn't deserved to win because he, Earl Graves, had the defendants in the palm of his hand. As the saying went within the office— where a conviction was more important than getting justice— it was more difficult to convict an innocent man than a guilty one. And Bernardi had warned him that the Mexicans were innocent; what a bastard he was! He yelled another curse, this time at the Kurd. Then, to make himself feel better, he turned and looked at the painting of the Indian chief staring down at him from the wall, just to the left of his desk. He imitated the wise old warrior's stoic expression. In this line of work you had to have patience, nerves and perseverance.

Miguel and Jose Ramos, the two missing Mexicans, are still suspects, he thought. *I'll let them be for the time being, and maybe something will come up.*

Then he picked up the dime store Louis L'Amour cowboy novel from his desk and threw it across the room.

* * *

Samuel's stories about the trial had gotten good play in the newspaper and in the Chinatown press, which cemented his reputation as a "News Bloodhound," as his companions had starting calling him. His editor congratulated him, but when Samuel asked for a raise, he said he'd have to think about it. A week later, he was still thinking about it. Samuel's latest success still wasn't enough to calm his doubts. Samuel felt uncomfortable with everything that had happened so, as usual, he sought advice at Camelot.

Melba's cough was getting worse and she now had a tank of oxygen by her side, but she went to the bar when she could. That night she was seated at her usual place at the Round Table, Excalibur at her feet. The dog had an attack of happiness upon seeing Samuel, repeating his choreography of jumps and rollovers before licking the reporter's face and chewing on his shoelaces. Samuel scratched his only ear and gave him the treat he always carried in his pocket just in case he went by Camelot. Excalibur would never forgive him if he appeared without one.

Melba inclined her head when she saw him. She stubbed her cigarette out in the ashtray and attached a tube connected to an oxygen cylinder to her nose. She was much paler than the last time Samuel had seen her. Her blue-gray hair looked like a bundle of yarn on top of her head and she had dark circles under her red, watery eyes. To control her cough, she took small sips of beer. She spoke in whispers, gasping for breath in between coughing spells. Busy with the trial and his work,

Samuel hadn't kept his promise to take her to Mr. Song's, but seeing her in such a bad state, he decided he couldn't postpone it any longer.

"You sound like you're dying, Melba! Tomorrow we'll go to consult with Mr. Song."

"I don't intend to die from a little clearing of my throat, my boy," replied Melba in a small voice. "I'm made of iron."

"Rusty iron, from what I can see."

"Congratulations, Samuel. You did a good job on that case. Is that Marchak lawyer, the one you introduced me to a few months ago, the specialist in chemicals?

"Yeah. But he's not a criminal lawyer."

"Maybe he should change to criminal law since he did such a good job for the Mexicans."

"Did Blanche tell you of my doubts about the case? We talked a lot about that last week. It was a real shame that you weren't here, Melba. You could have helped me clarify my thoughts."

"Your articles didn't suggest any doubts."

"I'm a reporter, Melba. I try to be objective. I didn't want to be prejudicial against Janak or his clients, but the evidence against the accused was pretty strong. I was sure they were going to be convicted. We were all surprised by the verdict, including Janak."

"Juries are very unpredictable, Samuel."

"That's what Janak says. You never know how they're going to react. And if that's the case, it's impossible to have confidence in our system of justice. It seems terrible to me that the lives of the accused depended on something as unexpected as the principal witness stealing money from the coffee shop."

"Do you still think those poor devils are guilty?"

"I don't know what to think."

"What worries you? Janak won the case; those guys can't be tried again. Period."

"I'm happy that they're free, but there are still charges pending against two of the other workers, Miguel Ramos and Jose Ramos. And they can't count on the same luck that Narcio Padia and Juan Ramos had."

He sighed. "At least they're still in Mexico. They'd have to be pretty stupid to come back and put themselves in the jaws of the wolf."

"I repeat the question, Samuel. Do you think the Mexicans committed those bloody crimes?"

"I feel bad because, in reality, I have doubts, Melba. It's possible they did it for revenge."

"Stop talking nonsense, Samuel! Your job is to expose the facts, nothing else."

"I sat with Janak on a bench at San Quentin when he was filled with doubts about his ability to even try the case, and now I turn out to be the doubter."

"I learned something a long time ago from some of the best criminal lawyers in San Francisco," said Melba. "It never mattered to them if a client was guilty or innocent, it only mattered that they got him off. That way they could collect a bigger fee from the next client. So forget about your doubts, Samuel. They're a waste of time."

"Janak is sure they're innocent and, if necessary, he'll also defend Jose and Miguel."

"For free?"

"Yeah, for free."

"Your friend Janak doesn't have a prayer!"

"That's why he's my friend, Melba. He's a good man. As Blanche says, even though he looks like a boxer, he has the heart of a golden retriever."

"Well, then," mumbled Melba, inhaling oxygen in gulps, "you need to get him hooked up with that French girl he's in love with."

"How do you know about her?"

"A bar is like a beauty shop. There are no secrets."

Samuel took the letter out of his pocket that he'd received from Paris that morning and gave it to Melba, who by that time had disconnected the oxygen and was lighting another cigarette.

"What's this?"

Samuel explained the details of his trip to Paris and how he'd asked Lucine to get information about Nashwan Aram, who turned out to be the star witness for the prosecution. "That's the guy who stole from the blind man in the coffee shop," he added.

"What does the letter say?"

"That he's dead."

"Dead? He was killed too?'

"No. There's a birth certificate with the guy's name on it and a death certificate three years later for the same person. You understand?"

"I understand that the D.A.'s witness was using someone else's identity."

"It sure sounds like it, but that's not all. Lucine also tells me that Armand Hagopian, the businessman who was murdered at the dump, had two wives. The first one lives in Paris and Lucine talked to her. She left him because he beat her. That never came out in the investigation."

"Hagopian had another wife in California?"

"Yeah, I met with her and the victims sister, but they never said a word about anything like this."

"Why would they say anything? In the majority of families, those things are kept under wraps. Where's the second wife now?"

"I don't know. She didn't show up for the trial."

"The D.A. didn't call her?"

"Nope."

"That means she has something to hide," said Melba.

"You'd better find out what it is, Samuel." She alternated between taking drags from her cigarette and gulps of oxygen while Samuel scratched Excalibur's head and looked around discreetly for Blanche, who was nowhere to be seen.

"So what are you waiting for?" asked Melba, coughing. "Get off your ass and get going. And if by chance you have an interest in seeing Blanche, you'll have to wait until next week."

"Tomorrow I'll come by your house at nine-thirty and take you to Mr. Song's."

"Can you guarantee he'll do for me what he's done for you?" Melba asked innocently, her eyes glued to the cigarette burn holes in the sleeves of his sports jacket.

* * *

When Melba and Samuel arrived at Mr. Song's shop for Melba's appointment, Buckteeth was behind the counter, dressed in her school uniform.

Samuel opened the door and Melba walked in under her own power, wheezing a little, but without her oxygen tank.

"Hello, Mr. Hamilton," the girl said, giving him a toothy smile. "I like your stories, which have been all over the Chinese press. When are they going to catch the real killer of the King of the Bottom now that the Mexicans got off?"

"I'll start working on it today," said Samuel, amazed at how much the girl knew. "Any suggestions?"

"That's Mr. Song's department. I just read the newspaper."

Samuel, now standing opposite her at the black lacquer counter, smiled. "We have an appointment with your uncle."

"Yes, I know. He asked me to escort you to him." She turned and walked the few steps to the blue beaded curtain and held it open, allowing Melba and Samuel to pass into the dimly lit room, where Mr. Song sat on a chair. Opposite him was an empty chair in front of a Chinese screen, which was lit by a floodlight. Mr. Song put his white hands together and bowed, then pointed to the empty seat. Melba took off her overcoat, puffed her blue-gray coif a bit and sat down.

Mr. Song mumbled something to his niece.

"Mr. Song says she makes noise when she breathes and that is not good. He wants to know how long she's been this way."

"About three months," said Melba.

"Mr. Song wants to know why she didn't stop smoking when this happened."

"You tell him that's why I'm here," Melba growled.

Mr. Song picked up a pendulum in his long, bony, white fingers and told his niece to have Melba watch it closely. He swung it back and forth slowly. After thirty seconds he stopped, shook his head and spoke rapidly to Buckteeth.

"My honorable uncle says that this person is not a good subject for hypnotism. Too strong-willed. She won't let her guard down. Session over."

Melba raised an eyebrow and smiled.

"Wait a minute," said Samuel, moving toward Mr. Song. "Surely he can do something for her."

Melba, who wasn't a bit offended, gave a sigh of relief; she'd only come to humor Samuel.

"Mr. Song will give her some herbs for her chest congestion," Buckteeth told them. "If she takes them as he directs, she should be better in two weeks. If she keeps smoking the way she does, she will die from bad lungs."

"Tell your uncle that everybody dies from bad lungs," answered Melba. "The dead don't breath."

She got out from under the spotlight, holding onto Samuel's arm. They walked to the front of the shop and stopped at the counter. In short order, Mr. Song appeared with two small paper bags. His niece translated his instructions.

"This one is ma huang and this one is gui zhi. They are both herbs for upper respiratory congestion. Soak them in hot water and drink the tea that results several times a day instead of water. If they help you, come back in two weeks and get more."

"How much for the herbs?" asked Samuel.

"Three dollars and fifty cents," said Buckteeth.

"No discount for friends?" asked Melba.

Samuel poked her in the side with his elbow, paid the money and thanked them. "Can I have a word with Mr. Song?"

Mr. Song nodded.

"You know what's going on with the case because you've obviously been following it through the Chinese press and whatever you've heard from Mae Ming. Do you have any suggestions for where to look for the real killers?"

Mr. Song stroked his thin, white goatee and looked at the ceiling. His pink eyes were magnified by his thick glasses.

"Right now, he is stumped. He thinks you did a very good job in getting the Mexicans off, but it seems that the trail stopped cold when the Kurdish man disappeared with the blind man's money."

"I wasn't the one who got them off. It was Janak Marachak, the lawyer who represented them."

"He says that you were part of the team. Didn't you find Mae Ming for him and write all those sympathetic articles?"

"I get what he means," laughed Samuel, thinking of how he got to Mae Ming in the first place. "Tell him I have more information for him to think about. I will come back later. Right now I have to get Melba home and then go and see the lawyer and the detective."

"My honorable uncle says that you should think about the Kurd."

"And I say that you should always look for the woman,"

interjected Melba. "*Cherchez la femme*, as the saying goes."

"What woman are you referring to?" asked Samuel.

"I don't know. I suppose any that are connected to the case."

"You don't have a very high opinion of your own sex, Melba."

"No, but I have a worse opinion of yours, Samuel."

Once outside, Melba told him with her usual frankness what she thought of the consultation. "That bullshit isn't for everyone," she said, coughing.

"At least we know you're not hypnotizing material," he said.

"You didn't have to pay the albino to discover that. Nobody's ever been able to fuck with my head. You know that, Samuel."

"Yeah, I know that, Melba," he said, shaking his own firmly. He hailed a cab for her and watched as it climbed the hill and made a left turn onto Stockton. He then started down the hill, headed for Janak's office on the corner of New Montgomery and Market.

* * *

It was a quiet afternoon at 625 Market. There were only two people in Janak's waiting room. Marisol, dressed in a dark blue suit that suggested a captain of the Merchant Marine, sat behind the reception desk. She gave Samuel a warm welcome.

"Mr. Marachak is expecting you," said Marisol. "Go right in."

Samuel smiled and clasped her hand as he passed. "I'll talk to you in a minute," he said.

He found Janak amidst the clutter of his small office. Samuel noticed, however, that the space was tidier than usual.

King of the Bottom

In addition to putting the papers that belonged to specific cases in their respective piles, Janak had stored all the Ramos and Padia files in boxes, which were now stacked by the door.

"Been thinking too hard, huh?" said Samuel.

"What d'ya mean by that," asked Janak, looking up at him.

"I can always tell when you're over-concentrating because the scar on your cheek becomes red."

Janak laughed and put the file he was working on aside. "Okay, I admit I've been working night and day since the case ended, trying to catch up and also trying to get some cash in the empty coffers."

"I guess it's tough to be out of the office for so long on one thing, isn't it?"

"Especially difficult when you don't get paid for your time," said Janak. "But I'm working on a big one here and it's almost ready to pop." He pointed to the chemical injury file he'd moved to one side. "It will take care of things for awhile, if it does. And the first thing I'll do is pay back my mother."

"What about Miguel and Jose?" asked Samuel. "Isn't their case still open?"

"Sure is, and with that crackpot Deadeye seething about his defeat and yearning for revenge, I can't let it go unattended for too long."

"Doesn't Miguel also have a problem in Fresno?" asked Samuel.

"Yes, he does. But let's deal with one problem at a time," said Janak.

"That's one of the reasons I wanted to talk with you," said Samuel, filling Janak in on the contents of the letter he'd received from Paris without disclosing that it had come from Lucine.

Janak didn't say a word during or after his presentation.

"What do you think about this?" asked Samuel.

"This is something we ought to take up with Bernardi. But I can't do anything about it until I wrap up the case I'm working on now. Do you understand my problem?"

"Yeah, I get your drift. You can't operate indefinitely without money. I'm supposed to meet with Bernardi today. I told him that I had some information to share with him."

"While you're there, try and feel him out about Miguel and Jose."

"I will, but I need some help here. Will you ask Marisol if I can borrow her car this afternoon?"

"You know her well enough by now," said Janak. "Ask her yourself." He got up and patted Samuel on the back as he escorted him to the door. It was clear that he had something else on his mind.

After Samuel had gone, Janak returned to his desk and sat down, trying to put himself into a state of absolute calmness, a technique that he'd learned from his mother. Only then would he be able to figure out the cause of the chemical explosion that had injured his clients. He knew it was futile to try and force his mind to work. He'd already organized the facts in the most rational way possible, keeping track of the connections that no one else understood. The final step, however, the one that would give words to the formula that would win the case, would come from intuition.

* * *

On his way out, Samuel stopped by the reception desk. "Marisol, I need a favor," he said.

"If it's in my power," she smiled.

"Will you loan me your car this afternoon for a couple of hours?"

"Can you have it back by three? I have an appointment."

Samuel gritted his teeth. "I don't think so. My appointment

with Bernardi isn't until then."

"Just a minute," she said, and went into Janak's office.

When she came back, she smiled. "It's all arranged. I'll take you over there right now, but you'll have to catch a bus to get back. I'm sorry, that's the best I can do."

Marisol drove to Richmond via Marin County, Samuel at her side. As they headed north on Highway 101, he stared out the window, mumbling to himself.

"A *córdoba* for your thoughts?" Marisol smiled over at him.

"What's that?" asked a startled Samuel, coming out of his reverie.

"My country's currency."

He blushed and turned to her. "I'm sorry. I was just thinking out loud. It's not important."

"No," she said, smiling. "Finish your thought."

"Are you sure you want to hear all this?"

"Samuel, get it out."

"Here's my problem: in order to expand the possibilities in this case, I need a connection in the Stockton area."

"What kind of a connection?"

"Someone who can give me information on the locals."

"I don't know what you mean," said Marisol, looking over at him again. "There are all kinds of locals in Stockton. Which ones do you want to know about?"

"Someone who knows the local terrain."

"I might be able to help you. My father is a deacon in a church outside Stockton. It's one of those evangelical Catholic churches. You know, the latest in the 'New Church' idea."

"Is he like a priest?"

"No. He's a lay person who helps the priest."

"Looking at you, I didn't think your father could be a priest," he said, laughing. "What does he do as a deacon?"

"He attends mostly to Mexican farm workers. He has a

pretty large following."

"I wonder..."

"Wonder what?"

Samuel was pensive. "I haven't thought it through."

By then they were approaching the gray stucco building with the radio antenna on top—the Richmond Police Department. Samuel thanked Marisol and got out of her car.

10

Find the Bug

WHEN SAMUEL WALKED INTO the building, Bernardi was waiting for him. He showed Samuel into his office and pointed to a chair facing the photograph on the credenza of his hundred-year-old grandfather. The detective, dressed in his standard brown suit, seated his heavy frame behind his desk.

"Cup of joe?" he asked.

"No, thanks," said Samuel.

"What can I help you with, Mr. Hamilton?"

"That's what I like, Lieutenant, a man who gets right down to business." Samuel pulled out the official documents he'd received from Paris and explained them to Bernardi.

"What do these papers mean to you, Mr. Hamilton?" Bernardi asked after a pause.

"Just what they say. This Nashwan person is a phony. He stole someone's identity. But in order to prove that conclusively, we need help from your department. You see these fingerprints on the birth and death certificates?" Samuel pointed to the respective documents. "I bet they don't match the ones you have on file for him."

"Finding that out is pretty easy," said Bernardi. "We can have an answer fairly soon. How'd you get these?" He shook his head in disbelief.

Samuel explained again, this time going over each of the documents in detail. Bernardi nodded, finally grasping the full extent of what Samuel had given him.

"Let's say the guy's a fake. That just means he's committed immigration fraud and that he assumed someone else's identity."

"It's more than that," said Samuel. "It's also more proof that he lied under oath."

"Yeah, we already knew that," said Bernardi, looking directly at Samuel. "I think that's why Deadeye's backed off."

"There's more. At the trial he said that he'd made his Air France reservation the morning of the murder. That was a lie. He made the reservation a month before."

"That's serious. It means he was in this mess up to his neck, doesn't it?"

"It sure does. So if you help us find out who he is, my hunch is that it'll lead us to the real killer."

"I assume I can have these?" asked Bernardi, grabbing the documents that Samuel still held in his hand.

"Do I have a choice?" The papers moved back and forth between them in a playful tug of war.

"Not if you want me to find out something about him."

"Sure," Samuel said, releasing the papers. "You'll give me a receipt, won't you?"

Samuel then explained that Janak wanted to know the status of his clients, Jose and Miguel Ramos.

"Are we on the record here, Mr. Hamilton?"

"What's best for you?"

Bernardi was quiet for a few seconds. "I can be more frank off the record."

"Okay, but sooner or later, I want to do a story about their innocence, including the lack of evidence against them."

"It can't be news to you that Deadeye still thinks he can win a case against them just on the fingerprints."

"And the fact that they're Mexicans?"

"He didn't say it, but, yeah, that's the way the guy thinks."

"Even if he knows they're innocent."

"What can I tell you? You've seen the way he operates."

"What's the answer?'

"Still off the record, right?"

"Yeah."

"I think it's pretty obvious they were framed," said Bernardi. "I've thought so from the beginning." He slammed the fist of one hand into the palm of the other. "I think the victim was killed somewhere else and then hung up at Point Molate. Marachak did a real good job of showing that at the trial. But Deadeye didn't give a shit about any of that evidence because he had the fingerprints."

"The case is back in your hands now, isn't it?' asked Samuel. "That makes a big difference, doesn't it?"

"Yeah, it makes a difference. My hands aren't tied like when Deadeye was in charge. I'm going to talk to the entomologist and see if I can get him to be more specific about what part of Stockton that bug came from."

Then it hit Samuel. Something had been nagging at him ever since the car ride with Marisol. "I may be able to help you," he said.

"What do you mean?"

"I'm not sure yet. Give me a few days."

"Okay. Should I hold my breath?"

"No, no. I mean it. I found out something on the way over here that may help us locate where that insect comes from. Just give me some time…Changing the subject, Lieutenant, do you remember the mud that was found on Hagopian's shoe?"

"Yeah, but we haven't been able to do much with that," said Bernardi, giving Samuel a wry smile. There's a lot of mud in Northern California."

"If we find out where the bug comes from and that the mud is from the same place, we may have something," said Samuel. "Is that the idea?"

"That's the whole cannoli."

"What about Hagopian's wife?"

"What about her?" asked Bernardi.

"You know she was his second wife, right?"

"I knew that, but not much else," answered Bernardi, suddenly interested. "Deadeye closed the door on us right in the middle of our investigation and hasn't returned the file to our office yet."

"We found out there was a first wife who left him because he abused her," said Samuel.

Bernardi's eyes widened and he sat down again. "Is that right? That's news to me. How'd you get that information?"

"The same way I found out that about Nashwan being a phony," said Samuel.

"We were never able to talk to wife Number Two again," said Bernardi. "After our initial interview with her, Deadeye sent her away so she wouldn't be available for trial."

"You mean she wasn't even in San Francisco?" Samuel grimaced.

"That's right. What's the face for?"

"Nothing. Just thinking about when I tried to serve a subpoena on her." Samuel remembered the discomfort of the itchy wig when he tried to fool Thaddeus Carlton. "Do you think Deadeye found out something about her that he wanted to keep secret?"

"If he did, he hasn't passed it on to me."

"I'd like to interview him about the case, but he won't answer my calls or let anyone else on his staff talk to me."

"I know," said Bernardi. "He told me not to give you any information." He turned and looked out the window, embarrassed.

"Does that mean you're holding back on me?"

"No, that's why we're off the record. Of course, you know we can't be seen together in public, especially in Contra Costa County."

Both men laughed, and Bernardi stood up.

"I'll see if I can convince the D.A. to drop the charges against Jose and Miguel, and you find out more about Stockton." He walked Samuel to the door.

"If I can arrange a trip out there, would you like to come?"

"Sure. Just give me some advance notice."

* * *

Samuel made arrangements for Marisol to take him to the church where her father preached the following Sunday. In the meantime, he filled Janak in on what Bernardi had told him. Samuel noticed that Janak's office was actually neat now and that his hair was combed. For once, he looked relaxed sitting behind his secondhand desk.

"Bernardi's information doesn't surprise me," said Janak when Samuel had finished. "I could tell he wasn't with Deadeye and that he felt the case was highjacked from him."

"That's probably true," said Samuel.

"But the Contra Costa and Fresno D.A.'s are in charge of dismissing the cases, not Deadeye or Bernardi," said Janak. "The most important thing right now is getting the facts." He tapped the eraser of his pencil on the desk.

"I'll get them," said Samuel. "Without them, I can't write the story."

Janak helped him pick out the best photographs of the blue beetle from the coroner's file. Then Samuel called Bernardi and gave him the name and the address of the Stockton church where they were to meet.

* * *

Sunday was one of those luminous spring days that put Samuel in a good mood. He was a night person and generally had difficulty waking up in the morning. But on seeing the sun coming through the dirty window of his apartment and thinking about all he had to do, he jumped out of bed, washing and dressing with more care than usual. He had already ironed his pants and shined his shoes in order to make a good impression on the people he was going to meet. After all, it was church.

He left his apartment with a spring in his step and went to the corner joint to buy his breakfast: two cups of black coffee and a doughnut that he devoured at the counter. The hot coffee reminded him how much he missed smoking. He'd more or less resisted the desire to smoke for a year, a desire that was always accentuated by coffee or a drink of Scotch. Those two drinks were inseparable from tobacco. He sighed and cursed Mr. Song under his breath.

When he got to Marisol's house, the young woman greeted him dressed in a flowered cotton dress that wasn't exactly provocative, but nonetheless accentuated her waistline and her breasts. Samuel couldn't help but admire the attributes of Janak's assistant. He decided that she couldn't be more different than Blanche—the true love of his life, even though she didn't know it—but they were both equally attractive.

What do I know about women anyway? Samuel smiled to himself.

"Let's go, Mr. Hamilton," said Marisol. "We have to get there early so we can talk to my father before the eleven o'clock service."

Driving Highway 4 on their way to Stockton, past the narrowing San Francisco Bay on one side and the lush delta farmlands on the other, Marisol explained to Samuel the origins of the evangelical church service they were going to attend after the Mass. It didn't make much difference to Samuel, who wasn't particularly interested in religion, but since she was doing him a favor, he felt obligated to listen.

The church was on the outskirts of Stockton, on the left side of the highway. A hand-painted sign in both English and Spanish identified it as a Catholic Church and announced that Mass was held there every Sunday at eleven in the morning. The building itself was of modest size and was covered in unpainted clapboard. The trim had once been white, but the paint was now flaked and peeling. There was a dilapidated cross on the top of a fake bell tower.

They pulled into the dirt parking lot at around a quarter to eleven. It was filled with pickup trucks, Mexican flag decals displayed in the back windows. Some of the trucks had boxes of vegetables in the beds, as if their drivers had stopped on their way either to or from a produce market.

Samuel and Marisol walked up the squeaky steps to the porch and opened the weathered door. Inside were several rows of collapsible wooden chairs on each side of the central aisle. An altar at the front was covered with a white sheet, four-by-fours protruding from the bottom. Behind the altar was a six-foot-tall statue of Jesus illuminated by a floodlight. Two guitar players strummed hymns and the congregation of mostly Mexican farm workers and their families were singing ecstatically. From several small windows high up on each side of the building, beams of light filtered into the room through the incense and candle smoke that emanated from the altar and drifted up toward the ceiling.

Samuel looked around, amazed by the noise level, and memorized as many details as he could for later use in his articles. He spotted Bernardi sitting in the last row, also watching the goings-on. Samuel came up behind him and tapped him on the shoulder, putting his hands over his own ears.

"Hi, Detective, thanks for coming," he shouted.

Bernardi, dressed in dark slacks and a brown windbreaker—a change from his usual uniform—turned around and smiled. His shirt was open at the collar and he looked relaxed, which, for Samuel, was something new.

"This is Marisol Leiva," yelled Samuel. "Her father's the deacon here."

"Nice to meet you, Miss Leiva," he yelled back, extending his chubby hand to meet hers. "My name is Bruno Bernardi."

She smiled and motioned for them to follow her down the aisle toward the altar. Although conversation was impossible, she stopped several times along the way, greeting acquaintances with smiles and gestures.

When they reached the wooden door behind the altar, Marisol explained—as well as she could, given the noise level—that they were going to meet both her father, the deacon, and the priest.

"*Entra!*" They barely heard the voice that responded to her knock. Marisol opened the door and ushered Samuel and Bernardi inside.

"*Hola, hija,*" said a tall, nervous man with hair so black it looked dyed. He and the priest stood next to a battered oak desk and matching chair, the only two pieces of furniture in the room. The deacon kissed her on the forehead. "*¿Estos son sus amigos, hija?*"

"Yes, Dad," Marisol responded in English for the benefit of her companions. "This is Detective Bernardi from the Richmond Police Department, and this is my boss's friend Samuel Hamilton, the reporter I've talked to you about several times.

"It's a pleasure," said her father, also in English.

Marisol turned to the visitors. "Say hello to Deacon Leiva and to our priest, Father Gonzalez."

"My given name is Antonio," said the preacher, who had a slight accent. He smiled, showing a set of even white teeth that were obviously false. "Forget religion for a moment. I understand from Marisol that you gentlemen want some help from our parishioners. Father Gonzalez and I have agreed that we will help you."

"Thank you, sir," said Samuel, showing him photos of the crushed but still-identifiable blue beetle. "Detective Bernardi is trying to solve a murder case and finding out where this insect comes from will help in a big way. We know it comes from somewhere around the Stockton area, and we're hoping your church members will be able to direct us to its specific habitat."

"It doesn't register with me, but I live in San Francisco," said the deacon. "What about you, Father Gonzalez?"

The priest shook his head.

"We'll show the photographs to the congregation before I start my sermon," said Mr. Leiva. "It always comes after the Mass."

"I'm afraid you'll have to stay for the Mass," said Father Gonzalez. "But don't worry, it isn't very long." This was the first they had heard from the priest and Samuel and Bernardi noticed he had a lisp.

"The most interesting part of the service is after the Mass, when Mr. Leiva speaks," continued the priest. "I'm not very eloquent, which is why I prefer that he take charge of the preaching. Mr. Leiva is famous around here. The people come from far away to hear him."

"That's fine," said Samuel, a bit intimidated at the thought of having to having to sit though an entire Mass. How long had it been since he had gone to church?

"It's probably not a good idea to tell them I'm a cop," said Bernardi. "Some people get nervous…"

"Yes. I thought the same thing," said Mr. Leiva, running a

hand through his hair, which was plastered with pomade. Our flock is sensitive about the police."

Marisol suggested that she pin the photos on a portable blackboard that she would place next to the altar when her father introduced the visitors. They all agreed, and Samuel and Bernardi followed the deacon and the priest out of the office to the church auditorium.

The church was full almost to the point of bursting. Samuel figured there must be at least sixty people filling the wooden chairs, and many more standing.

"Let's wait outside until the Mass is over," Samuel whispered to Bernardi.

"No. I always go to Mass on Sundays but I couldn't today because I left early."

"Are you sure you want to sit through a Mass in Spanish, Lieutenant?"

"Why not? A Mass is a Mass. Besides, I understand a little Spanish because I speak Italian."

"You don't say."

Bernardi participated in the Mass and Communion with the same fervor as the Mexicans. The service was much shorter than Samuel remembered and was greatly animated by the guitars and the singing of the congregation.

After giving the benediction, Father Gonzalez sat down in one of the folding chairs next to the altar and the deacon rose to stand at what looked like a fragile music stand. He was polished and professional in his tailored black suit, starched white shirt and gold cuff links. Samuel had to admit that the man looked persuasive without even uttering a word.

"¡Atención, por favor, hijos de Dios!" The deacon continued on in Spanish, explaining the matter of the insect and the photographs. "If any of you recognize the insect, you have a moral obligation to say so in order to help solve a crime. What do the Ten Commandments of our Savior tell us? Thou shall not kill! When these men—who are friends of my daughter, Marisol, and people we can trust—come back next week, we should be able to give them an answer."

Samuel noticed a distinguished elderly man seated at the back of the church, leaning on a cane. His snow-white hair and mustache stood out against his dark brown weathered skin. It was clear the man was paying close attention to the deacon's every word. Bernardi nudged Samuel, indicating that he too had noticed the parishioner's unusual attentiveness.

"I want all of you to come up here and look at the photographs before we start the sermon," said the deacon. "If anyone recognizes the blue insect, tell these two gentlemen right away." The congregation seemed hypnotized by his presence, and one by one the parishioners converged on the notice board. Samuel and Bernardi lost track of the old man in the shifting crowd. The parishioners studied the photos for several minutes but no one came forward.

"Very well, brothers and sisters," said the deacon. "I will leave this for the coming week but I want an answer by next Sunday. Remember, God wants this terrible crime solved."

The deacon paused and cleared his throat, preparing to change the subject. The congregation shifted in their seats in anticipation.

"And now," he announced, fire in his eyes, his voice taking on the tone and cadence of a radio announcer. "We shall start!"

At his gesture, the musicians began strumming a hymn on their guitars and the congregation stood and joined in singing. They pounded the floorboards with their feet, raising a cloud of dust. The deacon's voice rose with the force of a thunderclap as he called out admonitions and biblical passages, to which the people responded with equal fervor. The energy and enthusiasm grew and it seemed that at any moment the crowd would lose control; there were already two women pulling their hair, the whites of their eyes showing. Marisol motioned to Bernardi and Samuel, indicating that they should follow her to the door.

"It's better if we go," she said once they were outside. "When my father starts preaching, the people become crazy. Some fall into a trance and they roll on the floor. It can last a long time, and if a miracle happens, it can go on until nightfall."

"Miracle?"

"That's what they call it if someone feels an electric current when my father touches them."

"I'd like to see that!" exclaimed Samuel.

"Not me, Samuel. The truth is that I've been listening to my father's sermons for twenty years and I'm fed up."

"I don't blame you, Miss," said Bernardi. "But I think your father is a very interesting man."

"Perhaps you want to go back inside, Lieutenant?"

"Yes, but first I want to say goodbye to you."

Samuel saw that the detective couldn't take his eyes off Marisol. Even during the Mass Samuel had noticed Bernardi looking over at her furtively. Samuel was amused, though he couldn't help wondering if the detective was married. Didn't he have a photograph of his family on the wall of his office? Well, it wasn't any of his business.

"Do you mind bringing me again next week?" asked Samuel.

"Of course not," she answered.

"I'll come too," said Bernardi quickly.

"You'll come in your own car, Detective?" Marisol spoke in a tone of such studied indifference that Samuel's ears perked up.

"I'd prefer to come with you," said Bernardi, looking at his shoes.

"No problem," she answered and Samuel thought she blushed.

"You'll pick me up at the same time?" Samual asked.

"Whatever you want," she said.

Samuel turned his attention to Bernardi. "Can I ask a favor of you, Lieutenant? Would you be able to drop me off in downtown Stockton, over by the courthouse? I need to check something out early tomorrow. I'll get a hotel room there for tonight."

"Of course," said Bernardi.

"I can take you," offered Marisol.

"No, thanks. You've done enough. Maybe I'll see you in the office during the week. But I'll see you for sure next Sunday."

Marisol took the keys out of her purse, shook hands with them and went to her car, followed by the stares of both men.

"What about the fingerprints on the documents I gave you, Lieutenant?" Samuel's question brought Bernardi back to reality.

"They don't match the ones that we have for Nashwan."

"What did I tell you!" The reporter spoke with an air of triumph. "Now what?"

"First we have to find the bastard. I sent his prints to the FBI to see what they could dig up. Our hands are tied until they get back to us. They'll send a request on to Interpol. Who knows how long that will take."

After a moment, Bernardi spoke again. "Marisol isn't married, right?"

"You're kidding, Lieutenant," laughed Samuel. "I should ask the same of you."

"I'm divorced," mumbled Bernardi, escaping to his 1955 Chevrolet, closely followed by Samuel.

* * *

On the way to Stockton, Samuel asked Bernardi about the difference between the service they'd just attended and a more traditional Catholic one.

"I'm not really the one to ask," said Bernardi. "From what I've heard and what I saw today, it sounds like it's more evangelical than the regular church."

"Which means?" asked Samuel.

"There's more fire and brimstone."

"The preacher was on fire,' said Samuel.

"The congregation, too."

"I'll get more details from Marisol next week," said Samuel.

Bernardi proposed that they eat something and pulled off the road into the parking lot of an Italian restaurant. The large wooden sign on the front read Giuseppe's Tuscan Food.

"I come here a lot," said Bernardi. "Good home cooking. My whole family loves it."

"What's so special?" asked Samuel, who hadn't had a meal outside of Chinatown or down the street from the Contra Costa County courthouse since he'd gotten back from France.

"Giuseppe's from my parents' home town of Pistoia in Tuscany, and his wife knows how to cook all of their old favorites. It's pure nostalgia."

They walked into the crowded foyer of the restaurant. A middle-aged woman taking names saw Bernardi and reacted immediately. "*Ciao bello,*" she yelled over the din of the crowd. "You're table is ready, right this way."

Samuel and Bernardi made their way through the crowd until they reached the woman. She had strong features and was stocky, but Samuel thought she was good-looking. They followed her to a comfortable table by the window that was set for four. It was on an elevated platform and had a view of a pond at the back of the building, which appeared to be a nesting place for ducks returning from their southern migration. They also had a view of the kitchen, where several cooks scurried around filling orders and yelling at each other in Italian.

King of the Bottom

"I didn't know you made a reservation," said Samuel, sitting down at the table.

"I didn't, never have to. We're part of the family."

Within a minute, there was an open bottle of wine in front of them. When it was poured, Bernardi lifted his glass.

"*Cin-cin,*" he said. "This wine is called Badia ci Coltibuono, which is the region where my parents were born. Try it."

Samuel had never been in an Italian restaurant, and he wasn't exactly a gourmet, but he didn't want to appear ignorant. At that moment, he saw the waiter going by with what looked like a sure thing. "Spaghetti and meatballs," he said. "That's what I'll have."

"No! I'm going to introduce you to some real Italian home cooking, not that phony stuff they eat in…where you from?"

"Nebraska."

"Nebraska," laughed Bernardi. "Isn't that where they think that green Jell-O is salad?"

"Yes," admitted Samuel, red-faced, thinking of the terrible food his mother prepared in his youth, when he thought vegetables grew in a can.

"You've never eaten in North Beach, my friend? You have to go to the restaurants in the Italian section of San Francisco; they're famous. Let me choose from the menu. Are you very hungry?"

Without waiting for an answer, Bernardi motioned to the woman who had seated them and spoke to her in Italian. She smiled and patted him on the cheek, then grinned at Samuel. "You won't be sorry, *signore.* Have you tried our ribollita? Here we make it with black cabbage. It's not easy to get that, so we grow it in our own garden. Then I will bring some tagliatelle with porcini, which is today's special." She rushed off toward the kitchen.

The ribollita was a hearty soup that Bernardi ate with chunks of crusty Italian bread. Samuel imitated him, soaking pieces of the bread and chewing slowly between sips of wine.

"What're ya going to Stockton for?" asked Bernardi.

"Just following a hunch," said Samuel.

"You know a hell of a lot more about this case than you're letting on. Are you ever going to fill me in?"

"Just as soon as it all makes sense, Lieutenant. I'm still working on it."

The waiter brought steaming plates of tagliatelle, long, flat noodles topped with a porcini mushroom sauce. They ate in silence, almost with reverence.

"Here you eat as well as in France, Lieutenant," said Samuel.

"Don't offend me, man. Here you eat better. How can you compare Tuscan food with French?"

* * *

Samuel spent an uncomfortable night in the cheapest hotel he could find near the courthouse The next morning he went to the clerk's office of the Superior court for Stanislaus County and asked to look at the case register. He spent the next three hours going through it and then handed the clerk a form containing the case number of the file he was looking for.

When the file was turned over to him, the reporter copied what he needed, returned it to the clerk and asked that certain documents be certified as authentic.

"That'll cost you a dollar fifty for all three documents," she told him. "We'll have to mail them to you. It takes our staff awhile to compile and check them against the originals."

Samuel paid and asked for directions to the Greyhound bus station. On the way back to San Francisco, he read from an Earl Stanley Gardner detective novel before falling asleep. The next thing he knew, it was six o'clock and the bus was pulling into the San Francisco station.

King of the Bottom

* * *

The next morning Samuel was at the San Francisco Registrar's office as soon as it opened, where he perused the record of marriage licenses issued by the office for the last five years until he found what he was looking for. He made notes and again asked for a certified copy of the document he needed. From there, Samuel went to see Janak, who was waiting for him along with Bartholomew Asquith. The three men went over what Samuel had discovered over the last few days.

"Do you think I should go back to France now or wait until we find out where that bug came from?" asked Samuel.

"You should wait," said Janak. "Maybe something important will come up, which will make your trip even more useful. In the meantime, you can get hold of your contact and get things rolling over there."

"Are you sure you don't want to go this time instead of me?" asked Samuel.

The expression on Janak's face didn't change, but Samuel thought his ruddy complexion turned slightly pale. "This isn't the time for me to deal with personal stuff. We're in the middle of something big here. Let's just concentrate on it."

Samuel was about to make a joke about Janak's fear of confronting his past, but he thought better of it and decided that he shouldn't butt into his friend's life, especially since he had yet to give him an intimate peek into it.

"You're supposed to return to the church with Marisol on Sunday," continued Janak. "Let's see what comes of that."

"How much of this should I tell Bernardi?"

"Do you trust him?"

"Yeah," said Samuel. "He's helped us a lot. And frankly, we can't go any further without him. He gives us the power of law enforcement to investigate where we otherwise couldn't."

"You mean because we're broke?" laughed Janak.

"No. Because he can take us places we couldn't go otherwise."

"Just give me another week to think about it," said Janak. "When you've perceived someone as an enemy for a long time, it's hard to change that opinion."

"I hear what you're saying, but I need to share things with him so he'll share with us. You understand?"

"I understand."

Samuel left the lawyer's office and walked quickly down the street to his own office. He called Lucine in Paris, calculating that that the nine-hour time difference would find her at home after work. When she answered, he told her what he needed her to do, explaining that if she had any luck in finding the person he was looking for, he would return to Paris in a couple of weeks. Lucine took advantage of the opportunity to give him an update on her conversations with Hector Somolian. She then followed with an update on her personal life.

"Perhaps you would be interested to know that Janak sent me a letter."

"Don't tell me."

"Yes. We've started corresponding."

Samuel hung up the phone and laughed. He was not surprised that Janak hadn't said a word about Lucine since he'd given him her address.

* * *

The next Sunday, Marisol drove Samuel to Richmond, where they picked up Bernardi. He was dressed up, his hair had been recently cut and he smelled of cologne. Amused at the unexpected turn of events, Samuel sat in the rear so the lieutenant could have a better look at Marisol's legs.

They arrived at the church a half-hour before the service was to begin. They recognized a few faces, and the parishioners in turn greeted them as if they were now part of the congregation. As the guitarists warmed up, Marisol once again placed the photos of the insect on the blackboard. She also circulated a few copies among the parishioners.

"Is there anyone who knows where to locate the blue insect?" she asked in Spanish.

Several people in the crowd shook their heads. Samuel and Bernardi felt immediate disappointment, but she reminded them that it was still early and that they could ask again when the church filled up. Just then, the front door creaked open and the old man with the white hair and dark skin walked slowly toward the people surrounding the board. An odd silence gripped the crowd, and they turned to watch his approach as he shuffled up the aisle, his cane thumping as he walked. He murmured to those in front of him and they moved aside. When he reached the front of the crowd, Marisol addressed him directly.

"Do you know something about this, Don Silverio?"

"*Sí, niña*," he said, and spoke to her rapidly in Spanish.

"He says he thinks he knows where this beetle, he calls it, can be found. There's a creek on the other side of town and, if he's not mistaken, it lives there. He says he's spent a lot of time fishing those waters over the years."

"Can he tell us exactly where this place is and who owns it?" asked Bernardi.

Marisol repeated the question to the old man.

"He can't tell you who owns the property or give you directions on how to get there," she translated. "But he can take you there if you want to see it."

A murmur moved through the congregation. The parishioners had figured out who Bernardi was and they realized this was an important find. No one, however, was more excited than Samuel. Bernardi raised his arms to quiet the crowd.

"Will he come with us now and show us?" he asked.

"He'll be glad to," she said.

"Is it okay with him if he misses church today?"

"He says he has been thinking about this since last Sunday and, because he's taken this on as his civic duty, he wants to get it over with. He'll take time to pray later. But he wants to know why it is so important to you."

"I'll tell him when we get there," said Bernardi, not wanting to release too much information to the public.

Marisol took Don Silverio by the arm and led him out the door to the car. Don Silverio sat next to Marisol, with Samuel and Bernardi in the back. Don Silverio directed Marisol across the city and onto busy Highway 99, the north-south state thoroughfare. They exited the highway at Gage Road, one of the many country lanes that littered the area. It was divided into small plots that got larger the further away from the Highway they went. On the way, they passed several combination country store-gas stations.

Marisol and Don Silverio chatted in Spanish, paying little attention to their backseat passengers. Bernardi took the opportunity to ask Samuel what he'd found out at the courthouse the previous week. The reporter didn't want to lie, but he still wasn't ready to tell Bernardi everything.

"For the moment, it's a work in progress. I got some information that needs to be verified."

Bernardi, used to dealing with informants, knew Samuel was hiding something, but since he had other things on his mind, he let it pass.

After forty-five minutes, Don Silverio told Marisol to pull over near a clump of trees on the left-hand side of the road. Within the trees they could see a creek that ran hundreds of feet alongside a winding path before turning abruptly behind a stately Victorian manor surrounded by several outbuildings. Next to the creek was a paved driveway that ran the length of a large pasture dotted with grazing horses. At the top of the driveway was a black steel gate and a large mailbox with the number 11030 stenciled on its side.

They got out of the car and Don Silverio guided them to a railing that protected people from accidentally falling into the creek. He pointed in the direction of the manor and told Marisol that the creek was the home of the blue beetle.

"What can you fish for here?" asked Bernardi.

"Catfish," Marisol translated. "And you can also hunt for frogs."

"Frogs?"

"You haven't tried fried frog legs, Lieutenant?" she asked. "I'll have to prepare them for you one day."

"If you prepare them, I'll eat them." Bernardi smiled at her.

"Let's go," interrupted Samuel.

The two men climbed down the embankment and walked along the edge of the creek, looking carefully through the vegetation. From above, Don Silverio indicated that they should look in the trees. After a few minutes, Samuel found a blue beetle at the foot of a willow tree.

"Look, Lieutenant! Here it is!"

"Is it the same? All beetles look alike, don't they?"

"It has the same blue color as the one they found on Hagopian's pant leg."

"That color doesn't show very well on the photographs."

"I assure you, Lieutenant. It's the same."

Bernardi pulled from his pocket a wrinkled handkerchief that didn't look particularly clean and captured one of the insects. He folded the handkerchief carefully and put it back in his jacket pocket.

"What a break," he sighed.

"At least we have a clue. I wonder if there are other places where this thing thrives," said Samuel.

"Let's take it one step at a time, Mr. Hamilton. Our next

step is to go to the sheriff's office and find out who lives at 11030 Gage Road. Then we get a search warrant based on what we already know."

"How long with that take?" asked Samuel.

"Not too long," said Bernardi. "Judge Pluplot is already familiar with the case, so getting him up to speed will be easy."

"But this is Stanislaus County," said Samuel. "Don't you need a judge from here to issue the warrant?"

"That's true. But with a supporting request from Judge Pluplot, it'll happen a lot faster."

They climbed back up the embankment and rejoined Marisol and Don Silverio. Bernardi and Samuel thanked the old man for his help and explained the importance of the insect in solving the crime.

"Everyone at the church already knew that you were a policeman," Marisol told Bernardi. "They just wondered if you were after an insect or a man. Don Silverio said it makes more sense that you are after a man."

"How did they know I was a policeman?"

"By the way you walk, Lieutenant. And let me tell you—the only reason they helped you was because of my father. They don't have confidence in the police, but they do in him. Here, we all know each other. When I was a child, Don Silverio taught me to hunt frogs and fry them with garlic and pepper."

"Thanks for everything, Miss."

"You can call me Marisol."

"My name is Bruno."

"Well, Bruno, I hope that none of my friends will have problems because of you. You know what I mean."

"I'm not an immigration official, Marisol. Don't worry."

Marisol drove Don Silverio back to where he lived, near the church, and then took Bernardi and Samuel to the sheriff's office in Stockton. She explained that she wasn't in a hurry; all that awaited her was a Sunday afternoon with nothing interesting to do, so she would wait while they got what they needed. Bernardi insisted that afterward the two of them accept his invitation for dinner at Giuseppe's Tuscan Food.

* * *

After Samuel and Bernardi discovered who owned the ranch, it took the lieutenant several days to get the necessary affidavits prepared so he could get a search warrant issued by the Stanislaus Superior Court. On the morning of the day it was to be executed, the sheriff and Bernardi and his staff, including the forensic technology expert Philip Macintosh, gathered at the gate on Gage Road, waiting for the entire team to assemble so they could descend en masse. Bernardi had permitted Samuel to accompany them, provided that he say or write nothing of what was found on the property until Bernardi authorized it. It was a tough condition for the reporter but it would allow him to be the inside dopester, so he couldn't complain—at least not out loud.

When they were ready, the sheriff opened the iron gate and the caravan of vehicles proceeded down the paved driveway and parked in front of the Victorian house.

The sheriff and Bernardi knocked on the front door. A tall woman with bleached blond hair and dressed in a stylish spring dress answered the door. The two men identified themselves and explained that they had a search warrant against Rupert Chatoian that allowed them to search his entire property, including the outbuildings. "It also allows us to look for and confiscate items that Mr. Bernardi considers evidence in a criminal matter," concluded the sheriff, handing her the document.

"What on earth are you talking about sir? Mr. Chatoian is

not here and won't return for another week. Please come back when he is home." She tried to close the door but the sheriff blocked it with his foot.

"It doesn't matter if he's here or not. The warrant is still valid and we need to proceed with or without your cooperation, ma'am."

"I need to talk to my attorney. Please come back this afternoon when he can be present." She tried to force the door closed again. This time, the sheriff put his arm out to prevent it closing.

"I'm afraid not, ma'am. You can call him if you want to, but we're ready to proceed." He nudged her aside with his forearm and elbow so that Bernardi and the others could go in.

The sheriff cautioned the woman—everyone assumed she was Mrs. Chatoian—not to try to hide or move anything. "In addition, ma'am, if we don't finish today, you will have to vacate the premises until we do. Do you understand?"

"Yes, sir," she replied angrily. "I'm calling my lawyer."

Samuel took Bernardi aside. "This woman was in one of the photos that we took at Armand Hagopian's funeral. No one would identify her or the group that was with her."

"Not even the Armenian priest?" asked Bernardi.

"Not even the priest."

As the search commenced, the woman got on the telephone and the servants gathered in the kitchen, where they received specific instructions from the sheriff not to leave the room. When the team, under instructions from Bernardi, reached the living room, Samuel interrupted and called him aside.

"I don't think we'll find much inside the house, Lieutenant. I bet you if they have anything still here, it'll be in the outbuildings."

"It's okay," said Bernardi. "We'll go through the inside and catalog everything. After we look outside, we'll come back to see if they moved anything in the house."

The men spent hours in the house. The Chatoians' attorney showed up two hours into the search and he and the woman closeted themselves in a side room that had already been searched. After a long time going over the search warrant, the lawyer emerged to confront the sheriff.

"My clients have constitutional rights, which you are violating. I've called a criminal lawyer who will be here shortly. We demand that you cease and desist with this search until he arrives and we have a chance to consult with him."

"Not a chance, Mr. Attorney," said the sheriff. "Only a judge can stop us from what we're doing, and I haven't seen an order to that effect. I don't blame you for trying, though." The sheriff turned his back on the lawyer.

The teams had now moved outside and Bernardi told them they needed to see if there was a tree on the property where a man could have been hanged. Samuel said that the place was full of trees and a man could have been hanged from any one of them, but Bernardi assured him the experts knew exactly what to look for.

Several deputies fanned out over the large yard, looking for one that fit the bill. After a few minutes, Mac called Bernardi over to a patch of depressed ground near the creek that looked as if it had been turned over recently. Samuel followed.

"See this? It looks to me like maybe someone cut down a tree right here. See the condition of the earth and all these dead leaves?"

"I see," said Bernardi. "Take a soil sample so we can check it against the mud we found on Hagopian's shoe."

"Yeah, I'm also going to spray some luminol around here," said Mac. He went to his van and returned with a spray bottle of liquid and a small black canvas tent about three feet wide and a couple of feet high.

"What's that?" asked Samuel, pointing to the spray bottle.

"Luminol tells us if there is any residual blood," explained Mac.

"Couldn't they get rid of any blood by digging up the earth the way they appear to have done here?" asked Samuel.

"No, they couldn't. Some blood always remains."

"What's the tent for?"

"It has to be dark for us to see if anything glows," said the expert. "If there is a residual, it'll give off a blue-green light."

Mac sprayed the ground and covered the area with the tent. He then opened the flap and peered in. The ground gave off a blue-green light, indicating traces of blood.

"Holy shit, it looks like there is a lot of it," said an excited Bernardi. "Get some photos and take samples so we can test it to see if it's the same type as Hagopian's."

"It makes sense," said Samuel. "It's right next to the creek, and that's probably how the blue beetle got in the way of what was going on."

"Let's go to the tool shed," said Bernardi to Samuel. He motioned for a photographer and two officers from his department to accompany them.

They went to the rear of the property, where the creek made a left turn. Stacked against the outside of a small building was a four-foot high pile of firewood. Bernardi directed the officers to go through the pieces of wood, one by one.

"Look for a piece of wood in there that looks like it might have had a rope tied to it."

He and Samuel went inside the tool shed and began to rummage among the picks, shovels, rakes and machetes that were carefully stacked in a corner. They also found several jars of chemicals stored in a cabinet above the workbench.

"Don't you think it's odd to have a microscope in a tool shed?" asked Samuel, pointing to the one he'd found on the workbench.

"Not if you're checking items for fingerprints on various

objects," said Bernardi. "If I'm not mistaken, we're going to find Miguel's and Jose's prints on most of these tools."

He went to the shed door and called out to Mac. "Get prints off all the tools in here. After that, check the machetes for any blood stains."

Samuel, still digging around in the junk in the corner, pulled several old fence posts to one side and made another discovery.

"Look, Lieutenant," he called out excitedly. "Here's a rope."

"Check out that rope, too," said Bernardi to Mac and his assistant, who were now at his side. "See if the pattern matches the marks that were left on Hagopian's neck. And don't forget those jars in the cupboard. I bet you anything that the chemical liquids in them match what was in the bottles we found in Hagopian's pockets."

In the middle of all this, one of the men searching the woodpile came inside to show Bernardi a thick tree branch that had been severed from its trunk. The deep grooves in the bark indicated there had once been a rope tied around it.

"Okay, show me what part of the pile you took it from," Bernardi said. He then turned to his forensic expert. "Mac, photograph the piece of wood and see if the pattern of the rope we found inside the shed fits the marks on the branch. Then check for any residual tree bark on the rope."

"You don't even have to tell me, Lieutenant.

The crew finished its work several hours later, just as it was beginning to get dark. Exhausted, Samuel and Bernardi stood on the front porch.

"The evidence we uncovered today will blow this case wide open," said Bernardi.

"No question about it," said Samuel. "When will you be finished analyzing it?"

"We should have everything done within a week, except

for the chemicals. They take longer."

"Then you send it back to Deadeye?"

"No. The District Attorney wants me to report directly to him. Deadeye's no longer in charge of the case."

"When can I write my story?" asked Samuel.

"Not until the D.A. takes the case to the grand jury."

"How long will that take?"

"Minimum of two weeks, maybe longer."

"That will give me a chance to check out a couple more things," said Samuel.

"Like what?'

"Right now all I can say is that they involve my Paris connection, but I promise you that as soon as I get back, I'll fill you in on everything I know. Thanks for everything, Lieutenant."

11

Why?

WHEN SAMUEL RETURNED TO San Francisco two days later, he went directly to Janak's office and told him what they had discovered at the Chatoian compound in Stockton.

"This means my clients will be cleared, don't you think?" said the lawyer.

"I think you're right, especially since Deadeye's no longer handling the case. But there's still a bigger question here."

"What's that?"

"The question is why? What's the motive for these crimes?"

"We don't have a motive yet," said Janak. "They'll arrest the Chatoians and my guess is they won't talk. But if my clients are no longer suspects, it's not my problem. It's Bernardi's."

"Aren't you interested in justice?"

"Sure, Samuel. But I have to earn a living."

"But you can't wrap up Miguel or Jose's civil case until they're cleared. And you still represent them in the criminal case, so it's *still* your business."

"That's true," said Janak, biting his lower lip and looking thoughtful. "So I'm still involved. And I can't go forward with the civil case until they're cleared, because I can't take the chance on Miguel or Jose being arrested if they show up to pursue their cases."

"And I have to write my story," said Samuel. "We have to get to the bottom of this. I'm going back to Paris."

Janak laughed, clearly pleased with himself. "I told you to wait and it was worth it, wasn't it?" His expression became serious. "But it looks like we have a bigger puzzle than we did just a week ago. I can't imagine what you'll find in Paris that will clear it up."

"I admit it's a long shot, but there are all those unresolved questions that we've talked about," said Samuel.

"I want you to keep me informed."

"I'll tell you everything just as soon as I return. I'll only be gone for a couple of weeks, maybe less. Paris is very expensive."

Before leaving the office, Samuel thanked Marisol for her help in finding the blue insect.

"Always happy to help," she smiled. "My father will appreciate knowing the boys will soon be out of danger."

"It's not official yet, so don't publicize it," said Samuel.

"Do you think Lieutenant Bernardi will continue with the case?" she asked, trying not to smile.

"I'm sure you'll see him again," laughed Samuel.

* * *

After spending the day preparing for his Paris trip, Samuel went to Camelot in the evening to say goodbye to everyone, especially Blanche, whom he hadn't seen for a long time. He'd been so busy that he hadn't had time to visit his favorite watering hole.

Pulmonary congestion hadn't prevented Melba from coming to Camelot almost every day with her dog and her oxygen tank. Her usual spot at the Round Table allowed her to keep an eye on business and, at the same time, criticize every one of her daughter's efforts to help. Melba was bored in her apartment, where her only diversion was watching soap operas. She wasn't interested in the lives of television characters; she preferred the lives of her patrons, where she could have an influence. Besides, she didn't like to be absent on foggy days, such as this one, because the joint would be more crowded than usual. San Francisco's trademark fog had a depressing effect on office workers, and many of them liked to cheer themselves up with a couple of drinks before going home.

Melba looked better than the last time he'd seen her; she was coughing less and smoking more. Mr. Song's herbs really were a miracle. Excalibur received him with exaggerated happiness, behavior he only exhibited when Samuel was around. He sidled up to the reporter's side to be scratched.

Seeing that Melba's glass was empty, Samuel went to get her another beer and a Scotch on the rocks for himself—the first he'd had in several days.

"Come and tell this old friend what you've been up to, young man," she grumbled, pointing to the seat by her side.

Samuel sat down. Melba stubbed out her cigarette butt, took several gulps of oxygen and lit another cigarette.

"Hey, Melba, isn't oxygen flammable?"

"How do I know?"

"If that thing explodes, I don't want to be near you."

"Knock off the shit, Samuel. What's going on with the case of the Armenian?"

Samuel brought her up to date about what had happened over the last few weeks, including the letter from Lucine about Nashwan's false identity. He also told her he was going to go Paris again to interview Hagopian's wives, assuming Lucine could arrange it.

"It's pretty obvious that the Chatoians and the 'Turk,' whoever he is, are the culprits in this case," said Samuel. "The only question is why?"

Melba laughed. "I see you're following my advice: *cherchez la femme*. You think one of the wives will help you find the answer?"

"I think the second one is a key part of the puzzle, but I doubt she can give us the whole picture," said Samuel, looking around the bar for Blanche.

"Relax, man," said Melba. "She went to buy something to eat. She'll be back in ten minutes."

"Who?" asked Samuel, bending down to pet the dog so Melba couldn't see his face.

"Tell me what kind of a relationship you had with your mother."

"What a strange question to ask." exclaimed Samuel. "What's that got to do with what we're talking about?"

"You know what the psychiatrists say, Samuel. Men are always looking for women with whom they can have neurotic relationships like the ones they had with their mothers. It's what they know, so even though they're miserable, they're comfortable. Your mother must have ignored you the way Blanche does."

"Blanche doesn't ignore me!"

"Yeah, right, she plays hard to get so you'll notice her," laughed Melba.

"Don't change the subject," said Samuel, red faced.

"This time it's something much more complicated than a woman, Samuel. I'm referring to the case, not Blanche. *Cherchez la femme* doesn't always apply."

"Do you have any ideas?"

"No, but I advise you to follow the clues that we've talked about. Don't ignore anything. I want you to bring me news of the so-called Turk. How long will you be in Paris?"

"Depends on what I get from Lucine. Without her, I can't do much."

At that moment Blanche appeared from the rear of the

bar—she'd come in through the back door—and Samuel's face lit up. Every time he saw her, he thought she looked more beautiful, even though tonight her hair was greasy and she wore it in a limp ponytail. Her eyes were red from the smoke and she had round glasses that he'd never seen before perched on the bridge of her nose. Samuel was moved. He thought that he'd discovered something new about his love. She was nearsighted.

She waved hello distractedly and immediately went to work behind the horseshoe bar, attending to the patrons.

"Go," Melba pushed. "You don't have to stay with me, son."

Samuel didn't waste any time. He finished his Scotch in one gulp and approached the bar with the excuse of asking for another. Excalibur followed him, knowing that Samuel would secretly slip him the salty crackers that were for the customers, along with a few olives and hardboiled eggs. Melba had forbidden anyone giving eggs or olives to her dog because he always got sick and then it was left to her to clean up the mess.

"Hi, Blanche," said Samuel. "I've really been busy. That's why I haven't been around."

"Oh yeah? I hadn't noticed."

The reporter ignored the low blow. Perhaps the fog also depressed Blanche. Women were supposed to be moody, and Samuel knew she didn't like the atmosphere of Camelot. Ever since Melba had gotten sick, she'd had to replace her, but Blanche preferred her sports and the open air. She hated spending her afternoons in that closed space, breathing stale cigarette smoke and listening to the platitudes of sad drunks.

Samuel decided that Blanche's unfriendly tone wasn't personal. "Do you want to know more about the case?" he asked, eager to start a conversation.

"Which case? The one about the dump?"

"Yes, of course, Blanche. There isn't another one for the moment."

Samuel spent the next half hour going over the details of the investigation, patiently tolerating interruptions whenever Blanche had to take care of other customers. Finally, the bartender showed up, apologizing profusely for being an hour late, and Blanche was able to take a short break.

"I haven't eaten since breakfast," she said. "I have some Chinese food in the office. Accompany me? If I eat at a table out here, they won't leave me in peace."

The two of them went to Melba's small office, Excalibur at Samuel's side. They lit the lamp with the pink shade and took the only two seats available. Samuel liked the intimacy of that little room, and appreciated the soft light the absurd lamp gave off. He thought it was the perfect place for a romantic encounter. If his passions rose, he thought, Blanche couldn't escape. They were seated face to face, their knees touching, with him blocking the door. At the same time, Samuel knew his thoughts were pure fantasy. Athletic as she was, he realized that if Blanche sensed she was in danger, she could break his neck with one hand.

On the desk was a bag from a local Chinese restaurant. She took out a carton, a package of soy sauce, a pair of chopsticks, two fortune cookies and several paper napkins.

"Do you want to share this with me? It's vegetarian chow."

"No thanks."

"You haven't told me the most important part. What about Lucine?"

"It seems that she and Janak are writing each other, but that's all I know. Janak is being tight-lipped about it."

Blanche smiled coyly, the first real smile of the night, and picked up her chopsticks. "It won't be long now," she said, grasping a bite of food.

"What do you mean?"

"Mark my word, Samuel. It won't be long before they're together again."

"I have other things on my mind beside Janak's love life."

"Like what, for example?"

It was the opportunity Samuel had been waiting for for a long time. "My own love life!" he exclaimed, playing with one of the fortune cookies.

Blanche didn't respond; her mouth was full of food. She studied him, an inscrutable expression on her face as she chewed, while he breathed deeply and took an unusual interest in the fortune cookie.

Suddenly the reporter picked up a foul smell in the air, much worse than anything he could attribute to the vegetarian food. He blushed, thinking that Blanche had passed gas. He excused her immediately; she was human, after all. He looked up and in the pink light he could see that Blanche was also blushing. The girl was paralyzed, her chopsticks in midair and her food half chewed. She looked at him, intrigued.

"No!" exclaimed Samuel, horrified that Blanche suspected him. "It wasn't me."

Then they remembered Excalibur, who was lying at their feet with an air of absolute innocence. Blanche swallowed what she had in her mouth and they both laughed until the tears ran down their cheeks.

12

Unexpected Answers

AT TWO O'CLOCK SHARP ON the Sunday after Samuel arrived in Paris, Hector Somolian hobbled on his crutches up the stairs to Lucine's apartment, accompanied by the Armenian woman with the headscarf Samuel had seen in the hotel room some months before. Sunday was the only day the old man could keep the appointment, since he and his family worked long hours the rest of the week. And it was a good thing, too, because jet lag had knocked Samuel flat, as it had on his previous trip, and it had taken him awhile to recover.

Sasiska, dressed in a bright red silk dress, a white scarf covering her head, greeted them at the door. She propped the man's crutches against the arm of the sofa and offered her guests the low-slung chairs around the brazier. She then poured tea and made small talk until they were relaxed. After about fifteen minutes, Samuel and Lucine came into the room. Lucine reintroduced Samuel to Hector and explained that her American friend was going to ask him some more questions.

When Samuel first entered Lucine's apartment the day before, she helped him set up a hidden tape recorder behind the sofa, complete with an on/off switch on a cord leading to the seat he intended to occupy. Once the machine was set up, Samuel looked around the familiar room. He noted that although it hadn't changed much, now that the weather was warmer and sunlight bathed the space, the room was much brighter. He figured that since the old man lived in such a dark and dingy place, this would cheer him and make him more talkative.

Before beginning his interview, Samuel pushed the record button. He explained to Hector, with Lucine and Sasiska acting as interpreters, that there was all sorts of new information that had come out about the case of the Hagopians, which was why he needed to talk with him again.

"The first thing I'd like to know is your real name," he said, amazed that the diminutive but strong and hardworking man before him was ninety years old.

"Yes, I've been told by Mademoiselle Lucine that you would ask me that," said Hector. "I've had a long time to think about it. She is probably right that after all these years no one has done me harm, so they are probably not going to now. But the reason they haven't done me harm is that they don't know I'm alive. And it's not just me. What about my family? I want them to be safe, too."

"Without knowing who you are, I can't tell if you are in any danger," said Samuel.

The old man looked plaintively at each of the three women in the room and rubbed his calloused hands together.

"Very well, I'm going to tell you, but only since no one in my family carries the old name anyway, and I'm at an age where I'm beyond worrying about what could happen to me. My real name is Albert Gabedian. Gabedian was my family name in the old country. My whole family were servants in the Hagopian household for several generations."

Samuel wasn't sure if knowing the old man's name would bear any fruit, but he thought that Gabedian must trust Lucine very much to let go of such a long-held secret.

"Ask him if the name Chatoian means anything to him."

Even before the question had been translated, Hector and his female companion opened their eyes wide in astonishment.

"Where did you hear that name?" Gabedian asked.

"I'm following some leads and I'm just asking general questions. Chatoian is a name that's come up in the investigation. I see that it means something to you. Can you explain why?"

"The Chatoians and the Hagopian families were very close," said Gabedian. "They were both very wealthy and they did a lot of business together. Their children went to the same exclusive school. The Chatoians also suffered great losses at the hands of the Turks. The patriarch and his wife were hanged from the town square even before the attack on the Hagopians. The family lost almost everything they had. I understand that some of their children were killed. Luckily, others were able to flee for their lives, like the rest of us. I've never heard another word about them. That's why I was so surprised when you mentioned their name."

Samuel smiled. He'd gotten what he wanted. He pushed the switch to turn off the tape recorder. After Gabedian left, Lucine told him that she'd made arrangements for Almandine Hagopian, the young widow, to come to her apartment for tea the following Tuesday, without disclosing that Samuel would be present.

"She and I may have a pretty rough confrontation," said Samuel. "Aren't you worried that it will affect your relationship with her?"

"It's a little late to worry about that," she answered. "You obviously can't get the whole picture without her."

Samuel dawdled over a second cup of tea, wanting but not daring to bring up the question that was burning a hole in his tongue. Not surprisingly, Lucine guessed what was on his mind.

"Janak sent me a book of poetry," she said, showing him a

small volume with a blue cover that was lying on the table.

"Poetry? I can't imagine Janak reading poetry."

"*Twenty Poems of Love*, by Pablo Neruda. I had already read it. The verses are very passionate. The gift surprised me as much as it does you, Samuel. He promised that as soon as he could escape from work, he would come visit me."

"I hope that your encounter is as beautiful as those poems, Lucine."

Samuel examined the blue book, committing the title to memory. He decided he had to buy it and learn some of the poems by heart so he could whisper them in the elusive Blanche's ear, since everything else he'd tried had failed.

* * *

Almandine arrived punctually and sat in one of the low-slung chairs around the brazier, chatting in Armenian with Sasiska. Samuel watched her from another room. He thought she looked different—younger, prettier and more relaxed. She wore less makeup, and the stylish indigo dress she had on gave her a freshness that was missing when he met her in San Francisco. Almandine greeted her friend with a smile but froze when she recognized Samuel.

"This is a setup! This man is a reporter!" she exclaimed in English, struggling to pull herself out of the low-slung seat, but Lucine gently pushed her back.

"Please, Almandine," she begged. "Just listen to what Mr. Hamilton has to say."

"I can't believe you are doing this to me, Lucine. You have betrayed me!"

"I only ask that you speak with him. Your life may depend on it."

It took some time for Lucine's words to sink in. "What do you mean, my life may depend on it?"

"That's correct," Samuel told her, pressing the button on the recorder. "There are a lot of angry people after each other in this case, and you may be next on someone's list."

"Do you know that someone is after me?" she asked, clearly upset.

"Law enforcement may be the first, unless I get some answers here today. I never got a chance to talk with you after your husband's death and the picture's changed since then, which I assume you know."

"I didn't have anything to do with accusing the Mexicans," she blurted.

"That's what I want to talk to you about. Tell me everything you know about what went on last December."

"Why should I talk to you, Mr. Hamilton? I doubt you're here to do me any favors."

"I am here to help you, even if you don't believe me. You need to trust me so that things don't get worse for you, Miss Chatoian."

"What are you talking about?" exclaimed Almandine, getting to her feet.

"Just what you heard," said Samuel, pulling the certified copy of the Stanislaus court documents he'd obtained out of his briefcase. "It says here that your name was Margaret Chatoian but that a few years ago you changed it to Almandine Margolin."

Sasiska looked back and forth between them, trying to figure out what was going on. Lucine held a finger to her lips, indicating that she should be quiet.

"You have no proof that I am the same person. There must be hundreds of Margaret Chatoians, even Almandine Margolins. Besides, my name is Almandine Hagopian."

"Yes, I know," said Samuel pulling out another document from his pile of papers. "Here's your marriage certificate. It says that Almandine Margolin married Armand Hagopian in

San Francisco. Remember that?"

The young woman looked to Sasiska, who she felt was her only ally, and spoke to her in Armenian, sobbing from the depths of her being. Sasiska, beside herself, went to the bedroom and returned with a box of tissues. She sat down next to Almandine and patted her on the back to console her.

"What is she saying?" whispered Samuel to Lucine.

"She's asking my mother for help. She says you are badgering her."

They waited a long while until the woman's sobs subsided. Streaks of makeup ran down her face and her eyelids were red and swollen. Finally, she sat back in her chair, defeated, looking like an abandoned child.

"I'm very sorry, Mrs. Hagopian," said Samuel. "I assure you that I'm not here to harm you."

"What do you want to know?" she asked in a wisp of a voice.

"Please explain it to all to me, step by step."

"And who will protect me if I tell you?" She was obviously frightened.

"Your safety is not entirely in my hands," said Samuel. "I can tell the powers that be that you've been cooperative, and that is always worth a lot."

"Very well," she surrendered, giving a deep sigh. "I need to get this off my conscience anyway. I've lived with it too long."

Once she had answered all of his questions, Samuel decided his trip had been well worth it.

13

Is This Really the End?

THE MOMENT SAMUEL STUMBLED off the plane from Paris he rushed straight to Camelot to talk to Melba. Lucky for him, Blanche was there, too.

"You're back, Samuel!" Blanche exclaimed. "What news do you bring about Janak's girlfriend?"

"Is that all you're interested in? Don't you want to know how I got along over there?"

"Sure, silly," she answered, giving him a smack on the cheek that sent a jolt of electricity through his tired skeleton.

"What in the world happened to you, son?" asked Melba, looking at Samuel's wrinkled clothes and the dark circles under his eyes, all the while pulling on Excalibur's collar to keep him from slobbering all over the reporter.

"On the other hand, Melba," he responded, "you look great." He noticed that she wasn't coughing, that she had color in her face and that the oxygen tank was gone.

"Mr. Song's medicine did the trick," she winked. "But you didn't come here in the disastrous condition you're in to tell me I'm gorgeous. What d'ya want? Weren't you in Paris?"

"I just got back this afternoon and I really have some hot stuff that I have to talk over with you," he said, plopping down in a seat at the round table.

"First, tell me about Lucine," insisted Blanche.

"Janak sent her a book of poetry and wrote that he's going to see her as soon as he gets some free time."

"Poetry, huh? With a little luck and a good book of verses he'll conquer her again."

"I want to know about the crimes," said Melba. "The rest is pure soap opera. Have a drink and fire away."

"I don't need a drink. It would knock me under the table. Listen—"

Samuel told them all that he'd learned from Almandine.

"Pretty terrible, it seems to me," said Melba.

"Without a doubt. But what do I do with the woman's story?"

"You're asking me if you should disclose her role to the detective. Is that what you want to know?"

"I don't have much choice, do I? But I can't get her out of my head. Both Lucine and I think she's suffered enough, considering all she went through."

"I see it, man. You're dammed if you do and dammed if you don't. What happens if you give her a break and leave her role out of the report you give the cop and don't mention her in your article?"

"Impossible, Melba. I have to tell Bernardi, and I need Almandine for my story. She gives it a wallop that money can't buy. Besides, without her input there's no motive unless someone confesses. And as you know, the possibility of that is zero."

"A confession is only a technical problem," she said. "Motive isn't always obvious and sometimes never proved in murder cases. Besides, isn't there a lot of physical evidence the cops got from the Chatoian property?"

"Yeah, loads of it."

While she was thinking, Melba took a drag from her cigarette and exhaled slowly, clearly enjoying the sensation. "Okay, so the problem is a moral one. Can you get the D.A. to ignore what happened to someone in the process of carrying out her part in the crime?"

"Granted, she probably didn't know exactly what was going to happen," said Samuel.

"But she at least suspected it, unless she was stupid."

"She's not," said Samuel.

"You're lucky it's not up to you. Your job is to get the facts and present them. It's the D.A.'s job to decide if they require action."

"What are you trying to say?"

"Sometimes the cat doesn't get the rat."

It took Samuel a few seconds to get what Melba was suggesting. He slapped his hand to his forehead and let out a laugh. "They can't prosecute her if she's not here. I learned that from Janak. I'll tell Almandine that no matter what happens she should stay in France."

"Perfect," said Melba. "You tell the cops what you learned and then you give her the benefit of the doubt in your article."

"Like you say, I just present the facts."

"You're tired, Samuel, and you can't think straight," said Blanche. "Go to sleep."

"Thanks for your help, Melba."

"Thanks to you, son. I was half dead from boredom and you brought a circus to my very own table. There's nothing more delicious than a good murder."

"In this case there were two," Samuel told her on his way out. "And be careful, woman! Don't smoke so much."

* * *

Samuel handed Bernardi several typewritten pages of his draft on the Hagopian murders, explaining that he wanted to publish it in the next few days, as soon as he had the detective's go-ahead. Bernardi took the pages, sat back in his chair and perused the document, occasionally nodding his head in agreement or grunting in surprise. Samuel, who spent the time looking out Bernardi's office windows, thought his surprise must have come when he encountered the revelations about Almandine.

When the detective finished reading, he twirled his chair around, slapped the article down on his desk and smiled.

"Some of this is unbelievable. How in the hell did you get her to tell you all of this stuff?"

"On some of it, I had the goods on her. As for the rest, my connection in Paris made all the difference. She created the conditions."

"I can't tell you not to print any of it. I would add that Rupert Chatoian has just been indicted in both Contra Costa and Fresno counties, and the two D.A.'s are just waiting for Mr. Marachak to make motions to dismiss the charges pending against the Ramos boys."

"Does Janak know this?" asked Samuel.

"I'll leave it to you to give him the news. When you say you had the goods on her, does that mean you have this documented?"

"No only that, I have a tape recording of her talking to me. Do you want to hear it?"

"Sure," said Bernardi. "Let's go down the hall to the conference room."

Several minutes later the tape recorder was plugged in and Samuel explained to Bernardi how he'd gotten Amandine to say what they were about to hear.

"Did she actually know you were recording her?" asked Bernardi.

"Of course not," said Samuel. "If she had, she wouldn't have said a word."

"Okay, let's hear it," said Bernardi.

"The first voice you hear will be that of Almandine," Samuel explained. "I had just asked her to tell me everything. The other voice, of course, is mine." He hit the play button.

"You're right. I am a Chatoian. The Chatoian and Hagopian families go back a long way. They were business associates and family friends for many generations in Erzerum, long before the genocide began. When the killing started, something strange occurred. Deep suspicions arose among the Armenian families in the region and terrible things transpired between trusted friends. For instance, we know for a fact that the Hagopian family bought its freedom by betraying the Chatoian patriarchs to the Turks and telling where their treasures were hidden. But it backfired. While the Turkish authorities allowed the wife and children and the brother to escape, they killed Hagopian Senior, as well as every Chatoian they could find. In the end, they confiscated what the Hagopian patriarch thought was protected."

"Did that include killing the Gabedians?"

"Where did you get that name?"

"Wasn't that the family name of the servants who took care of the Hagopian family?"

"Yes, but they were all killed by the Chatoians. They went after everyone connected with the Hagopians as a way of getting even for the betrayal. They accomplished all this while the remnants of both families were still in Erzerum, before they escaped to France."

"The Chatoians also made it to the United States."

"You already knew that, Mr. Hamilton."

"So what was your role in all this?"

"Like the rest of my family, I grew up hating the Hagopians. It was made worse by their success and by the wealth they amassed. My family felt that those were achieved as a result of the betrayal of our family. That's why Rupert Chatoian planned his revenge."

"But that was years ago!"

"So what? 'An eye for an eye, a tooth for a tooth' Mr. Hamilton."

"I understand, ma'am."

King of the Bottom

"The rumors started flying around the Armenian community that Armand and his first wife were divorcing, and that he had a reputation for liking young, attractive women. That was all we knew, so we assumed that he was a womanizer and that his wife got fed up.

"I was sent to court to change my name and make myself available in all the places we knew he would frequent. He took the bait and, surprisingly, after only a few dates, he asked me to marry him.

"My job was to spy. But I admit that at first I was confused, as Armand initially conquered me. Although he was no longer young, he was still handsome and strong and he was a very good lover. He seduced me. I wasn't prepared for that. I was supposed to seduce him, although I had no knowledge or experience of how to do that. I suppose that in the end what he liked about me was that I was young and naive."

"Did you learn that the reason his first wife left him was because he abused her?"

"I was just getting to that. It didn't take long for his true character to come out. Armand started with little things—caustic remarks and, later, cutting sarcasm. I could have handled all that but what I didn't expect was the physical abuse and his cruelty. He started to beat me. At first it was random; as time went on, though, I could count on beatings twice or even three times a week. In the beginning, to make amends, he showered me with expensive gifts. At the same time he told me that it was my fault, that if only I hadn't said such-and-such a thing, he wouldn't have lost his temper. Toward the end, it didn't make much difference what I said or did. When he became jealous or enraged he beat me and then refused to talk to me for days, until he wanted sex. If I resisted, he'd rape me and beat me again."

On Bernardi's signal, Samuel stopped the tape.

"What a bastard the guy was," said Bernardi. "And to think he walked around Richmond like a big shot."

"You should have seen her face when she was talking about all this stuff," said Samuel. "Her expression was harsh and angry, and she looked ten years older. Remember, this is a young woman in her early thirties. I knew what she was saying was taking its toll on her, but I also knew I couldn't stop until I got it all."

Samuel started the recorder again.

"As I said, I was the spy. So I began to pay attention to everything that went on in the Hagopian family. I carefully prepared the way for Nashwan, so he could come to work at the company. I reported back to Rupert Chatoian weekly and worked on Armand to get him to trust Nashwan. That was fundamental to the plan."

"What about Nashwan? We know that wasn't his real name. Who is he?"

"He's a Chatoian, too."

"Really? What's his first name?"

"It's John. John Chatoian."

"Do you know where he lives?"

"He's a Parisian. I have no idea where he is now. He disappeared after his court testimony and I doubt that he will ever show his face again. The family was very angry with him for ruining the trial."

"You mean for stealing from the blind man?"

"Yes, of course. That resulted in the acquittal of the Mexicans."

"What was Nashwan's—or John's—role in carrying out the plan?"

"I honestly don't know. Although, from what happened, I can guess. Rupert Chatoian knows the answers. I was just supposed to soften up Armand so Nashwan could get the job."

"Does that mean that you were kept in the dark about the details of what the Chatoians were up to?"

"That was the men's secret. I knew that they wanted revenge, but not how it was to be achieved."

"What about the emasculation?"

"It's a very old form of revenge. That's what the Turks did to the Chatoian patriarch."

"And that's why your family wanted all the Hagopian men and their male servants to suffer the same fate?"

"Exactly. I suggest you read a little history, Mr. Hamilton. In the Armenian culture, that's just a way of getting even. One tribe learns it from another."

"I see. Getting back to your husband, ma'am. Didn't you expect his abusive behavior when you got together with him in light of the way he treated his first wife?"

"I had no idea about the reasons for his divorce and I didn't ask. It was something that was never mentioned. I had a mission. As a Chatoian, I was supposed to spy on him and not complain, but there was a point of no return. He became sadistic and he hurt me—seriously hurt me—so I just wanted to get my part over with and escape. I feared for my life."

Samuel stopped the tape again.

"You should have seen her when this was taking place," he said. "Her voice became grave and she had an icy look in her eyes. Lucine put her arms around her but Almandine shook her off."

"What do you mean he seriously hurt you? Please excuse me for insisting, Mrs. Hagopian. It's obvious this is painful for you but I need to know."

"You really want to know what that bastard did to me? Well, look…"

"At that point she stood up," said Samuel, stopping the tape again. "She opened her dress, took off her bra and exposed her breasts. Instead of nipples, there were two ugly scars."

"This is what my husband did to me, Mr. Hamilton! He mutilated me! Take a good look!"

"We were all speechless. We just sat there staring at her until Almandine put on her bra back on and buttoned up her dress."

"Jesus Christ," said Bernardi. "I'm going to be sick."

"The interview is almost over," said Samuel, turning the recorder back on one last time.

"Why didn't you go to the police, for God's sake?"

"Because Armand would have killed me. And besides, I had a way of getting even. After that, I fully accepted my mission. I could perform the tasks assigned to me by my family."

Samuel turned off the recorder.

"How much of this stuff did you know before you left?" asked Bernardi.

"I only knew that she was a Chatoian, and that Nashwan was a phony," said Samuel. "The rest was a total surprise."

"You found that out the day you went to Stockton, didn't you?"

"Yep, but I had to keep it quiet until I had all the facts."

"This stuff about Nashwan being a Chatoian should buy him an indictment," said Bernardi. "We found his fingerprints all over the tools in the shed. And now that footprint that matches his shoe size becomes very incriminating, especially since he lied about making the plane reservation to France."

"What about Hagopian's wife? What do you intend to do about her, Detective?"

"It's not up to me. It's up to the D.A. What I can do is suggest that he give her immunity if she's willing to testify."

"What do you think her life would be worth if she took him up on that silly idea?" asked Samuel.

"I don't get what you mean."

"If the Hagopians don't kill her, the Chatoians will," said Samuel. "I'll have to explain tribalism to you later, Detective, when you invite me again for an Italian meal." Samuel was anxious to leave and get his story to his editor.

"I think I see the problem. I'm just a public servant; my job is to pass on the information to the powers that be. They make the decisions."

"I thought it wouldn't matter much because she was in France, so she could avoid the long arm of the law. Then I thought about Nashwan. You said, in effect, that you're going after him."

"There's a big difference between the two," said Bernardi. "She's only an accessory to murder. It looks like he's one of the perpetrators. You've made that very clear, Samuel."

"Let me tell you the rest of the story, Lieutenant."

"Shoot, Samuel. I'm not the one with a deadline to meet."

"What was left of both clans escaped to Paris, but the thirst for revenge wasn't forgotten. The Armenian priest had to know and that's why he was so uncomfortable when I showed him the photos of the Chatoians taken at Armand Hagopian's funeral and why he pretended not to recognize them. What's amazing is that it simmered all these years until Rupert Chatoian figured out how to get even. He sent Almandine into enemy territory with orders to carve out a place for Nashwan at the dump. After he set up the Mexicans, Nashwan lured Hagopian to Stockton, where he was tortured and murdered. His body was then moved to the dump and strung up with Juan Ramos's knot on the rope.

"Nashwan, because he was a chemical engineer, also knew what chemicals to use in the Coke bottles. All he had to do was read the civil complaint. And in order to complete the revenge, Rupert arranged to have Joseph killed in Fresno."

His story finished, Samuel got up to leave, shaking the Detective's hand on his way out the door. They'd worked well together, he thought.

"If you're going back to San Francisco," said Bernardi, "say hello to Marisol for me."

"Sure will, Detective. But why don't you pick up the phone and do it yourself."

"I may just do that."